THE WORST PART IS NOT that I am alone and terrified, but that I am helpless. I understand why Bree broke down when she was isolated in Burg's tunnels. Helplessness weighs on a person, and in tight quarters, it's downright suffocating.

When I wake, I see I am in an unadorned room, a mirrored wall opposite me. I look far less tired than I feel.

"Morning, Gray," my reflection says.

Also by Erin Bowman

Taken

Frozen

Stolen: A Taken Novella
Available as an ebook only

A **TAKEN** NOVEL

FORGED

ERIN BOWMAN

An Imprint of HarperCollins*Publishers*

HarperTeen is an imprint of HarperCollins Publishers.

Forged

Copyright © 2015 by Erin Bowman

Rock photograph by Daniel J. Grenier/Getty Images

www.epicreads.com

Library of Congress Cataloging-in-Publication Data
Bowman, Erin.
   Forged / Erin Bowman. — First edition.
      pages cm. — (Taken ; 3)
   Summary: "After learning the truth about the Laicos Project and surviving
betrayal by a Forgery in their midst, Gray Weathersby and his group of rebels
plan their final attack on the Franconian Order"— Provided by publisher.
   ISBN 978-0-06-211733-5
   [1. Science fiction.] I. Title.
PZ7.B68347Fo 2015   2014026696
[Fic]—dc23   CIP
                                                                             AC

Typography by Erin Fitzsimmons
16 17 18 19 20   CG/RRDH   10 9 8 7 6 5 4 3 2 1

First paperback edition, 2016

For my sister:
who was my very first fan,
and for all the fans that followed.

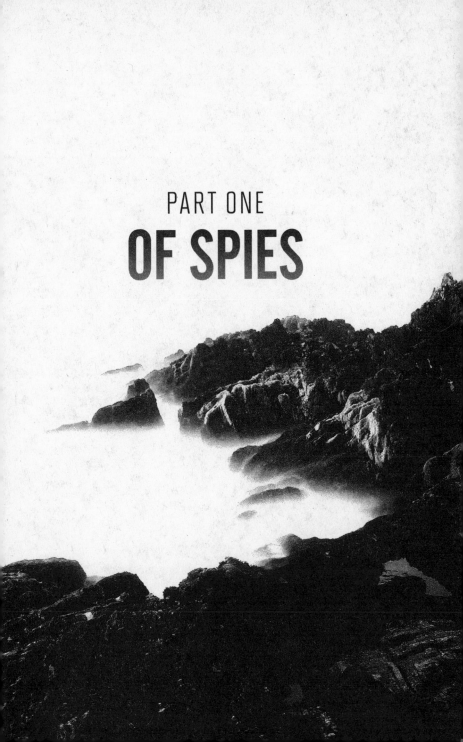

PART ONE
OF SPIES

ONE

MY SURROUNDINGS ARE BECOMING FAMILIAR. I never expected this to happen. I thought we would have done something by now, made progress, marched on Taem, lobbed a threat Frank's way. *Anything.* But no. There's been no forward action, not that I can see at least. We are falling into routines and growing comfortable in them. We are letting the days drift by like we have time to waste.

I've complained—politely at first, bluntly after that. They keep telling me the same thing: *We're planning. Planning takes time.* As far as I'm concerned, the longer we sit around, the more advantage we give Frank.

"I'm saying something again tonight," I tell Blaine. "This

is ridiculous. We should be out there *doing* something. Not sowing crops."

He stops breaking up the soil he's working on and rests a forearm on the handle of the rake. "You're just gonna stir the pot."

"Maybe it needs to be stirred."

He raises his brows knowingly, then stretches, arms reaching toward the gray, segmented ceiling of the greenhouse. It looks like the notches of a giant pill bug. Sterile. Unattractive. The hum of artificial lights fills the space between us.

"It's been two months," I say, "and all we've done is sit in a few meetings and pull weeds."

"And what do you think we should be doing? Marching to Frank's door? Knocking and asking him if he'd mind stepping down and letting someone else give things a go?"

"It would be better than doing nothing."

"It would be reckless." He goes back to hacking at the soil. "And a death wish."

"Dammit, Blaine. His Order only gets stronger while we sit here. Screw whatever Adam and Elijah are dreaming up with Vik. I'm ready to swipe a rifle from the stores and round up my own team to head east."

"I don't remember you being so bloodthirsty."

"And I don't remember you being so content to coast. To let

everyone else make decisions for you. Especially important ones. Don't you miss Kale?"

"Of course!"

"Well, you could have fooled me."

Blaine doesn't take the bait about his daughter. Doesn't snap or yell or even give me a good shove. He just frowns. "Do you want to talk about it yet?"

"*It?*"

"Whatever happened during your mission with Pa that caused this rift between us."

I catch Sammy and Bree in the corner of my vision. They're working two rows away and have both paused, eyes drawn by my raised voice.

"There's nothing to say," I mutter to Blaine, and return my attention to the soil.

He doesn't argue. At least his hatred of confrontation has remained constant. It feels like the only thing I can count on these days.

We were fine the first few weeks following our reunion at Sylvia's—an Expat safe house west of the border—blinded by the joy of being together after so much time apart. Then friction started to surface. Awkward silences. Moments when I realized I had no clue what he was thinking. Situations where I could have used support and he didn't bother backing me up. Like with all this stalling, this inactivity. We used to read each other so well, and even if we didn't always agree, we understood. The way only brothers—*twins*—can. But now I catch him looking at me sometimes—eyebrows drawn, mouth twisted in a puzzled pinch—and it's like he's regarding me as a stranger. In the time that passed between my departure from Crevice Valley and our reunion, something changed. Something drastic.

I probably shouldn't be so surprised. How *could* Blaine understand? He didn't see Pa take a bullet and go down with the *Catherine*. He didn't have to kill a Forgery of his own brother or watch friends fall around him. He doesn't wake up every morning knowing that half of Group A's people died on account of his decision to strike an allegiance with the Expats.

It's no wonder I find myself relating better to Sammy these days. And Bree. Always Bree, though she's been as forthcoming as a brick wall since we left Sylvia's for Pike. Still, they understand because they've been through it with me. They know the true extent of Frank's ruthlessness, the way a Forgery can be merciless and sly. It's practically a part of us now, those horrors. It's like witnessing it made it crawl beneath our skin and leech on to our souls.

Emma as I last saw her flashes through my mind—Forged, her eyes narrowed, her gun pressed to the back of Xavier's skull. Frank still has her—the *real* her. He has Emma in his grasp, and Claysoot under his palm. Maude and Carter and Kale. Kale with her blond curls and small nose and pudgy fingers. I don't think I appreciated how amazing it was to be her uncle until I was separated from her.

I hack at the earth beneath my feet. A hard chunk of soil crumbles into finer particles. The bond between Blaine and me isn't fully broken, because he senses my temper.

"Just hold off on saying something 'til tomorrow, okay? Today's Clipper's birthday. Let's enjoy it."

A reminder of the date—the last day in February—only unsettles me further. We've been in Pike working with the Expats for two months and have nothing to show for it. Although I *am* farming in the middle of the winter. That would impress anyone in Claysoot.

"I'll even back you up when the time comes," Blaine offers. "But give the kid a show for the night—smile, be *pleasant* if you can manage. Everyone would probably appreciate it, not just Clipper. What do you say?"

I give him a long look, then go back to raking the soil.

"That wasn't a *yes*," Blaine says.

"It wasn't a *no* either."

We work in silence, the clink of tools creating a rhythm for our labors. I watch Bree out of the corner of my eye. She's stopped to massage her left shoulder.

"Hey, guys!" A voice echoes through the greenhouse. I

straighten to see Jules, Adam's niece, running to meet us. She's gorgeous and she knows it, and even though I've only seen her in a few meetings, scribbling down notes at Adam's request, she seems to think we're best friends.

"Hey," she says again, breathless as she finally reaches us. Her dark hair is sticking to her neck. "You've gotta come quick. Adam's called a meeting."

This gets everyone's attention.

"What for?" Sammy asks.

"No clue. It's something big, though. He told me to get you all fast, everyone on Elijah's team."

"Maybe we're finally going to *do* something," I say, gathering up the tools.

Jules laughs like I've made a hilarious joke. Throws her head back and everything. She may be eighteen, but I swear she acts ten most days.

"You joining us for drinks later?" Blaine asks her. "Clipper's a man as of today. We're all going to celebrate."

"Poor kid," Sammy chimes in. "He's been through more crap than any thirteen-year-old I know. Talk about loss of innocence."

"How sentimental of you," Bree deadpans.

"Sentimental? I'm just saying I assume he can handle his alcohol like an old-timer, given all he's been through. How many rounds do you think he'll hold down?"

Blaine shoots Sammy a look. "He's *thirteen*."

"And you're the one who just said thirteen marks manhood. Pardon me for wanting to be sure he gets a drink. Or seven."

They go on arguing about rites of passage as we stow the tools. After two months of afternoon greenhouse duty, we're skilled at making everything fit in the exceptionally small storage shed. All Expats are expected to carry some weight in exchange for a room, and not a day goes by that I don't wish I'd been assigned to a task at the base. Sure, we spend our mornings training—target practice and drills—but working soil every afternoon has left me out of the loop. Apart from the few meetings we've been invited to, all I've managed to learn is that my leathered hands aren't so tough that they won't blister from working a hoe, and that artificial lighting can make a person sweat just as impressively as the sun can.

By the time the tools are stored away, Sammy is taking bets for how many drinks Clipper will hold down tonight. We make for the exit, and Jules nudges me with her elbow. "You joining Clipper's party?" she asks. She has the longest lashes I have ever seen.

"I haven't decided."

"Come on. Live a little." She grabs my wrist with both hands like it will convince me. She's sticky from her run. "I'll buy you a drink. Two even." She leans in, drops her voice. "Unless you're after something else altogether."

I shrug her off. Probably a bit more aggressively than needed. She doesn't seem to like that.

"I'll let Adam know you're on your way," she announces to the others. Then she turns and sprints out. She reminds me of a deer, all lanky limbs, eager. But with the tenacity of a hawk.

"Way to spook her off, Gray," Blaine says. I take one look at him and know what he's implying.

"I'm not interested." My eyes drift to Bree, but she's busy smacking dirt from her pants. "Besides, I don't know why Jules wouldn't cling to you instead," I say to Blaine. "We're identical, and you're at least nice."

"I think she likes the brooding ones."

"All girls like the brooding ones," Sammy interjects. "I think the only type they like more are the charmers. Humorous. Good-looking. Tall and toned, with green eyes and killer biceps and—"

Bree snorts at Sammy's description of himself.

"What, you don't like that?"

"Arrogance is such a becoming trait."

"Who said anything about arrogance? I was describing physical features, Nox. *Attractive* features. If anything, that's vanity." He flashes a smile. "You can't really blame me though, right?"

Bree rolls her eyes. "So what do you guys think Adam wants?"

"No idea," I say. "But I know what I *hope* this meeting is about."

"Me, too. I'm sick of sitting around."

I watch her rub her sore shoulder again and wonder how it is possible for the two of us to want the same things and think the same way, yet not be together. But Bree's stubborn. She's kept her word since telling me she was putting herself first. She's stood at a friendly distance. Said friendly things. Smiled but never flirted. Turned down everything I've thrown her way, be it apologies or advances or shameless begging. Even still, I haven't stopped trying. She forgets I'm as stubborn as she is.

It's been years since citywide climate control was used in Pike, and while the protective dome keeps the streets free of snow, cool winter temperatures hit us as we step from the greenhouse. Cut off from the east, the Expats had to decide which assets were necessary to power and which they could go without. Their trolley system hangs inanimate, cars hovering on their tracks in random locations throughout the city. Instead of being plastered with electronic signage, the walls are plain cement and brick and wood and glass. But the biggest difference between Pike and Taem is the lack of the Order. There are no black-suited soldiers here, no forces storming through town with the Franconian emblem on their chests. Nearly half of Pike's citizens consider themselves Expats, members of the group that years ago waged war on the East and still looks to eliminate Frank today. The others just shuffle along, wishing their people would finally accept defeat. *We cut ourselves free years ago*, I've heard them muttering. *Why can't we keep it like that?*

Pike has a smell about it—salt from the sea that finds its way beneath the dome by clinging to people's clothes. What can't be grown within the city itself is hauled from the ocean and land beyond its doors, then sold in an open market. As we pass the street lined with vendors, I watch a boy not much older than Clipper wrap a fish in brown paper and toss it to a customer. She thanks him and carries on her way. I can see why some people here just want to forget Frank. They are set in their ways. Almost content.

And *this* is why I fear how idle we've been lately. If it weren't for Emma or Kale or Claysoot, I could see myself forgetting the need to fight, happily uncurling my fists.

The Expat base comes into view ahead—a drab, sprawling building checkered with windows. The only sign of color on the entire facade is a red triangular flag hanging above the main entrance. Inside the triangle is a blue circle, and inside that, a white star. The Expat symbol. Not too different from the emblem Frank uses for his Order.

"Frank chose a red triangle for obvious reasons," Adam said when he first showed us to the base, like we'd asked him for a history lesson. "A color of power and strength, and a shape with a sturdy base, near impossible to topple. Good in theory, but dangerous when you think that it is one man who rises to the top of it, and labels the whole as his own." I thought of the cursive *f* in the center of the Franconian emblem differently after he said that. "So the Expats put a circle within that triangle, to represent balance and equality, and we chose a star rather than a label. All nods to our past, to what Frank's forgotten."

I've seen the symbol throughout town, sometimes a smaller version of this flag, other times a haphazard carving on a door, but always making the same announcement: *This home/business supports the Expats*. It seems silly to oppose the Expats—they're largely responsible for keeping the city of Pike running—but unlike in Taem, people here don't fear for their safety because they disagree with people of power.

Sammy stops just outside the base's main doors to fish a pebble from his shoe, and we all pause with him. Bree again rubs her shoulder. I look at the spot she's still massaging. I used to be able to touch her whenever I wanted—she welcomed it, even—and now, when she's what I want more than anything, she's so far away. Bree catches me watching and frowns.

"I miss you," I say.

"I'm right here," she responds sharply. "I've *always* been right here. That's half the problem."

The base is huge: an old military facility made up of training fields, weaponry stores, vehicle garages, barracks, and meeting and communication offices. We head for the smallest of the conference rooms, which is where Adam and Vik hold all their meetings. Or at least the ones we're invited to.

"You might want to make yourself comfortable," Vik says when we file in. He's sitting on the far side of a long table, legs crossed. "The others are on their way, but I have them double- and triple-checking a few things first. Want to be sure."

Vik is Adam's opposite in nearly every way. Clean-shaven. Polished. Willowy and pale haired and charismatic. He's a man of many words, with a bounce in his step that is almost graceful. When we first landed in Pike, I was surprised to learn that *he* leads the Expats. Adam is second-in-command and reports directly to Vik, but Adam looks the part in a way Vik doesn't: rugged, worn, ready for a fight. I guess Vik's pristine appearance could assure people that he's organized and professional, but his build reminds me of Harvey—a touch delicate—and it's surprising so many have put the fate of their battle behind someone who looks so . . . *nice*.

Vik stands when Adam strides in. "Well? Is it confirmed?"

Adam hurries over and they embrace the way they always have—a hug as intimate as if they were siblings. When they step apart something is passed between them in the silence, told with just the shifting of their eyes. Elijah and Clipper are in the room now. I didn't even hear them come in. One look at them, and I know this meeting is not about taking action. It's about something much, much worse.

Adam scratches the stubble on his chin. Vik smooths his pressed pants.

"I'm afraid we have some bad news."

TWO

WE WAIT WHAT FEELS LIKE an eternity.

"We lost contact with Rebel headquarters earlier today," Vik says finally. "A little before noon."

"And you're just telling us now?" I say. "It's nearly dusk!"

Elijah pivots toward me. "We didn't want to worry you if it was only a temporary communication issue."

"You knew about this, too?" Sammy says.

Elijah doesn't answer. By the look on Clipper's face, I'm guessing the boy also knew. Of course he did. He's been allowed in the com offices with higher-ranking Expats on account of his tech skills, and if it weren't for our ridiculous greenhouse schedule, he likely would have told me by now. Clipper keeps no secrets from me. I realize then that he's crying. Silently. The tears paint two glistening rivers down his cheeks.

"Don't be too hard on Elijah," Vik says. "I didn't loop him in until very recently. Not until after Clipper was able to help us confirm a few things."

The boy nudges his twine bracelet—a gift from his mother— with his forefinger. It swings lazily around his wrist.

"What the heck is going on?" I demand.

"Clipper tried everything, but we can't get through to the Rebels' technology wing. He doesn't think it's a connection issue either. It seems more like . . . well . . ." Vik sighs.

I know what happened. I know it and it's slitting my chest open.

"Will you just spit it out, Vik?" Bree snaps. "We're all thinking it. Put us out of our misery."

"We think they've been hit," he says after a moment. "It was only a matter of time, to be honest. I'm half surprised it didn't happen sooner. Frank has always suspected the Mount Martyr Range as the general location of the Rebel headquarters. It's possible he took a risk and decided to level the whole of the mountains with an air attack."

Our group is silent, numb. The only sound is Clipper, who has finally started to cry audibly. His mother is still at Crevice Valley. Or was. And he couldn't get through to them. Couldn't confirm or deny anything. All this on his birthday.

Sammy is right. I don't know a single thirteen-year-old who has worn heavier burdens than Clipper.

"Last we talked to Ryder was 1900 yesterday," Vik continues. "He didn't mention any suspicions regarding a possible attack, nor had he received any warnings from his Taem spies. This strike seems unprompted, unless Frank was responding to Rebel antics Ryder didn't share with us. We're holding out hope we'll hear from him soon, but it's not looking good."

Blaine and I make eye contact. Ryder didn't want to send Blaine west. It was supposed to be only Elijah overseeing our new alliance with the Expats, and if Blaine and I hadn't demanded otherwise, my brother could be dead right now. And all those people still at Crevice Valley . . . The entire goal of teaming up with the Expats was to grow our numbers, and now every single Rebel who sought shelter there is potentially gone.

Unable to bear it anymore, I jump to my feet. "Can we finally do something? Fight back? Or are these casualties not large enough?" Blaine tugs at my sleeve, urging me to sit, and I shake him off. "Over two thousand of our people are potentially *dead*. What else needs to happen before we act?"

"We *have* been acting," Adam snarls. "Bleak's traveling to Expat safe houses and trying to rally any fellow Burg survivors who want to join our fight. We've got a bunch of our own men along the Gulf working with September to tip loyalties in Bone Harbor. Rebel and Expat spies are gaining numbers within domed cities. We are waiting for the pieces to align—for the moment when we can strike, all at once, in multiple locations. Any offensive attack before we are truly ready could backfire and set us back indefinitely."

"You can dress your logic up however you want, Adam," I say. "It doesn't change the fact that Frank is getting stronger while we do nothing. That more of our people suffer while we tiptoe around miles from the fight, using the excuse of *planning* to calm our consciences."

"We all want the same things here, Gray, so don't imply this loss doesn't hurt everyone. Or that the Expats aren't as invested as you."

I catch Bree in the corner of my vision. She's shaking her head, a tiny movement that is not reprimanding, but cautious. A warning. Like she means to say she agrees but now is not the time. I clamp my mouth shut.

"Gray does have a point," Vik says. Adam, who was leaning toward me from his side of the table, stiffens.

"I only mean that if Frank did indeed attack, it cannot be shrugged off," Vik explains. "If we don't counter in *some* manner, what message will that send? Clearly, Frank's comfortable going after any lead that might hurt us, no matter how vague his information. He didn't have direct coordinates for Crevice Valley, and it appears he acted anyway. He has resources to spare and is fighting dirty." Vik turns to address Elijah. "We will shuttle you east immediately to survey the damage with a small crew."

Elijah nods. In moments like this, I forget he isn't much older than me. Other than the flask he keeps sipping from, he looks completely unfazed.

"As for everyone else," Vik continues, "I want you back in this room first thing tomorrow morning. 0700. We have a lot to discuss."

He escorts Elijah out, one hand on the captain's shoulder, the other splayed across his own heart as he offers sympathies. This is why Vik is in charge and not Adam. This nurturing side, this ability to make people feel loved and cared for.

Heidi—Adam's sister, Jules's mom—sticks her head in the room. "Can I steal you?" she asks Adam.

Adam grumbles something and stalks off, leaving our original mission team—the few of us left from the trek to Group A in December—alone with Blaine. Ten of us set out from Crevice Valley and only four of that group made it to Pike. September, our cook and weapons expert, stayed behind in Burg. Everyone else is dead, two of them lost directly to Emma's hands. Well, her Forgery's. The same Forgery who reported information about Rebel headquarters to the Order. Nearby coordinates, not direct ones, but in the end, it didn't matter. Frank suspected a certain location and Emma's last tracker transmission was close to it. He took a chance, and the Rebels' defensive grids couldn't stop an air attack.

"So . . . ," Sammy says.

He's never been good in situations like this—too used to cracking jokes and delivering sarcastic comments. Then again, I'm not in my element either. Clipper is still struggling to gain control over his tears, and it hits me again: He is only thirteen.

"It's still not confirmed, Clip," I say. "She might be okay."

"Some birthday gift, huh?" he says between sniffles.

The idea of a party—drinks and darts—suddenly seems ridiculous. "Hey, if you just want to head to bed tonight, we all understand. Whatever you need."

"No," he says, sitting up. "Don't change the plans." He wipes his cheeks dry. "I want to keep things as normal as possible. Let's have that party. I think I could use a drink."

"I don't know if—"

"You just said anything I want," he snaps.

I glance at Sammy, who looks like he wants to take back his

comment about treating the kid to several rounds.

"You got it, Clipper," Bree says. "Come on, I'll get you your first."

After grabbing dinner from the mess hall, everyone makes their way to the bar. Everyone but me. I can't bring myself to celebrate a birthday with the fate of Crevice Valley still unconfirmed. I pace the halls, head to the barracks and shower just to keep my mind occupied. In the end, being anxious alone seems even more absurd than being anxious with friends. As it is most evenings, the bar is packed when I finally arrive.

I find Clipper and Jules facing off against Sammy and Bree in a game of darts, the others watching. When Clipper spots me, a dumb grin streaks over his face.

"How much did you give him?" I ask Bree.

"Enough."

"Great, he's just drinking so he can forget."

Bree examines the tip of her dart, then glances up at me. "That's why everyone drinks heavily, Gray: to forget."

"You know that's not what I . . . Look, he's just a kid. I think—"

"Treating him like a kid is what's dangerous. He's one of us. If he thinks we don't see him that way, it will be nothing but trouble."

"He's gonna be passed out in—"

"Relax. I let him have one drink and then switched him over to watered-down stuff. He doesn't know the difference, and if he does, he clearly doesn't care. Point is, he *feels* like he's included, that we're not babying him, and I'm pretty sure that's what he needs right now."

Clipper throws his last dart and turns to us, the grin still on his face.

"You need a drink," he says to me. "I want a birthday toast."

"We'd have initiated that in the end," Blaine says. "You don't have to demand it."

I wave a thumb over my shoulder, letting Blaine know I'll visit the bar.

"Grab one for me, too?" he asks, and goes back to teasing Clipper.

In many ways, the bar reminds me of Crevice Valley's Tap Room. This place has cleaner edges and uniform tables, but the energy is the same. Music is seeping from a far corner—the strum of a lazy guitar. The lighting is dim and the space around the many tables crowded. After a day of work and a lifetime of worries, the Expats here are seeking out a little merriment, trying to forget the grim uncertainties for a while.

Forget. Just like Bree said. Does that girl have to be right about everything?

I raise two fingers for the bartender and tell him to charge the drinks to Adam. It's worked every other visit, and I don't think Adam is going to start complaining now. In fact, I'm starting to wonder if this is his way of bribing us: drinks at night in exchange for another day of pointless work in the greenhouse.

The bartender slides two glass mugs my way. I'm gathering them up, a palm cupping each, when I'm hip checked playfully.

"You were supposed to let me buy you one," Jules says. "Remember?" She leans into me until we're touching from shoulder to elbow. She's so tall she barely has to look up at me as she blinks those lashes.

"Guess it slipped my mind."

"Then why don't we just talk awhile? I'll drink my drink"—she waves for the bartender—"and you can drink yours. I mean, you owe me after all."

"I don't owe you anything. And aren't you in the middle of a game of darts with Clipper?"

"Riley took my place."

I glance over and sure enough, there's Riley, a miniature Jules of fourteen, only skinnier and still without curves. Clipper sure seems pleased about the change in partners. I didn't think it possible, but as Riley shows Clipper a better throwing technique, the dumbstruck expression that was previously only on his lips moves into his eyes.

"See? No need to rush back. In fact, we are perfectly capable of celebrating Clipper's birthday from here." Blink, blink, blink. "Or elsewhere." She touches my forearm.

I pull away.

"What? You honestly don't want to get out of this place with me?" She gives me the most seductive smile she can muster. She *is* pretty. "Well?"

I raise one of the mugs in Bree's direction. "You see that girl, Jules? She's the only person I want to leave this bar with. She's the only girl I want, period."

"And you've told her that? Because she doesn't seem all that interested in you. Actually, I can't help but notice she doesn't seem to give you the time of day."

This, like she knows Bree. Like chatting occasionally at dinner makes them best friends. Like offering Bree special Expat meds for her cramped gardening muscles or whatever they were going on about a few weeks back makes Jules an expert on Bree's desires.

"Doesn't change the fact that she's still all I want," I say.

Jules's expression hardens. "Maybe you should start thinking about what you want if you can't have her, Gray. Who are you on your own? Because it looks like you're going to stay that way."

She snatches up the drink the bartender delivered and heads back to the group.

I'm glad she didn't wait for an answer, because I don't have one. The truth is I never imagined much of my life beyond eighteen. For so long, that marker was a foggy, black void, a milestone draped in unknowns. The only thing I believed for certain was that my Heist would be the end. I've lived longer than I ever thought I would, and now that there's more beyond eighteen—a possibility that we might actually beat Frank and I could carve out the life of my own choosing . . . Well, I don't know what to do with that sort of prospect.

"Damn, if that's not a look that scares me." Sammy is standing beside me, ordering another round.

"Huh?"

He points at my face. "You went all serious." He scrunches his nose in disgust.

"What do you want to do with your life? After all this is over?"

He rests an elbow on the bar and leans his weight into it. "Be happy. Get old. And maybe fat. But only if I've got a girl by my side and a bunch of children running around and no reason to still look like a catch." He winks a green eye. "I'd probably try to learn a few guitar chords, too. My dad used to play before he . . . Well, you know. What about you?"

"I'd want to settle somewhere quiet," I say, trying not to overthink things. "I'd want woods nearby so I could still go hunting, and I'd want a small house. I guess something simple like what I grew up in. I wouldn't mind privacy either, so long as Blaine was around. Oh, and Kale, too. She grew so fast in the two and a half years I knew her." Sammy is staring at me like I'm a stranger, but I keep right on rambling. "I'd take up whittling, because my father always was fond of it. And I'd try to enjoy it all—every last moment, the highs and lows, even the people who drive me crazy. I'm starting to see life's too short to hold grudges and judge everyone, you know?"

Sammy glances at the two drinks I'm still clutching. "How many have you had?"

I shake my head. "None, but I must be drunk anyway, because I somehow want you around, too. Even though you're a pain in the ass."

"Likewise." Sammy's eyes drift back toward the game, where Bree is taking aim at the dartboard. "How come she's not in your story?"

"I'm still working on those details. Which is probably the same reason Emma wasn't in yours."

His face pales. We haven't talked about Emma recently. Not for at least a week. We both still worry about her, both still love her, even, but in different ways. My feelings for Emma are unconditional and irreplaceable, but they've settled in a new territory since escaping Burg. I love her the way I love Blaine, or Kale, or Clipper. Even Sammy. She's someone I'd die for, but for completely different reasons than why I'd also die for Bree. It's so obvious now, these feelings, that I'm not quite sure how I was ever confused.

Sammy forces a smile, clinks his glass against one of mine in agreement. "For what it's worth—and pardon me because I'm about to get painfully serious—I don't think you should give up on her."

Bree throws her dart. It strikes a thumb's width from the bull's-eye.

"I was never planning on it."

We toast Clipper and celebrate late into the evening. Everyone has a bit too much to drink. We try not to think about what's awaiting us tomorrow or what Elijah might find when he reaches Crevice Valley. I wanted a reason to resume forward momentum, but not at this cost. Plus, now that our meeting with Vik looms, I'm starting to worry about what he has planned for us. The last mission I was a part of saw over half our team die.

Sammy has Riley in a fit of giggles from a napkin he's rolled up and scrunched between his upper lip and nose—a ridiculous white mustache. Bree and Clipper are attempting to re-create the look themselves. The boy looks especially determined to make Riley laugh as Sammy does. Nearby, Jules is sitting on a tall stool at an even taller table, talking with Blaine. They're laughing about something, their proximity dangerously flirtatious. Blaine brushes the tip of her nose with his knuckle and she bats those eyelashes. Better at him than at me.

I keep wishing my buzzing head would warm to the merriment surrounding me, but when I look around, all I see are faces that might not make it. The odds have never been good. Not in anything the Rebels have faced.

I don't want to lose any of them, and what stings most of all is the very real possibility—a deep, unyielding fear—that I won't possibly be so lucky.

THREE

DESPITE THE FACT THAT ADAM is missing and Sammy can barely keep his eyes open, the meeting begins promptly at 0700.

With the exception of Blaine and Jules, who disappeared from the bar well before midnight, the rest of us didn't retire until closer to two. By that time, Clipper was dozing off on a shabby couch, Riley out cold with her head on his shoulder. After a lot of nudging he grumpily followed us to bed. When I collapsed on my bunk, I couldn't help but notice that Blaine's was empty.

He sits beside me now, looking a lot more agreeable than he has the last few weeks. His hair is wet from a shower he didn't take in our bathroom. I raise an eyebrow at him and he just smiles. Good for him. Maybe he'll be carefree enough to finally side with me in these meetings.

Vik kicks things off unceremoniously, announcing that there still hasn't been any word from Ryder. He promises more details as soon as Elijah is able to survey things and contact us.

The doors bang open, and Adam walks in, looking a bit disheveled. "Sorry I'm late. Did you tell them yet?"

Why are we constantly a step behind?

"You're well aware that we have forces gathering in various areas," Vik says to us, completely ignoring Adam's entrance. "And if your group is still anxious to play a part, we've got an operation you can help with."

Vik glances at me, waiting. I realize I'm somehow in charge again.

"I've made it clear we're ready."

He slides a glossy piece of paper across the table: a bird's-eye view of the New Gulf. I saw maps bearing the same visuals aboard Isaac's ship. AmEast and AmWest are divided by a blue chunk of water, which spreads north through two-thirds of the land before splitting into two thin bays. Vik touches an island in the dead center of the Gulf.

"You know what this is?"

"The Compound," I say automatically. Isaac told me, my father, and Bo about it. I can feel the group's surprised eyes on me. "It's a water treatment plant."

"Wrong," Vik says. "About its purpose, not its name."

"They're working to purify salt water there," I say. "I'm sure of it."

"That's just what they want everyone to think. We've got reason to believe this place is far more important."

"What could be more important than water purification?" Sammy asks.

Adam grins from where he's standing, slouched against the far wall. "Frank's got enough water. He's *always* had enough."

Sammy shakes his head. "But it's rationed. You need water ration cards. And my father . . ." He swallows, letting the statement fade out. His father died—was executed—for forging them in Taem.

"There was a time, right after the Continental Quake, when water was in short supply," Adam says. "But our numbers are fewer than they were before the War, and this country is rich in forests and streams and lakes. There is water—plenty of it—if you venture beyond a dome to seek it out.

"The truth is that Frank's convinced his people they need his protection. He controls what they know and what they read. He fabricates stories and with the right delivery, they are accepted as fact. Remember what we discussed when you first arrived here?"

I think back to the moment. Adam introduced us to Vik,

who immediately assigned us greenhouse duties. Only Elijah and Clipper would be working directly with the Expats. I'd been furious, yelling about how the Expats were using us for their own needs, how I shouldn't have been surprised given that they'd attacked Taem—a city filled with thousands of innocent citizens—just months earlier.

It was then that Adam had laughed.

"We live beneath a dome of the same exact strength," he said. "If we were going to use precious resources to flatten Taem, don't you think we would have known exactly what to drop?"

The attack as I witnessed it flashed through my head: planes flying in formation, the sirens blaring through town and inducing panic.

"Was it staged?" I muttered, barely believing my own words.

"Not quite," Adam said.

"We act only when we have a chance for success," Vik explained. "That's meant small things. Along the border, on the Gulf. We've got some spies in Haven. But the last time the West truly attacked the East, it was our distant relatives, ages ago, with an engineered virus. And we will do everything in our power to not watch so many innocent lives fall again.

"We knew the attack last fall wouldn't breach the dome, but

I had to send Frank a message. He was tossing threats our way, growing land hungry along the border, and I needed him to know that I wouldn't stand for it. I wasn't going to submit or crawl back under his rule. The only united country I want to see is one without him in it. I should have known how he'd twist everything—broadcasting that the Order barely held us off, that Taem had been just moments away from annihilation at our hands."

Another lie. Another brilliantly altered tale Frank passed off as fact. And now . . . with the water . . .

He's always had enough. Years of water rationing just helped him create a constant state of uncertainty. It gave civilians another reason to rely on the Order and never leave the safety of a dome. The world outside might have been deadly once—during the War, when the West's virus spread rampant—and Frank's made sure that fear never died.

"So if the Compound isn't a water treatment facility, what is it?" I ask.

"That's exactly what we want you to find out. If you're willing to take the job."

A handful of problematic details surface: how far we are from the place, the way it's surrounded by water and heavily fortified, Isaac's comment about the number of guards patrolling it night and day.

Vik senses my hesitation and goes into compassion mode.

"I understand your concern. Truly, I do. It's a lot for us to ask, but we wouldn't ask at all if we didn't think it could mean something huge for our side.

"We'll arrange transportation for you and assign a specialist to guide the team. But Frank—the Order—is up to something there. We need to learn what, and plan our defenses accordingly. Maybe we can even use whatever he's hiding to our advantage."

Blaine and Sammy glance sideways at each other, looking skeptical.

"This idea that the Compound is more than the Order lets on . . . ," Bree says. "Where did it come from?"

"What do you mean?" Adam looks insulted, like Bree's questions are a personal attack on his character.

"I mean," she drawls, "if we're heading to a seemingly unbreachable location and being asked to breach it, you had better tell us what led you to believe it's worth checking out."

"Some of our spies on the Gulf have been suspicious of the place for a while," Vik says. "They claim boats come in and out, but not frequently enough to be handling mass provision shipments of drinking water." Vik pushes another photo across the table, this time of a man I've never seen. "That's one of our best spies, Nicholas Bageretti. Sells water to AmEast under the alias *Badger*. He says he's found a way in."

For me, it's enough. More than enough.

Clipper and Sammy don't hesitate when I tell them to get ready. Even Bree refrains from being difficult. But Blaine has yet to pack a single possession.

"I think it's a death wish," he says as I toss clothes into a bag.

"I think it's a great lead."

He stops pacing between the bunks. "A lead? How? Vik's asking us to approach a heavily patrolled area and stick our noses inside. I bet all we find is a bunch of weapons and war provisions. I don't see how that can help us."

I take a deep breath and squeeze the handle of Pa's carving knife, pressing the etched shape of our last name—*Weathersby*—into my palm.

"We blow the place up. Or steal the supplies. Sabotage it. It doesn't matter what we do so long as it's some sort of setback for the Order."

"We're not prepared. The whole thing is—"

"Blaine!" I turn on him, let his name come out of me like a whip. "Look," I say as evenly as possible. "Badger claims he knows a way in, and Vik is going to exploit that with or without us. If we don't take the job, he'll just send someone else. This is our chance to *do* something. Be a part of the big strike he's planning."

"The strike he's planning but hasn't shared any details

about," Blaine mumbles. "What do we really know about this Badger guy? He could get us all killed."

"I read about him in some underground papers in Bone Harbor. He's been selling water to AmEast citizens right under the Order's nose. Badger's good and he knows what he's doing. He'll get us in. And anything we need to plan further, we'll figure out before we get to the Compound."

Vik has a chopper set to bring us to the small Expat settlement of Pine Ridge west of the Gulf. From there, we'll get in touch with Badger. We need to be ready within the next hour, which means packing fast, and asking questions—the detailed questions—later.

"I still don't like it," Blaine says. "We shouldn't go. We—"

"Do you even care that Pa is dead?" I erupt. "I'm trying to make his sacrifice worth something. Trying to get us back to Emma, Claysoot, *Kale*. Remember your daughter, Blaine? Or are you fine pretending she doesn't exist either?"

His fists grab the front of my shirt, his momentum sending me backward. My shoulders hit the wall, followed by my head.

"Don't you dare," he hisses. "I think about her every damn second."

"Sure doesn't seem like it."

"Just because I don't say something aloud doesn't mean I'm not feeling it. But this is so like you—jumping to conclusions, saying whatever comes barreling into your head."

This is the closest we've come to a fistfight in years. I half want him to throw a punch, but he won't. I know he won't.

"I used to think you were so much better than me," I say, staring him down. "I'd always beat myself up over how selfless you are, putting everyone else first, being so sickeningly *decent*, and it's like I don't even know you anymore. Because this isn't decent: wanting to sit around and do nothing but work soil and fool around with Jules. It's cowardly."

"You arrogant—"

"Pack or stay, Blaine!" I grab his wrists and tear myself free. "I don't care what you decide so long as you don't stop me from doing what's right."

A muscle ticks in his jaw. We stare at each other for a painfully long moment. Then he picks up his bag, throws a few things into it haphazardly.

"You're an ass, you know that?" he says. Dark shadows linger beneath his eyes, and he's squinting slightly, almost as though looking at me blinds him.

"I've always been an ass."

He either doesn't hear the teasing tone of my voice, or he chooses to ignore it.

"I love you, Gray. I always will. Which is why I get so riled up by the fact that you can't see how losing you would kill me."

He snatches his bag and leaves, and I realize for the first time that all his hesitations could be for different reasons—ones that have nothing to do with not wanting to remove Frank from power or returning home to Kale.

He's still trying to keep me safe. Just like he did when we were kids—shielding me from a slingshot blow with his own body, or pulling my curious hand away from a flame. Blaine is never going to outgrow playing big brother.

I stop by the female quarters and find Bree making her bed like the room is more than a temporary home.

"Here goes nothing," I say.

She straightens, turns to face me. "It'll be a breeze, I'm sure. Getting in off-limits places always is." Her eyebrows are raised with the joke, the corners of her lips curled in a smile.

"Can't go much worse than Burg, right?"

She swings her bag onto her shoulders. "Don't tell me to hand over my gun when I need it, and we should be fine."

The reminder of how she took a beating at Titus's hands because I convinced her to lower her weapon makes me cringe.

"Oh, don't give me that look. I bounced right back. Even have a nice battle scar as a result."

She's speaking of the thin mark above her left eye, a pale

echo of where stitches once held together split skin. I reach out, my thumb eager to trace it, and she pivots away from me. It's quiet for a moment, the air heavy with how things once were between us.

"We should go," Bree says. "They're probably waiting."

She attempts to squeeze by me and I grab her elbow before she can escape into the hall. "I'm not going to stop trying, Bree."

"Then you're an insensitive jerk who doesn't respect me," she snaps. "Or what I want."

"You really don't want us to talk? Ever?"

"That's not what I said." She's scowling, looking at her feet, the doorframe—anything but me. "It's complicated," she says finally.

"Explain it, then."

Bree stares down the hallway. Licks her lips. Finally, she glances back at me. "I still trust you on missions like this, I do. I still want us watching out for each other. I just don't want to be anything more."

I don't believe her. Not for a second. But then I wonder if that's because I'm doing exactly what she said: not respecting her decision, choosing my own feelings as a greater, more worthy truth. I let go of her arm and the tension in her body dissipates. Her shoulders relax. She peers at me, as if she's trying to read my thoughts.

"Come on," she says, but I feel like I've managed to pull her closer by letting her go and the concept is so bizarre that I stand there smiling, my feet fused with the floor.

"What's the matter with you?" she asks.

"You," I say. "You make me a mess."

She rolls her eyes and *hmph*s. But she also gives my chest a light shove before walking away. Contact. That she initiated. The first since Burg.

FOUR

UNLIKE BONE HARBOR, PINE RIDGE sits along a narrow inlet
instead of a cove. We fly over a long stretch of dry earth and
rust-colored rock to get there, and when we arrive the tide
is out, making the town look impressively dreary. From
the sky, the community is a horseshoe around the empty
trench, pockets of water still pooled in the deeper areas,
with bridges spanning it at various intervals.

We touch down well inland, where the inlet is fed by a
small river butting against a narrow ridge of pines—the
landform that likely gave the town its name. The smell of
salt hits me when we climb out of the craft. We haul the gear
from the helicopter and Heidi disappears almost immediately. She must have her own orders to attend to.

The outer edge of town is marked by a failing wood fence, and it is here that a young man reclines, hip against a post and ankles crossed. When he sees us approaching, he pushes off the fence and tosses his rolled smoke in the dirt.

"Adam?" He gives a hesitant wave, then presses a fist to his heart, three fingers splayed out so they almost look like a capital E given the angle he's holding them. "You're here for Nick?"

"It's that obvious?" Adam says, mimicking the Expat salute.

A smile flickers across the guy's face. "Chopper kind of gives it away. So, what were the plans again?"

"We never said. Can't be too careful in gulfside towns these days. I'm sure you understand . . ."

"Gage," he finishes. "Man, I'm sorry, rattling on and not introducing myself. I've been working the waters with Nick for about a year now." He pulls out a new smoke and lights it. "We were competitors before that, but Nick bought me out, which was a blessing, really. It was only a matter of time before he'd have run me under. He's a hardnose, Bageretti. But that's why he's the boss, not me."

"And does the boss have an address for us?" Adam asks.

"Oh, right!" Gage slaps at his shirt pocket, jacket pocket, then finally his pants. He pulls out a scrap of paper, and with his smoke still bobbing between his lips, reads, *"Our third choice.*" He exhales smoke from the corner of his mouth, expression puzzled. "I swear, this is right from Nick. He said you'd understand."

"I do." Adam swings his gear back onto his shoulder. "Thanks, Gage. We're good."

Curt, direct, a man of few words. That's Adam.

Gage doesn't look fazed, though. He takes another drag of his smoke and tucks the scrap of paper into his pocket with a shrug. Maybe Badger always saddles him with these sorts of message deliveries.

"You all set with the rig?" Gage asks. "I'm supposed to see to getting you refueled."

Adam says, "She's all yours."

As Gage passes by the group, he takes us in for the first time. The smoke nearly falls from his lips when he sees me and Blaine. He looks between us, confused, and asks, "Gray?"

Blaine shakes a thumb at me.

"As in Weathersby?" Gage continues.

"Yeah," I say.

"Damn!" he says, clapping my shoulder. "God damn!" He punctuates it with another clap. Up close, he's younger than I first guessed. Maybe Sammy's age. "You've been giving the Order one heck of a time. Well done, my friend. Well done."

"How do—"

"People are whispering on the water. Plus, your face is strung up back east, on wanted posters with a list of crimes as long as my forearm." He holds his up in illustration, eyes gleaming with approval. I think I like this guy, all wild enthusiasm. Optimism's been hard to come by lately.

"Well, we're all giving the Order a hard time," I admit. "It's not just me."

"It doesn't hurt that they're putting your face—and only your face—on everything," Bree says. "Helps the rest of us stay unrecognizable."

Gage's gaze drifts over my shoulder.

"Hello," he says to Bree, only he manages to draw the vowels out for so long that he has time to eye her from head to toe in the process.

"Do you need glasses," Bree says, "or should I come closer?"

Sammy chuckles as Gage stumbles to recover, but Bree is already stalking after Adam.

"Aw, come on," Gage calls after her. "I didn't mean anything by it. Let's get a drink later or something. Give me another chance. I promise I'll behave." She's well out of earshot now, and Gage acknowledges defeat. He gives a disgruntled exhale and turns to me, Blaine, and Sammy. "If you feel like a few drinks tonight, I'll be at the Wheelhouse— along the inlet. Come if you can get away."

He takes a long drag on his smoke and heads for the

chopper. We dart after Adam and the others.

As the inlet widens, the buildings go from spotty to cramped, and begin climbing in height, as though the town has been extended vertically in order to keep residences as close to the Gulf as possible. Rarely less than three stories, they seem to lean on one another, weary gutters and roof tiles intimate friends.

A gull screeches overhead. The last time I heard that cry, I was standing on a beach with Bree and staring at a rough patch of water where the *Catherine* had sunk the previous night, taking my father with her. There are days when I still don't believe he's truly gone. He stepped into my life over the summer, and out of it before winter could thaw. Our time together barely equates to two seasons. I'm not sure which would have been worse: never knowing him, or only knowing him the few months I did.

". . . not even to other Expats," Adam is saying when we catch up. "Where we're staying, the details of the plan—that remains between our team and the one Badger's assembled. This close to the border it's always best to err on the side of caution. Ah, this is it."

He points to an establishment as skinny as the rest. A bookshop, according to the lettering on the window. We stagger our entrance so as not to draw attention, which seems like overkill. The only activity in the street is a group of kids playing catch.

Inside the shop, two chairs flank the doorway, and a patch of light from a window above each dusts their cushions. Walls to the left and right are overflowing with books—leatherbound, clothbound, hard and softback. I've never seen so many. The shelves continue along the back wall as well, where a lanky man of about thirty stands behind a counter. He's so engrossed in what he's reading that he doesn't acknowledge us. Not even with the bell above the door chiming every time it's opened.

"Charlie," Adam says, leaning over the counter and plucking the book clear out of the man's hands. "Is Nick in?"

Charlie snatches the book back. "You've some nerve, Adam, getting between a man and his read."

"We're on a schedule. Is Nick here or not?"

Charlie returns to reading. "I don't know who you're talking about."

"Don't pull that with me. I don't have to prove myself."

"You absolutely do after interrupting this action scene."

Adam puts a hand on the book and pushes it onto the counter, forcing eye contact with Charlie. "I'm looking for Nicholas Bageretti, who goes by Badger on the market, and Nick among friends. The real patriots are Expats." Adam makes the same fist-and-E salute he had when greeting Gage.

"That wasn't so hard, now was it?" Charlie says.

"It was annoying."

"So think twice before interrupting a reader." Charlie grapples with something on the wall of the bookshelf behind him, and an entire section of the bookcase swings inward to reveal a hidden room. "Badger's in the back."

"Some rumors about Badger and his work have made it to the Order," Adam explains to us. "If spies come 'round asking for him, he's good and hidden. Charlie doesn't let anyone past the storefront unless they're on first-name terms with Nick and know the Expat slogan and salute."

Adam raises a hinged section of the counter, and we all skirt through to the back room. It's loaded with jugs of water: on shelves, on the floor, in crates piled on top of one another. The bookcase closes behind us with a heavy *shwack*, and at the far end of the room, a man jumps. He's small and scrawny, sitting in a leather chair that practically swallows him. Maps and ledgers litter his desk.

"Nick," Adam says in greeting.

They shake hands vigorously and mutter about clientele numbers they can't keep up with. The rest of us stand there, a bit confused, until Adam finally introduces us.

Nick has skittish eyes, beady and eager looking, and seems to start at the smallest noises. Bree sneezes and I swear he almost falls over. I remember something Isaac said about the man being "shifty," and I see it now, the animalistic edge to him, like he's trying to sniff out danger. His alias is certainly fitting.

"So this is the team?" he says, taking us in. "The girl's perfect—right age, small, spry, can probably get in and out of tight places—but I don't know about the rest of you."

"I'm flexible," Sammy says, looking highly offended at being told he is not spry.

"Is being small important?" I ask. "We weren't warned about that. Probably would have picked the team differently if we'd known."

"It's not a necessity," Badger says. "Just a preference."

"Well, in that case, we're all coming and that's the end of it."

Badger's hand goes to the gun at his hip. He doesn't draw it, but I can see the defensive nature of his stance. It's odd that someone so twitchy could be a spy. Or maybe that's a casualty of the job—always on edge, never fully trusting.

"He's okay, Nick," Adam insists, putting an arm on Badger's shoulder. "They're good, all of them. I promise you."

"What would be good is knowing the plan," I say. "When do we go over details?"

"I've got to follow up with one of my crew this evening," Badger says. He checks the ammunition in his gun. Pulls a second from the back waistband of his pants, checks that one, too. Satisfied he has enough rounds, Badger opens the bookshelf door. "I'll brief you all tomorrow, and we'll hit the water the morning following."

Then he exits the bookshop, bell chiming in his wake.

"Well, I sure feel great putting our lives in his hands," Bree deadpans.

"No kidding," Sammy says.

"He's one of the sharpest men I know," Adam says. "He has his reasons for ducking out. Badger never does anything without a plan."

"So y'all want to see where you're crashing for the night?" Charlie sticks his head into Badger's office. Now that he's not absorbed in a book there's a lot more life to his face. He seems happy we're here, rather than inconvenienced by our presence.

We follow him out of the hidden room and back into the bookshop. He motions to a spiral staircase I hadn't noticed before, and we head up to a spacious second-floor apartment. A small bedroom and bathroom sit off to the right, but otherwise, the floor plan is open, with the kitchen and sitting areas overlapping. A fire burns in a woodstove. This seems downright dangerous given the number of brittle pages below our feet.

"I sleep in the loft," Charlie says, pointing to another spiral staircase that leads up to a third level overlooking the common rooms. "You guys can fight over my sister's room 'til she gets back." Sammy and Clipper immediately bolt for the bedroom. "Everyone else is going to have to crash on the couches or floor. Should be cozy given the extra guests that are coming."

"Guests?" Sammy echoes, pausing enough to give Clipper the advantage. The boy slips into the private bedroom, whooping triumphantly.

"I need to play catch-up while in town," Adam explains, "and that starts here. Tonight."

Downstairs, we hear the bookshop's door chime. A moment later there are feet pounding against the stairs. A flash of copper tears into the room, a small boy trailing after.

"Rusty!" he shouts. "Calm down, boy!"

September appears next, grinning at the sight of us. She has such harsh features that something about the expression looks wicked.

I haven't seen either of them since our mission to Burg and I'm so shocked at the sight of them—here, in Pine Ridge—that I can barely get my mouth to work.

"I thought you were supposed to be finding him a home?" I point at Aiden, who is still chasing Rusty through the apartment, hands outstretched as the dog's nose explores every last floorboard.

"That was the plan. But I got attached to the kid and let him stay with me when I found a safe apartment. And he's come in handy. The Order is inspecting every vessel leaving or arriving in Bone Harbor these days. Something about having a kid and a dog with me when I travel makes the lie that we're visiting relatives more believable."

Aiden and September could not look more unrelated—his complexion is nearly as dark as my hair, whereas September is fair—but there's an undeniable innocence pouring off the boy and his dog. It must be enough to draw eyes away.

"Where's Jackson?" Aiden asks. He's finally given up on chasing Rusty and has paused to assess the group. "And Emma?"

Dead. Both Forgeries are dead.

Jackson bent his will to help us escape Burg, only to be murdered at the hands of my own Forged counterpart. Emma betrayed us, although Aiden never knew her true nature. He adored her, just as he did Jackson. What should be a cheerful reunion is shaping up to be anything but.

"Are they coming later?" Aiden asks. "I want to play Rock, Paper, Scissors with Jackson."

"I'll play," I offer.

"Okay. And then Jackson when he gets here."

I bite my lip. It's all Aiden needs to know the truth.

"They're not coming, are they?"

I shake my head.

"Not ever?" A tear trails down his dark cheek.

"No. I'm sorry, Aiden."

He crumples to the floor and dissolves in tears. "It's so unfair," he gasps out. "I hate it and it's not right and it's not fair."

"That's life, kid," Bree says, which only makes his tears come faster. She drops to a knee and touches his elbow. "Aiden?" He coils into himself. "Aiden, look at me." Finally, he glances through teary lashes. "Life is rarely fair," Bree says. "It's hard. Really, *really* hard. Sometimes terribly cruel. But the bad stuff isn't worthless because it makes us stronger, and you are going to be so strong, Aiden. Understand?"

He blinks a few times, then throws his arms around Bree's neck. The look on her face is priceless—first shock at the hug, then pleasant surprise as she envelops him in return.

It was what he needed to hear. Not that everything was okay. Not even that everything would *be* okay, because who can promise that? Bree spoke the hard, honest truth, and somehow, it pulled the world back beneath his feet.

Charlie says something about dinner, and the tension dissipates as we shuffle into the kitchen.

FIVE

AFTER EATING, MOST OF OUR group drifts away from the table. Clipper stumbles off to bed, exhausted, and Blaine and Sammy disappear downstairs after swiping a bottle from Charlie's liquor cabinet. He dozes on one of the couches, blissfully unaware of their theft. Camped out on the second couch, I'm in the middle of a game of Rock, Paper, Scissors with Aiden, but most of my energy is spent listening in on Adam's conversation.

He's sitting at the kitchen table with September, discussing the state of Bone Harbor and the number of supporters she's rallied. Somewhere else in Pine Ridge, Heidi is having a similar discussion with Bleak. I sort of wish it was happening here. I miss the guy. Want to ask him if his outlook on life is still . . . *bleak*.

From what I pick up, September has been busy in Bone Harbor. She's assembled a team to forge inspection slips so vessels carrying freshwater can slip in and out of harbor more easily, and she's also struck up a friendship with the woman who runs the *Bone Harbor Harbinger*, an underground newspaper aimed at exposing Franconian lies and providing tips and insider info for struggling AmEast citizens. The paper now serves as an additional Rebel recruiting outlet—if read from front to back, taking in only the corner words on each page, locations and times for meetings September holds can be deciphered. But most notably, September is using the paper to combat the lies spread on Franconian signage. The *Harbinger* prints stories about how I stole a vaccine to ensure the Rebels' safety last fall. How I freed Burg from Frank's clutches, eluding an entire squad of Order soldiers in the process. How I fled to AmWest—to people who are *not* the enemy—and am currently rallying Expats to aid in the East's fight for justice.

The pieces sport slogans like *Lead the way, Gray*, and *The wanted Expat: a fugitive for freedom*. I see Bree's point—how focusing on my face and name keeps everyone else safer—but I'm not the miraculous, one-man hero these stories paint me as. I'd have been a goner in any of those past situations had it not been for the help of numerous others, and everyone deserves to know that.

As the discussion shifts to technology, it sounds like September's been spending a lot of time in a basement lab similar to the one Sylvia had beneath her Expat safe house. September's been using this place to communicate not only with Ryder, but with fellow supporters in the domed cities of Haven, which I've heard of, and Lode, which I have not.

"We lost touch with Crevice Valley around the same time you did," she says to Adam. "We had started sending digital files of the *Harbinger* to Ryder a few weeks earlier, and he was working to spread those around Taem. I'm guessing one of his crew got caught, because the day before our lines died, the Order ran a search and seizure effort in Bone Harbor looking for the press. They tossed our place good, but didn't find the trapdoor. Maybe when Frank couldn't crush the paper at its source, he just retaliated on Crevice Valley? Leveling it would at least cut off the supply of the paper to his city."

"It's possible," Adam says. "Makes a heck of a lot more sense than him striking out of the blue. Especially when he's already suspected the location for months."

Aiden covers my fist with his palm. "Paper beats rock. *Again*. Are you even trying, Gray?"

I nod enthusiastically.

"We're still hoping for the best," Adam continues. "And Elijah should know more about the damage soon. Actually, he might have already reported back, but I haven't reached out to Vik yet. Now about the key cards . . . Were you able to get them squared away?"

Aiden clunks my two exposed fingers with his fist. "Gray, you're bad at this."

"Maybe you're a supergifted, mind-reading cheater," I tease.

I try to make out what's being said about the key cards, but Aiden won't quit jabbering.

"That's what Jackson always said: that I was reading his mind." The boy tenses up at his mention of the Forgery. "I'm glad you're here. And everyone else. Even Bree. She had that gun when I met her in Stonewall, but she's just not as bad as I thought."

"No, she's not bad at all," I agree. "She's pretty awesome."

Aiden squints at me. "She's pretty? Or she's awesome?"

"Both."

"You *like* her," he says, eyes wide like he's accusing me of a heinous crime.

"Well, I wasn't trying to keep it a secret."

"Yuck. Girls are gross."

I wrap my palm over his fist—I've finally won a round—and give it a playful shake.

"Just wait, kid. You might change your mind."

"Never. And if I do, I've got at least"—he looks at me, counts our age difference on his hands—"ten years still."

I raise an eyebrow. "Try more like four or five. *Tops*." His nose scrunches up. "Don't believe me? Ask Clipper about Riley."

As if on cue, Clipper emerges from the bedroom, yawning and mumbling about being thirsty. Aiden scrambles off the couch and tails him into the kitchen.

"Clipper, how old are you? And who's Riley?"

I head downstairs, grinning. It's dark in the bookshop, but I can hear Blaine ranting to Sammy about something as I descend the stairs.

"I just don't understand what happened," Blaine says. "I know he's been through a lot, but he's acting like I'm a stranger. It's like he can't stand to look at me."

"Well, he did shoot a Forged version of you," Sammy responds. "That probably messed him up a little."

"He what?"

"I thought you knew."

"No!" Blaine practically shouts. "He didn't say a thing. He didn't even—"

They see me now, because I haven't slowed or bothered to stay quiet. Blaine's holding the bottle in one hand, and it's obvious he's had too much. His eyelids are heavy, his mouth hanging open.

"Why didn't you tell me?" he demands.

"Because I knew you'd never let it go. That you'd ask every single day if I'm okay. And I am. I'm fine! Things are hard enough already without adding more guilt and grief to the situation."

"So it's better to act like it didn't happen? To keep me in the dark? No wonder I can't help you."

I hate when Blaine sounds disappointed like this. He acts like all I've ever done is inconvenience him. To him, I'm a child. A small, helpless thing he has to take care of.

"If you were truly concerned you would have *demanded* answers, Blaine. But that would have been too hard, standing up to me, butting heads. So you drag Sammy into it and dance around the issue from a safe distance. Where you won't hurt or upset anyone. Well, guess what, Blaine? I'm upset. It backfired and I'm so upset I'd throw a punch if I didn't think you were too wasted to slug me back."

I knock into his chest as I storm onto the street. If I were a better person I'd take a few deep breaths and shake it off, accept that Blaine is drunk and talk to him about it in the morning. But even then it won't change the heart of the problem. I now have what I never wanted: Blaine's pity. Blaine worrying about me more than he already does. Blaine acting like the damn parent when I've already had and lost two and what I really need is my brother. Someone who talks to *me*, instead of running off to chat about the things that haunt my nightmares with others.

I hear the door bang open.

"You're acting like a child, Gray." I walk faster, not sure where I'm going, but happy so long as it takes me away from Blaine. "Gray! Don't you dare—"

I twist. "What? Speak my mind? One of us has to."

"I was going to say don't you dare leave," he shouts back. "You're running away from your problems because you're too scared to face them like a man."

That does it. I'm on him in a heartbeat, my left hand clutching the front of his jacket, my right curling into a fist. Sammy forces his way between us, shoves me backward.

"Go cool off!"

"Stay out of this, Sammy!"

He shoves me again, so hard I stumble. "Now, Gray!" With his other arm around Blaine, Sammy pulls him toward the bookshop. "Inside," he orders. "Gray will be back when he's ready."

And then they are both gone, the door slammed in my face.

I stalk down the unlit street, fuming, my legs moving fast enough that I eventually break into a jog. The cool night air feels good in my lungs, helps Blaine's words merely sting rather than burn. Sammy knew what I needed more than my own brother. How is that possible?

I run for a few blocks, and slow along a street that runs parallel to the inlet. The squawk of a rowdy crowd can be heard ahead, where a patch of light streams from an establishment. It's a pub. The Wheelhouse, according to the sign hanging above the entrance. Two patrons stand just outside the door. It's not until I'm closer that I recognize them. Gage and Bree.

"What are you doing here?" I ask her.

"Sammy told me Gage had invited us all for drinks, and I needed to get out," she says. "That place was suffocating."

"You gonna join us?" Gage asks. "It would be a real shame if you passed, know what I mean?" He jerks his head toward Bree and winks at me.

I don't think I like this guy anymore.

"We should go," I say to Bree.

"Nah, the fresh air's been good."

"Bree, I'm not suggesting it."

"I think she can speak for herself, Ace," Gage says. "And besides, the night is young. You want a drink? I'll go grab a couple." He shoves off the wall and heads inside.

I move to follow, and Bree blocks my way. "What is your problem?"

"You honestly don't see what he's after?"

"I can see just fine," she says. "But he's been perfectly civil since I got here, so how about you have a drink with us instead of babysitting me like I'm five?"

She takes her hand off my chest. I could walk after Gage now, but it all feels like a test.

And I don't intend to fail.

SIX

I LEAN AGAINST THE WALL and try to pretend like I couldn't care less that Bree's been out here talking with Gage all night. Tilting my head back, I survey the stars. A whole blanket of them. Pinpricks of light. Small, yet stunning.

"They're phenomenal, huh?" Bree says, even though I haven't commented on them out loud. She's got her head back, the arch of her neck bared to the evening. The night sky reflects off her pupils, which are massive in the moment—as wide and eager as they should be under such poor lighting.

The day we arrived in Pike, I told Adam about the telltale sign we'd discovered for identifying Forgeries—how their pupils don't dilate properly—and suggested we check everyone after the betrayal Emma's Forgery committed right beneath our noses. Bree pitched a fit, claimed I was walking a line that toyed with our faith in one another at a dangerous level. Clipper also sided with her, but in the end, because Adam said the entire thing was voluntary and that it would only look suspicious if they *didn't* participate, they yielded.

Vik had everyone in the Expat base pair off, and Bree and I ended up together. She stared at me blankly as I passed the beam of a small flashlight before her eyes, watched her pupils expand and contract. A Forgery's would, too, according to what we'd learned, just very subtly. An unnaturally minimal change.

"We should be coming up with safety questions," Bree said. "They'd be more effective."

"How's that?"

"What Forgery is going to let you get close enough to shine a light in their eyes? *Oh hi, I'm not sure if you're human, so would you mind submitting to this eye test real quick?*" She scoffed. "It's ridiculous. We should be asking questions that have answers a Forgery would never know."

I lowered the flashlight. Owen had asked the Forged version of Blaine personal questions when he first found us in Stonewall, and we both saw how that panned out.

Sensing my reservations, Bree sighed. "Look, when you see me, if you ever doubt that it's actually me—even for a second—just ask what my favorite bird is. Growing up on Saltwater, it was herons. They were the most graceful animals I'd ever seen, and I was obsessed with them. Thought they were magical, even. A Forgery will answer wrong based on those memories."

"And the right answer? Now?"

She took the flashlight from me. "Loons."

I was deeply puzzled by that choice, still am. Why would her favorite bird be associated with one of the ugliest moments between us? That night on the beach, when I said things I wish I could take back.

"What about you?" she said as she began to check my eyes.

"Ask what the biggest mistake of my life was, and I'll answer that it was doubting us. That I told you we wouldn't work."

She lowered the flashlight, scowling. "Why do you insist on making this hard? Isn't there another question? *Anything* else?"

"Probably, but that's the deepest, truest thing about me right now. It's one of the only things I know for certain."

She snapped the flashlight off and stood so aggressively her chair skidded back. "Congratulations, Gray. You're not a Forgery." But she left like I was: quickly, hurried, as though she couldn't put enough distance between us.

Bree turns to face me now, the starlight disappearing from her perfectly human pupils. "Will you stop staring? It's creepy."

I smile and look away. "Sorry."

"No, you're not."

I smile wider and her elbow prods my side. More contact. Initiated again by her.

Gage returns with a pair of mugs and hands one to Bree. "I only had enough for two," he says to me.

How convenient.

I stalk inside to get my own, then realize I have no way of paying for it. When I come back out, Gage is talking about his work with Badger. He rambles about shipment schedules and various clients—some of which keep getting busted by the Order, but there's a waiting list a mile long to get on Badger's route, so it never hurts their business. Every detail is shared solely for Bree, Gage's frame angled so that I'm cut out of the conversation. When he tires of his own stories, he starts asking about our plans—when are we acting, what are we after, why?—and Bree keeps her answers vague. *Soon. Information. Because.*

"Well, Nick's a real genius," Gage says. "Doesn't miss a beat. You're in good hands, whatever that job of yours is."

He winks at Bree and my patience dissolves.

"I'm going to head back," I announce. "You coming?"

"Don't," Gage says to Bree, and points at her near-empty mug. "I was about to get us another round."

Now he magically has enough money for extra drinks?

Bree shrugs and nods in one motion. "Okay," she agrees. "One more." Then she jerks her head in the direction of the bookshop and says, "I'm fine, Gray. Really."

A nudge for me to leave.

I know there's no winning this one, so I say goodnight and head out, trying to ignore the jealous sting in my side. I get only a few steps away before Gage touches my shoulder.

"It's obvious you care about her," he says in a low voice, "so I just wanted to say don't worry. I'll get her home safe."

I force a smile. "I didn't doubt you would."

"You, Gray Weathersby, are a terrible liar." He takes a drag of his smoke and exhales out the corner of his mouth. I realize my right hand has curled into a fist and stalk off before he can notice he's gotten under my skin.

Back at the bookshop, I sit on the front stoop. I'm not ready to go inside and face Blaine, and I can't stop thinking about Gage, the way he winked at Bree and nudged her shoulder. I know his intentions, could read them in his sly smile. And even though Bree's tough, she's also small, no match for a guy twice her size if he gets aggressive. I should go back there in case . . . No, like she said, she doesn't need someone to babysit her. She's smart. And competent. And completely capable of taking care of herself. Heck, maybe she even *wants* Gage to make a move. Maybe that's why she stayed for another drink. The thought of him kissing her—of her kissing him back—makes my blood hot.

I hear footsteps. A figure storms around the corner. Bree.

"That ass!" she says, and I scramble to my feet. "He got all grabby as soon as you left. When I told him to stop, he just tried harder, so I kneed him in the groin and bailed."

My blood's nearly boiling at this point.

"You want me to go back there and hit the message home?" My hand is back in a fist. "I'll do it, Bree. Gladly."

"I could do it myself if I thought it was necessary. So thank you, but no." Bree sighs, her expression suddenly tired. It's this that makes me relax. She's annoyed and furious, but not hurt.

"Why are guys like that?" she says after a moment. "I didn't give him any sign that I felt like making out in a filthy pub."

"A girl like you—confident, gorgeous? Can you really blame him for trying?" She gives me a look. "At least the first time," I clarify. "The second advance was uncalled for."

"Which is why I kneed him."

"Naturally. He deserved it. Probably worse."

She grins at that. "He *definitely* deserved worse. I think he put something in my second drink. It tasted off. You sure read him better than I did, huh?"

I clap a hand to my chest. "Are you admitting that I was right for once?"

"Sadly, yes. But if you keep rubbing it in, I'll never do it again."

"You know, I could get used to this feeling. Being right. I think I only need about"—I make a show of counting my fingers—"a million more outcomes to go in my favor for us to be even."

"A million? When on earth did I rack up all these points?"

"I think it started when you told me I was fighting us."

The street seems to grow incredibly quiet as she turns toward me. Her expression is curious, her brows raised.

"You also said we challenged each other in a good way. Correct again. And that I hadn't given you everything . . . that I was distracted . . . that the fire was good . . . Correct, correct, correct. Should I keep going?"

"Yeah, I kind of like this list." She moves nearer, just one step, but our proximity changes from friendly to something more. There is mischief in her eyes, a playful twist to her lips. She hasn't looked at me this way in two months and suddenly I can't think straight. I open my mouth, but no words come out.

The scar above her left eye is brilliant in the moonlight. Brilliant and my fault. I reach for it, and this time, Bree doesn't recoil or twist away. She lets me touch her. I trace the scar with my thumb, and when I finish, she leans into me slightly, presses her cheek into my palm.

A small sigh escapes her.

A *yearning* sigh.

The sound sends a flare of heat through my chest. I grab her face with both hands and press my lips to hers before my nerve vanishes. She flinches with surprise, then relaxes, opens her mouth to mine. She kisses me back, desperately, rushed, and it's so perfect—us pressed together, breathing each other in like it's never been any other way—that my blood nearly dries in my veins when she whispers, "Stop."

I open my eyes. She's staring at my chest, how her palms lie against it.

"I . . . I can't," she says, drawing them back like she's been burned.

"You just did."

She shakes her head. "I want to be friends."

"Friends don't do that, Bree. Friends don't kiss like that."

"I want to be friends," she says again.

"And I want to be *more*. I want to be so much more and you're killing me."

I can feel the moment slipping away, sense her refortifying her wall. What is she battling? Her pride? Some promise she made to herself?

"Please don't do this, Bree. Please don't start fighting us when I've finally decided to stop."

"This was a mistake," she says, refusing to look me in the eye. "I'm sorry."

She slips into the bookshop and I stand there, struck through with shock, the taste of her still burning up my mouth.

SEVEN

WHEN I STUMBLE INTO THE kitchen the following morning, Badger is already frying eggs. I don't know when he returned to the bookshop, but the smell of breakfast is so intoxicating, I'm easily convinced to focus on eating over asking questions. In fact, I haven't said a word since Bree left me on the stoop last night. It was easier to crawl straight into my sleeping bag and avoid my problems than to face them. Now, it feels like my dispute with Blaine has doubled in size overnight, become just as glaring as the sunlight streaking through the apartment windows.

Blaine doesn't say a word as I sit down at the table, doesn't even look my way. This is so wrong, us fighting. Nothing lingered between us in Claysoot. We'd argue or wrestle or throw a punch, and then we'd be laughing two minutes later, rebounding so quickly we could barely remember what we were fighting about to begin with.

Still, tensions with Blaine might be preferable to dealing with Bree, who acts as though nothing happened last night. She asks me to pass her a plate and then smiles her thanks like the gesture won't slit my chest open. Soon the kitchen is buzzing with activity, which is a relief. Hands reach and overlap, plates are filled, mugs are clung to. The table is surrounded by yawns and bedhead and casual chatter. Aiden still hasn't stopped pestering Clipper about Riley.

"I told you, Aiden. I hardly know her."

"That's not what I'm asking," the boy says. He slips a piece of bacon to Rusty beneath the table and Clipper shoots a murderous look my way. *I hate you*, he mouths. I stifle a laugh and shovel some eggs down so I have an excuse to avoid speaking.

"Everything go okay yesterday, Nick? With your crew member?"

Badger twitches at the sound of Adam's voice, sharp in the rowdy kitchen. "It was . . . uneventful. Probably could have skipped the whole thing."

"Well, that's not vague," Sammy says through a mouthful of egg.

"It was a personal matter regarding water shipments. If I

wanted you to have the details, you would."

"And yet we're putting all our trust in you to run this mission. The guy who refuses to give a straightforward answer."

"I don't need a wise mouth on this team," Badger snaps. "You have a problem with me, you can walk right out that door." He jabs the spatula for emphasis.

"All right, Nick," Adam says. "You've made your point. How about we talk logistics rather than arguing?"

Badger grumbles something unintelligible and dumps the last batch of eggs on the serving plate.

"The Compound," he says, tossing a handful of sketches onto the table. "From what we've gathered, the entire first floor is a shipment center. A channel of water drives right into the island, and we've watched boats come and go, docking beneath the building itself."

In an aerial depiction, I can see what he means. The island is oblong: round at one end, and split by water on the other. Part of the Compound hovers over the channel, its foundation set in the land on either side.

"Most of the boats frequenting the place are commercial cargo vessels. But 'round nightfall on the first Friday of each month, an inspection team stops by on a small rig. They are in and out in the course of an hour. We will be that crew for March's inspection, arriving two days early on account of a scheduling change."

I shift in my seat. This is not going to work. There is no possible way this will work.

"September's just delivered ID badges, plus key cards to get us through locked doors. The latter won't be a problem if we're escorted during the inspection, but we wanted to be prepared either way." He shoots a thankful look September's way and she raises her fork as if to say, *my pleasure.*

"Charlie's sister should be returning later today with our ride. She and her husband spent the last week tracking down a matching boat model from an Order scrap yard on the eastern shores of the New Gulf. Last we heard they found one in almost perfect working condition. They're just looking into a few spare parts."

"And it needed a paint job," Charlie says, emerging from the loft. He rubs his eyes with a fist as he descends the stairs. "Colors were all wrong and she had to get the Franconian emblem on its side."

"True," Badger says. "But that was four days ago, and they're due back today. I'm confident everything's been seen to. So that just leaves uniforms, and I've got Mercy over on Mooring Street whipping up three sets."

"Three?" I echo.

"One for me," Badger says, "and a pair for the rest of the team." He points at Bree and Sammy. "They are the only two setting foot inside. You and your brother are too recognizable given the way your face is strung up across AmEast—half the time on Order wanted ads, the rest in this crazed string of new propaganda. And the kid"—he nods toward Clipper—"is young, could raise suspicions. You can come on the boat if you insist, but the only way I do this mission is if you stay on it."

"I came so I could *help*, not sit around," I say.

"You want to help?" Badger tilts his head, blinks his beady eyes. "Go pick up the uniforms with your brother. They should be ready."

"Great. Running errands. What would you do without us?"

"How is Mercy making uniforms when she doesn't have our measurements?" Bree interjects.

"I gave them to her," Badger says.

"How?"

"By using my eyes."

Twitchy and skittish as he may be, Badger doesn't miss a thing.

"Why are all the eggs gone?" Charlie asks, surveying the spread on the table.

"We ate them," Adam answers seriously.

"All of them?"

Sammy makes a show of inspecting the empty serving plate. "Looks like it."

"I'm the host! I'm supposed to be able to eat in my own house."

"You should have gotten up with the rest of us then," Adam says. "Or were you too busy reading?"

"Course I was reading. Those fictional characters are way more fun than you."

This opens up the floor for a bunch of friendly jabs. Bree: "The characters are probably better looking than Adam, too." Sammy: "Wouldn't take much to be smarter, either." Soon, the group seems to have forgotten all about the mission awaiting us, or the fact that Blaine and I are supposed to sit around like ducks during it.

When Aiden starts asking about the dogs in Charlie's book, claiming none can possibly beat Rusty, Badger leans across the table.

"You said you wanted to make yourself useful, so why are you still here?" I glare at him, and he slips me a piece of paper bearing Mercy's address. "Bring a case of water to cover the payment."

The crate of water is even heavier than it looks and the handholds boast rough edges perfect for wedging splinters in even the toughest skin. Blaine and I carry it awkwardly through the streets, trying not to bang it against our thighs. The address Badger provided is meaningless to us, so we stop to ask directions from a few local kids kicking a ball outside the bookshop. We've got hats on, and scarves wrapped to cover half our faces because of Badger's paranoid nudging. I doubt the kids can even tell we're related. They point us toward the Gulf and instruct us to head north along the water.

"It's a really skinny building," the shortest kid says, as if they aren't *all* narrow. "Painted bright red. Mercy's shop's on the fourth floor."

The thought of lugging the crate of water up four flights is enough to make me want to drop it here and now, but we carry on in silence.

The harbor is busy with boats. Most are modest rigs, the vessels of fishermen who are supporting their families and selling the extra catch in town. Nothing like the massive Order ship that chased the *Catherine* in December. The water laps at the barricade dividing the street from the Gulf, providing a steady rhythm for our march.

"Why you didn't tell me?" Blaine asks.

The pain of the crate driving into my palm is more preferable than his words.

"There's no easy answer," I say, tugging the scarf below my chin so talking is easier.

"I can't understand or relate or help if you don't *tell* me anything, Gray."

I stop, and he does, too, the crate swinging between us.

"You *can't* understand, period. That's the problem. Our lives used to be exactly the same—same routines, same fears, same end waiting for us on our eighteenth birthday—but then we got separated and started living different lives and . . ."

Is that all life is? Growing apart from people? I haven't seen Emma in months, Kale in even longer. My own brother feels like a stranger. We've always been opposites, but now it's something else, something far more complex than having conflicting personalities. It's like the more you grow to know and accept yourself—to find your own way in life—the more distant and mysterious everyone else becomes.

"We'll get through it," he says. "When this is all over, everything will go back to normal."

"You know it's not that simple, Blaine. There's no going back to how things were."

No longer able to bear the stricken expression on his face, I glance away. Between the shoulders of bustling townspeople, on the far side of the street, I spot a girl standing in the mouth of an alley.

Not any girl.

Emma.

She's wearing a white sundress despite the cold, her hair hanging over her shoulders in tangled waves. She looks exactly the way I remember her the day we went to Claysoot's lake and talked about birds. The shock I feel at spotting her here is mirrored on her own face. She backs down the alley, almost fearfully, shaking her head like she doesn't want me to follow.

"Emma?" I call.

A group of teens pass by, momentarily blocking my view. When they clear, the alley is empty.

I drop the crate. "Emma!"

Blaine grabs my arm, but I shake him off and break into a run, the crate of water forgotten. Blaine's shouts that I'm seeing things are swallowed by the wind.

I sprint down the alley and spot her at the next intersection. Her white dress is a beacon, screaming against the dreary shades of winter attire. I keep her in my sights, push my legs faster. I'm gaining on her—lost among the grid of streets given the number of turns she's made, but gaining.

I round another corner. This road dead-ends. Emma spins to face me, eyes wide, then skirts into a building to her right. It's a textile facility, or was. Looms tower, dusty and skeletal. Cobwebs cling to my face and limbs as I race after her. Beneath my feet, glass crunches, and a breeze drifts through the empty windowpanes.

I hear Emma trip on something. I duck between two looms

to cut her off, and find her on the floor, one palm bleeding from the broken glass. She scrambles to her feet, but I'm faster. She cries out in surprise when I grab her arm and push her backward, but I don't ease up, not even when I've got her against the far wall with nowhere to go. Her face is just inches from mine, and it looks exactly like her—that beauty mark on her cheek, her brown eyes gleaming—but so did her Forgery.

"When was the last time you saw me?"

She twists. "Gray, you're hurting—"

"When was the last time you saw me!"

"In Taem. Outside my room. After Craw . . ." She trails off.

From my belt, I grab the flashlight I no longer go anywhere without. With a click it's on and aimed at her eyes. She blinks rapidly, tries to shake me off. I keep her pinned there until I see what I need. Her pupils shrink under direct light, then expand when I move the beam away. Drastically. It's her. I let go, and she pushes me off, rubs her sore arm.

"What is the matter with you? You weren't supposed to follow me! Didn't you see me shaking my head?"

"Gray?" Blaine's voice echoes through the building, and a moment later he stumbles upon the two of us. His expression is nothing but shock—that Emma really is here, that I wasn't imagining things.

"You have to go," she says. "Before they come. They're

using me to get to you and you need to leave. Both of you. Right now."

"You heard her," Blaine says.

But I'm still staring at Emma, confused, bewildered. "Why did you even show yourself if . . . I don't . . ."

"They've had me in town for a few days, hoping I'd make contact with you. I thought they were crazy—why would you be in some random AmWest town?—but they were holding my mother's life over my head, so I played along. And then there you were, today, out of nowhere, just standing along the Gulf." She pauses for a moment to really look at me. Tears pool in her eyes. "Please go. You can't be here."

"Gray," Blaine urges, tugging my arm.

"I'm not leaving you again," I say to Emma. "Come with us. We've got people that can keep you safe."

She shakes her head. "They're watching me. You have to leave." The tears are streaming freely now, down her face, her neck.

"Dammit, Gray!" Blaine actually hauls me backward. I turn and shove him as hard as I can. He stumbles, and when he catches his balance, he is furious. "Will you separate your heart and your head for one minute? Use your brain! This isn't right. We need to get out of here. Finish the trade and head back to the bookshop."

"Screw the damn trade, Blaine! Screw the trade, and screw you."

I turn back to Emma, but she is no longer alone. There's a man restraining her, his grip tight on her wrist. I don't know where he came from. I didn't hear anyone else enter the building, but then again, I was yelling like a madman.

A second man steps between two looms. Like always, a smoke is pinched between his lips. He exhales in my general direction, then smiles.

"Gage?" I don't mean for it to come out as a question, to sound so obviously stunned.

Emma is screaming for us to run, but there are two more men already bearing down on Blaine. I wish I had a knife, or a gun, or *anything* other than a worthless flashlight. All that's left is my fists, and I don't even have a chance to use them. When I pivot to face Gage, his arm is already swinging, a club barreling at my head.

The world snuffs out like a candle.

EIGHT

I THINK WE'RE ON WATER. It feels like the floor beneath my feet is moving separately from me. My hands are bound in my lap, but I'm able to reach back and check where I was clubbed. I find a massive welt and wince.

I'm lucky it's not worse. I'm lucky I'm not dead.

"How are you feeling?"

Gage.

We're in a cramped bedroom with an extremely low ceiling. I'm on one bed, and he's on another, both feet planted on the skinny patch of floor that separates us. No longer in the dimly lit factory, I can see he has a black eye and wonder if Bree managed to clock him last night. The thought almost makes me smile. Then I hear the unmistakable sound of waves against a hull. We must be on water after all. Going who knows where.

"You're a snake, ratting us out like that."

"You act like it was easy," he says, "but you've seen how Nick operates. He had me deliver your lodging instructions in *code*, for God's sake! It took months of eavesdropping before I even caught wind of his vague plans to infiltrate some Order facility, how the infamous Gray Weathersby and a few Expats might play a part. So I passed along what I heard, and that pretty brunette got planted in town as a lure."

Gage draws a smoke from his jacket pocket and lights it.

"But then," he continues, "this is the best part: I was sent to meet your team! No one was very forthcoming with information—Nick's got everyone worked into a paranoid frenzy—and the chopper had exactly zero useful information stashed onboard, but I wasn't concerned. The team was finally in town. I knew you'd be moving soon, so I had the lure transferred closer to the docks. And when that blond fireball showed up at the Wheelhouse last night, I figured she'd spill everything if I buttered her up enough, showed her a good time. But she turned out to be quite the bitch. Called me a pig and everything."

"I'm sure you deserved what she dished out and then some."

He leans closer, blows a cloud of smoke directly into my

face. "Let's remember who's tied up and who's calling the shots. Show a little respect."

"Right, because you're clearly so deserving of it."

"Your brother and the brunette are above. If you want them to stay alive, you'll watch your tongue." He smiles at my newfound silence, the expression wicked. Why did he seem so likable yesterday when I first met him?

"Nick and his codes," Gage muses. "The funny thing is he thinks they'll save him, but whether it was the first, third, or *thirtieth* option your team decided on, it would still have been one of his hideouts: the restaurant, the bookshop, his sister's, that new post he's working to set up above the Wheelhouse." He taps his smoke against the rim of a near-empty glass between his feet. Ash swirls into the liquid. "But thanks to your brother spouting off about getting *back to the bookshop*, I don't even have to visit Nick's places one at a time. That twitchy moron won't suspect anything until it's too late, leaving the perfect window for me to visit the shop when I get home and finish the job. You will be back in Order hands, the man they know as Badger will be dead, and I'll retire a rich man of twenty-two."

"Why?" It's the only thing I can manage to get out. "You're from AmWest. Why would you *help* the Order?"

Gage stands, hunched slightly on account of the low ceiling. "I'm not helping anyone but myself. Nick ran me out of business and then had the nerve to act like he was doing me a favor by taking me on his crew. Bossing me around. Paying me next to nothing. Acting like I was too stupid to handle anything important. I can't wait to see the look on his face when he realizes I worked against him. His last thought before I squeeze the trigger will be that I pulled this off right from under his pointed, greasy nose."

I see everything in that moment: Gage talking about clientele falling to the Order, because he is the leak. Badger being so skittish and on edge. How he stepped out immediately after we arrived so that he could visit one of his crew. Armed. Ready to stop the leak. *It was uneventful. Probably could have skipped the whole thing.* Badger went after the wrong guy.

"He knew something was up," I spit out. "Badger knew someone on his team was defecting."

"Ah, but look who's on a boat about to hand a fugitive to the Order, and look who's still back in Pine Ridge with a slightly smaller crew."

The boat's motor slows before Gage visits me again. He secures a blindfold over my eyes and hauls me above deck.

We are shoved and shuffled to the edge of the boat. I assume *we*, but it's possible Emma and Blaine aren't heading where I am. Or that they're already dead. I strain to hear anything of use, but only Gage's voice is audible over the wind. Mist from the Gulf blows onto my front, icy pricks against my nose and neck.

"I'll report back when Badger's taken care of. If the others are with him, do you want them alive?'

An answer I can't make out.

"No, that's fine. I have no problem wiping the place clean. Happy to be of service."

Something mumbled.

"Tonight," Gage says sternly. "I'll do it as soon as I'm back. And then I get the rest of the pay? Good, good."

I'm shoved over the edge of our boat and hauled onto another. My shin bangs something. Hard. I keep waiting for the blast of a firearm, but it never comes. That would be too easy. They didn't go through all this trouble just to kill me.

Gage's boat roars to life, then fades out across the Gulf.

In the darkness beneath my blindfold, I picture Charlie complaining about eggs, and Aiden chasing Rusty, and Clipper's blushing face at the mention of Riley. Sammy cracks a joke about my tardiness, saying Blaine and I can find our way through a forest but manage to get lost among marked streets. Bree is unamused. She turns to Badger, scowling, and says something is wrong. Adam agrees.

They sweep the town and find the dropped crate of water. At Mercy's, they learn Blaine and I never arrived. When they get back to the bookshop they put an armed watch at the door and start weighing their options, discussing what might have happened, devising a plan.

These are the things I tell myself to dull the twisting sensation in my stomach, to ignore the bile scratching at my throat.

Their executioner is coming, but they'll be prepared. They have to be. I repeat it, over and over, not sure if I'm lying to myself.

We're moving again. I crouch on the deck to shield my face from the frigid air. Nearby, someone laughs, shrill and in tune with the clawing wind.

Far too soon the engine slows, then dies out completely. I'm lugged to my feet, off the boat, toward whatever—and whoever—is waiting.

PART TWO

OF COMPOUNDS

NINE

I CAN'T SEE A THING, but the rhythmic lull of the water and the soft thump of our boat against an unseen structure tells me we are in some kind of port. The strain of pulleys and the clank of cargo suggests a large one. Surrounded, somehow, given the echo. By mountains? Rock? Someone shoves me between the shoulder blades, forcing me forward. The ground beneath my feet is sturdy. Not dirt or mud like the streets of Bone Harbor or Pine Ridge, but man-made. Even and level. Slick with a sheen from the ocean.

"No, that one's going to Lode," I hear someone shout. "To Lode, you idiot! Dock 3B."

"What about the Haven shipment?"

"It went out yesterday, with the other cargo for Taem and Radix."

Radix. Another domed city? I tuck the name away and breathe deep. It smells different here than the other gulf-side ports I've been in. There's the normal salty air and the lingering stench of diesel engines, but there's also something cool and sharp about the place. I'm tugged along by an escort I can't see, and I start to feel like we're walking into the belly of a cave. A cave with damp, bloody walls, if the metallic tinge to the air tells me anything.

The *swoosh* of a door sliding open reminds me of Union Central, Frank's base of operations in Taem. The commotion and smells are cut off as the door closes behind us and the lighting—even from beneath my blindfold—changes. It is bright here.

I try to keep track of my path, but there are too many turns, plus a few levels. My escort pushes me—hard—and I fall to my knees. A door slams. It's pitch-black now. Even after I use my still-bound arms to pull the blindfold off I can't see much. I feel my way around the room. Maybe two wingspans by another two. Windowless. One door, locked.

Not a room. A cell.

I shout for a while, but no one comes. I wait, and that does no good either. I sit with nothing but my thoughts and the welt on the back of my skull.

I should have listened to Blaine's warning, should have known Emma being in Pine Ridge could mean nothing good. But I couldn't walk away. That was the beauty of her as a lure. Frank—the Order—knew this. After seeing Emma, I couldn't *not* investigate.

I rest my head against the wall. I wonder if Gage has made it back to the bookshop yet. I wonder if the team is ready for him.

My throat clenches.

The worst part is not that I am alone and terrified, but that I am helpless. I understand why Bree broke down when she was isolated in Burg's tunnels. Helplessness weighs on a person, and in tight quarters, it's downright suffocating.

I fall asleep leaning against the wall, and the unadorned room is lit when I wake, pale on three sides, a mirrored wall opposite me. I look far less tired than I feel.

"Morning, Gray," my reflection says.

I flinch, knocking my head against the wall. There's no mirror, just something—someone—far worse.

Forged Me stands.

"Where are the others?"

"They're safe," he says. "And they'll remain that way so long as you cooperate."

My insides curl. Blaine. The last thing I said to him. The

way we spent the past few days fighting.

Forged Me plucks at a fraying thread along the cuff of his uniform. An *Order* uniform, which means we're likely in an Order facility.

The Compound.

I wasn't on either boat for long, certainly not long enough to travel across the whole of the Gulf or get to any domed city. The place we docked, the way the noises echoed and boats were loaded—that must have been the shipping center, the channel of water cutting inland and slipping beneath the Compound itself. I feel foolish for not putting it together sooner.

I assume I slept through the night, that it is now Wednesday, two days prior to the first Friday of March, the day of our planned inspection. If Gage didn't get to the team, could they be on their way to me right now?

"Now I want you to listen to me very carefully," Forged Me says. "Gage gave us some disturbing news. He said Badger was planning to infiltrate an Order establishment and that you would be involved. He believed the strike would happen this week. Do you know anything about that?"

He looks so much like me. Identical. Down to the shape of his nose and the shade of his hair and the way his colorless eyes are veiled in shadow from being so deep set. The last time I saw this Forgery, our team was fleeing from Burg.

He slit Jackson's throat and then went crazy when our team slipped free. The image of him screaming as our car tore away from Burg's wall—back arched and arms outstretched— is seared into my memory. There is nothing I can do to sway his beliefs. Unlike Jackson, he is a newer model, an F-Gen5 like the Forged version of Emma we encountered. Forever loyal to Frank, a slave to his orders.

"It would be ironic if your goal was *this* establishment," he says, "seeing as you'll never leave it."

I keep my face as blank as possible.

"I will get answers from you," he snarls, "and it won't be pretty. Are you sure you don't want to speak up while you're still in possession of all your limbs?"

Is this what I sound like when I speak? Harsh? Emotionless? Threats bound to every syllable? I stare up at him, attempting to appear indifferent. I can't let him see that I'm terrified or he's as good as won.

"Fine. Just remember that you picked this."

He winds up and kicks me in the stomach. I'm still coughing when he leaves.

Someone reblindfolds me so that I can be moved. We ascend two levels, but I can't keep track of all the turns before or after the stairs. Now, with my legs and arms strapped to the corresponding parts of a chair, the blindfold is torn off.

The room is excruciatingly bright, but windowless. One wall is made of mirrored glass, and overhead lights glare, bouncing off it and the honeycombed floor tiles. I blink a few times, adjusting to the brightness. Behind me, I can hear someone shuffling through cabinets, and when I glance at the mirrored wall, I see the back of a white lab coat, its wearer hunched over to study something on the counter. A tray of menacing-looking tools waiting beside my chair catches my attention next. The restraints holding me in place seem suddenly tighter.

Directly in front of me, my Forged counterpart sits with one foot resting against his opposite thigh. A notebook is propped against his bent leg.

"Let's try this again," he says. "I want the details of whatever mission you were about to attempt with Badger, and I want the names of everyone involved."

I say two words to him, one of which is a swear.

"Now really, Gray. There's no need to be so hostile. Here, I'll even compromise with you and table that question for now. Fair? Let's start with something smaller: the location of the press that keeps printing papers with our face on the covers."

For once, I'm happy Adam kept so much information from me. I can't answer this question even if I wanted to.

"Nothing?" the Forgery continues. "How about one measly

name? An Expat or insurgent AmEast citizen. Anyone you want. High ranking or low. You give me the name, and I'll jot it down."

He is so smug, so relaxed. I can tell he's not going to drop the interrogation. *Interrogation.* I'm in an interrogation room. The tray of tools at my side becomes much more ominous.

Delay him, I think. *Just keep him talking.*

"You're not actually in charge of this place, are you?"

"Of course not. We just thought I might intimidate you most." He writes something down in his notebook, only to glance up at me in a manner that makes his eyes look like slits beneath his brow. "It's working, right?"

I grunt, worried that if I speak the truth will be evident in my voice.

"I'm waiting," he says.

"Well, keep waiting! I'm not telling you crap."

He waves a hand to whoever is behind me. "Gray's going to need a little convincing."

I hear footsteps, the snap of gloves being put on. The bindings on my limbs feel like they are tightening. My fight-or-flight instincts are screaming and yet I can't even lift my wrist off the armrest.

The white lab coat appears. Sits on a stool on wheels. Slides in front of me. And time slows.

I know this man.

His glasses are different—wired rims instead of thick black frames—but his eyes are the same: dark, a bit vacant, chilling. It's him, from his brittle-looking build to his slouched shoulders to his gaunt, hollowed cheeks.

"Harvey?" I say, and there is not an ounce of recognition on his face when he looks into my eyes.

TEN

"GO ON, MALDOON," FORGED ME urges. "Remind him why he should cooperate."

Harvey's fingers trail lazily over the tools and the only thought I can form is that this man should be dead. I saw proof of it, a visual projected above Taem the evening I fled back to the Rebels with Bo, Bree, and a Forged version of Emma. Harvey had been strung up like a scarecrow in Taem's public square, the Franconian emblem painted on his chest. His eyes had even been gouged out.

But the man before me has eyes. They are blinking, surveying his options on the medical tray. Maybe I saw it wrong. Or maybe that visual was a fake.

Has Harvey been alive all this time, stuck working for

Frank—a man he hates—because we deserted him?

Harvey selects a scalpel, then switches to a pair of pliers. He pivots toward me, the tool held out.

"Last chance, Gray," Forged Me says from his chair. "A name. Any name."

"Harvey?" He lowers the pliers toward my left hand, my pointer finger, the nail itself. My pulse jumps frantically. I start writhing in my seat. "Harvey, you know me, dammit! It's Gray! We worked with Ryder and the Rebels. We're friends. I'm sorry we left you, but we're—" The mouth of the pliers closes down on my nail. "Harvey!"

He looks directly at me, and I realize he doesn't care. There is no compassion on his face, no sympathy, no trace of the scientist I once knew. This is a man fueled by revenge.

He adjusts his grip on the pliers, and I know what's coming.

"Harvey, please! Don't do it. I'm so sorry. I'm so—"

He yanks his arm back and my nail goes with it. I scream, and scream, and in the flashes of red pain shooting before my eyes a memory also resurfaces: a hallway in Union Central. Harvey is ushered into a room by medical staff. His shoulder hangs limp and dislocated. His nose is bloody. They nursed him to health for his execution, just as I'd suspected that very day, but they also did more. I see it now, because the real Harvey—even one left for dead—would never go this far. Those Order members took what was necessary that day, did whatever they needed to set the wheels in motion, to create the thing in front of me now.

Why would Frank want the rebellious version of Harvey to resume work on the Forgeries when he could have a loyal one instead? Same brains, same skills, but programmed to follow any order. No chance for mishaps. No fleeing or backstabbing or abandoning his post.

This is not Harvey.

It is Harvey, Forged.

He drops my nail in the medical tray. My finger throbs, wet with blood. I can't get my pulse to slow, can't stop choking on my own ragged breaths.

"That was so quick," Forged Me remarks. "And to think you were having issues with orders in December. Take your time with the next one, Maldoon, and make it a finger."

Harvey sets the pliers aside and picks up a knife. I'm begging shamelessly now, stammering over the pain, screaming for him to reconsider. This is not the Harvey I knew—gentle, patient, *good*. If he remembers me at all, he's been told what to do and how to think, which pieces of his own past to forget and who to serve. His grip tightens on the handle. My skin breaks from the pressure of the blade, and as the white-hot spark of pain jolts through me, I panic.

"There's a safe house," I sputter, the place appearing to

me out of nowhere. Harvey pauses, my nailless finger now bleeding in two places.

"Where?" Forged Me asks.

"Near Group A, but west of the border," I gasp. "I don't know exact coordinates. The woman running it is named Sophia? Sally? She harbors people crossing the borders."

I've been as vague as possible—even changed her name—but I feel like scum. I deserve the pain, am not worthy of being spared it. Sylvia took our team in when we fled Burg. She saw to my wounded leg, patched up Clipper's arm. She fed us and clothed us—strangers—and I've handed her over like cattle for slaughter.

Forged Me makes a note in his book. "That wasn't so difficult, now was it?"

I am going to rot for all of eternity.

I'm back in the cell.

I have nine nail-bearing fingers, and one naked one. Its bandage is stained with my blood. Light pink near my knuckle where Harvey's blade sliced skin. Black where his pliers did worse.

I still haven't seen Blaine or Emma. I don't know if they're going through similar interrogations. All I have is a less than reassuring statement from Forged Me before he locked me in: He's going easy on me for now, but expects better results next time I'm questioned.

Nerves threaten to overwhelm me. The little food I'm given tastes like ash because my mouth is so dry. Any water I drink rolls in my stomach, waves on a stormy ocean.

There was a time when I thought I hated the sea. It made me feel trapped. But now I am trapped on an island in the middle of the sea, truly without hope. At least on the *Catherine* there was the illusion of escape, a possibility to flee and reset our course.

I trace the burn scars on my left forearm, thinking of Bree, who traced them first. I hope she's okay. That they're all okay.

The room is completely silent, and it's deafening.

A few hours later, I'm brought back to the interrogation room, only this time for an examination. I'm strapped down to a table, and Harvey inspects me from head to toe, the butt of a pencil tracing the scars on my body before he flips it nimbly in his fingers to record his findings.

As he moves to a puckered scar on my chest that I've had since I was a kid, I'm hit with a crushing realization. Harvey—not Emma—is probably the reason Crevice Valley was compromised. A Forgery retains all memories of their source; it's the programming that forces them to ignore certain details. Frank would want Harvey to forget *why* he helped the Rebels, but not *where* he helped us from. But then why did it take so long for the bombs to drop?

My Forgery's earlier comment echoes in my mind: *And to think you were having issues with orders in December.*

Frank didn't pluck Harvey from one world and insert his Forgery into another. He re-created Harvey, put him back to work doing the same tasks, and hoped the programming was strong enough to sort out the rest. Maybe Harvey's life now is so similar—the labs, the code, the research—that it took him weeks to settle into his Forged skin. He might have even fought giving up Headquarters, or at the very least, his memories could have been so rattled that the location was temporarily clouded. It would explain why the Forged spies sent after our team in December were still trying to get Headquarters' location.

If Harvey had trouble adjusting to his Forged state, maybe his mind-set can be shifted again. Jackson helped us, after all. Climbing the Wall into Burg had been too personal, too closely tied to his childhood in Dextern, and it caused something in his programming to flicker. But Emma's Forgery was a Gen5, and she joined our group the same night Harvey left it. If he was created in the following days, it's likely he's a five as well.

Any hope I was clinging to disintegrates.

Harvey makes a note of my chest scar, then moves to inspect the burn scars on my left forearm.

"What's this for?" I ask.

"A security measure. So that when we're done with you, ours will match."

"You'll mark the Forgery? Reproduce every scar?"

Harvey's pencil scratches over paper.

"And then what? Send him back in my place? Why would I give you *any* information now that I know this?"

"You gave me a name to save a finger," he says quietly. "Imagine what I'll get in exchange for your brother's life."

I pull at the restraints over my wrists, my ankles. I could claw his eyes out for that threat.

"This will be easier if you don't struggle," he says, but I go right on thrashing, creating as much of a disturbance as possible.

Harvey sighs and moves away from the table. A moment later music engulfs the room—sweeping chords and crying strings. The melody is layered and complex, so rich I feel it in my bones. I've heard music like this before, when Harvey was still Harvey. *Mozart*, he called it. A composer he'd always been fond of. Frank had outlawed such art in AmEast, but Harvey was granted the privilege of listening because it helped him focus while working on the Forgeries.

Old habits, old ways, now both alive in his Forgery.

When he reenters my vision, his arms are extended, swaying like tree limbs in a breeze. The butt of the pencil arches as the music swells and lulls. His wrists elegantly mirror each motion. If it were the real Harvey, this dance would be something beautiful, but knowing those hands put a blade to my finger changes everything. You can't unsee a truth. Not even if you want to.

The song ends and a new one surges to life. Not just any piece, but the same music we used to stage a diversion in Union Central. Clipper helped Harvey select it.

"Do you remember what you said when we met?"

Harvey raises an eyebrow, bored.

"You told me you hoped joining the Rebels was a step in the right direction. You said you hoped that someone like *me*, a victim of the Laicos Project, might be thankful for at least some of your work.

"Well, I'm not thankful for this. This is so opposite what the real you would want. The real you was willing to die so that I could live. The real you *hated* the work he did for Frank and he spent the last days of his life trying to undo the damage."

"The Harvey you remember was a criminal and a traitor." He says this like he's reciting it from a book. "And it doesn't matter what I wanted in the past. I know what I want now."

He's still conducting the music, an eerie smile on his lips as the notes build to the finale.

"I hope Clipper never sees you like this," I say. "That kid loved you, and this would kill him."

"Clipper?" He drops his arms to his sides and backs away from me, head shaking. He trips over a chair and ends up on the floor. The music continues to swell around us, and now Harvey's cringing at the staccato beats, flinching as though the horns and strings are causing him physical pain. He scrambles to his feet, rushes to turn off the music. As the room is thrown into silence he gasps like it's his first breath of air in ages.

His gaze drifts back to me, wide and fearful. For the briefest moment I think he heard me, that something about the music or my mention of Clipper resonated. But then his eyes narrow.

"You," he says, looking like he wants to slit my throat. "We'll finish this later."

I'm brought back to my cell because Harvey has other work to do, or so the guard says. Tomorrow I'll be questioned again.

Tomorrow, tomorrow, tomorrow.

I'm only focused on today, the first Wednesday of March,

and how it's nearly over. Today shouldn't end without them arriving, because that was the plan: two days early, disguised as the Order inspection team, with key cards from September and uniforms made by Mercy.

But the hours pass.

The day ends.

And they don't come.

ELEVEN

MY BREAKFAST ARRIVES BEARING A gift. It is unintentional, I'm sure. Someone very foolish didn't think of the sort of damage that can be done with something so small.

I pull the toothpick out of the fruit and hide it in the palm of my hand. I need the wood dry, sharp. I eat my breakfast with my fingers.

When a guard finally comes for me, I have to fight the urge to spring into action. Unless I somehow manage to get my hands on his gun, I'm doomed, and my arms are still bound. The odds wouldn't be good. I've never been a patient person, but I force myself to cooperate, letting the guard blindfold me and drag me into the hall.

Once again, I lose myself in the turns. We go up two flights of stairs. More dizzying direction changes. I'm handed off to my Forged counterpart. I know it's him because our gaits match perfectly.

When the blindfold is ripped off, I find myself back in Harvey's interrogation room. The tools are laid out, waiting beside my chair, but no one else is present.

"Are you doing the honors today?"

"Harvey is preoccupied."

The toothpick feels like even more of a blessing now. I'm not sure what it says about me when I know my own Forgery will be more ruthless than any other interrogator.

He moves me toward the seat, and as he reaches to adjust one of the straps that will soon tether me in place, I twist. Thrusting with both hands, I aim for his throat. He barely gets a hand up in time, and the toothpick lodges in the web between his thumb and forefinger. He yells with surprise, staggers. In that flash of his panic, I grab the nearest tool from the tray—a wooden mallet—and swing. He tries to dodge the blow but isn't quick enough. The wood connects with the side of his head, and the light winks out of his eyes.

My chest is pounding, but my hands are steady as they work. I grab a knife from the tray, and with the blade pointing toward my stomach, saw through my bindings. Then, when my hands are free, I strip the Forgery of his uniform.

It fits perfectly, and soon I look like an Order member, and him, like me.

I struggle with his limp body but manage to strap him into the chair. I doubt this room is free of cameras, which means someone, somewhere, is probably watching. I can only hope they missed our fight, that when they next look at the feeds, they assume my Forgery stepped out and left me in the chair.

I momentarily consider killing him but know a dead body will look too suspicious. The Forgery was trying to get answers from me, not kill me, and I need to buy myself as much time as possible.

I toss the mallet on the tray and wrap the blindfold around the blade of the knife before tucking it into my waistband. Then I dart into the hall.

Two Order guards stand a little ways ahead, one of whom may have even been my escort earlier. They each have a handgun at the hip and an Order-issued rifle in arm, the barrels resting against their shoulders. I walk confidently. They nod as I pass by, assuming I'm my Forgery.

I pick up my pace after rounding a corner. The window for escape is shrinking even as I walk down this hallway, and I need to find stairs. The shipment center—the docks—was below the Compound itself. If I locate it, I might be able to hop a boat, flee back onto the Gulf, but only after finding

Blaine and Emma. If they're being held anywhere near my cell . . .

Two flights down.

With luck, I find a stairwell. There's another armed guard stationed here, and I slow my gait, try to appear as calm as possible as I pass by. I descend two levels. The door on the landing won't open until I fish a card from the pocket of the Order uniform and swipe it for entry.

The room I step into is massive. Pillars support the ceiling at various intervals and the only light source comes from row upon row of what look like glass coffins. They sit on waist-high tables that extend as far as I can see, their contents filled with teal liquid, murky like pond water. It's the liquid, I realize, that's glowing just slightly, casting a halo of green-blue light around each unit.

Two flights. This should be the holding cells. Or at least a hallway leading to them. The levels between my cell and the interrogation room are the only detail I'm sure about.

A wave of panic hits me. The Compound is large and probably has multiple stairwells. Just because I counted two flights between my cell and the interrogation room does not mean that all stairwells will bring me between the two.

I consider backtracking, but worry the stairwell guard might be suspicious. Maybe I can go through this room, find another set of stairs. Maybe the cells are even waiting just beyond this room.

Too many maybes. I'm going to get caught.

I push the thoughts aside and move forward just as lights along the lab's ceiling begin pulsing. A silent alarm. Someone found Forged Me or I was seen fleeing. Regardless, it isn't good.

I spot a glass box mounted on the wall, holding an Order rifle. I throw my elbow into the case and the pane shatters. I've held this model only once before, when I was tasked with executing Harvey in Taem. In the end, I didn't pull the trigger—Bree made sure of that—but the shape of the weapon feels startlingly familiar in my hands now.

Clutching it, I skirt up the nearest row of glass coffins. Tubes run in and out of each, connecting to equipment below the table. I catch a shadow of something in the murky liquid to my right and can't help but pause. I bend at the waist, peer closer. There's something behind the glass, small and pale. It vaguely reminds me of a stillborn calf I once saw birthed in Claysoot.

I twist and examine the coffin behind me. The shape in this one is much larger. I lean until my nose is against the glass and almost cry out in shock. There is a body suspended in the murky liquid, the nub of his nose pointing toward the surface. He looks dead. Sallow skin is pulled tight over his frame. Fingers are no more than bones. I can see every last one of his ribs. It's like he's decaying, but somehow I know it's the opposite. He's growing. He's being born.

They all are.

I'm in a lab. I'm in a lab in a production facility.

I thought the Forgeries came from Taem, and at one point, they must have. Maybe some of them still do. But the Compound is producing them in far larger numbers, shipping them out from the docks somewhere beneath my feet.

In the bottom right corner of the tank, a display reads *Subject #C317, 21 days*. I twist and check the first tank I peered into. *Subject #C317, 5 days*. I tear up the aisle. *C317, C317*. Over and over. Every single Forgery in this row has the same origin.

And right then I know that Harvey has accomplished what Frank always wanted: a Forgery that can be created again and again, off any previous version of itself. The original subject no longer matters. Frank is no longer limited to one Forgery from every human. He has his limitless model now, and he's growing his army. An army that can have a new soldier in roughly one month's time, given the tank I've paused next to. Inside is a boy with my build, his skin smooth and youthful, his muscles clenched even in sleep. His display reads twenty-nine days.

Snippets of the conversations I overheard when first stepping off the boat flash through my mind. Shipments to Radix and Haven and Taem. Others still heading to Lode. Domed cities. Frank is manning them with Forgeries.

But for what? What is he planning?

I hear footsteps at the far end of the lab. I'm about halfway up the aisle with nowhere to run. Stupid curiosity. I shouldn't have stopped to examine the tanks. Shouldn't have stopped for anything but Blaine and Emma.

The footsteps grow louder. Harvey steps into view at the end of the aisle. He sees me and his face goes blank.

I pull the rifle up, the butt against my shoulder, the sight trained. "Freeze right there!" I say. "Point out the way to the holding cells. Then get down on your stomach and let me pass!"

The silent alarm cuts out without warning, throwing the room back into an odd state of glowing, iridescent blue. It's harder to see now. It feels vaguely like twilight—depth is difficult to discern—and everything seems suddenly familiar. Harvey at the end of my narrowed line of vision. My finger on the trigger. A palpable tension in the air.

I'm going to have to shoot him.

I need to do what Bree prevented that day in Taem.

"You couldn't just wait," he says, glaring.

Wait for what? To be tortured, inspected for scars?

"I had a plan," he says, "and you're ruining everything. I could have—" Harvey flinches, bringing the heel of his palm to his temple. A half dozen armed Order members spill into the aisle behind him. I turn to flee, but my Forgery is already there, thrusting an arm out. He's holding something small and compact. My body seizes up. There's a burning sting—everywhere and relentless—and then the sensation of falling.

TWELVE

I'M IN A NEW ROOM, with a panel of glass separating me from my Forgery. I'm only vaguely aware of the guards behind me because I can't take my eyes off Blaine and Emma. They are sitting on wooden stools, each bound and blindfolded. I pound on the glass, yell Blaine's name. They both flinch at my voice.

"Do you think this is a game, Gray?" my Forgery asks. I can hear him as clearly as if he were in the room with me. I reach for the knife I tucked into my waistband only to find it gone.

Forged Me draws his gun and motions between Blaine and Emma. "Pick one. Who lives?"

"What?"

"You seem to think there aren't consequences for your actions—for attacking me, for threatening Harvey's life, for trying to *escape*. Not the case, and I want to make that crystal clear." He jerks the gun again between Blaine and Emma again. "So choose."

There's a dull throb in my side from where he shocked me earlier, and while I've heard his words, I can't seem to process them. *Choose?*

"I'll select for you then." He takes a step toward Blaine.

"No! Wait!" I slam a palm into the glass. I hate him, this version of myself, this horrible thing I can't believe is somehow built from *me*. I hate myself even more for what I have to say. Because there is no choice. I knew the answer the moment he first made the threat. I feel a tear trail down my cheek.

"I'm so sorry, Emma," I whisper.

I can see the shock on her face even though her eyes are covered by the blindfold. Her entire body tenses.

I hate myself.

"Okay then," Forged Me says. "The girl goes."

But he doesn't move toward Emma. He turns on Blaine, puts the weapon to the back of my brother's head, and pulls the trigger.

The stool kicks out from beneath him and I'm screaming before Blaine even hits the floor. My fists are against the barrier, banging, punching, willing the glass to shatter. But there is so much blood beneath his head. It's done. It's done and no matter how many times I blink, it's not changing.

"This was a reminder," Forged Me says. "You cross me, and I cross you. But if you work with me, Gray—if you are honest—I'll be sure to keep my word. Here: an example." He turns the gun on Emma. "Tell me what the man named Badger was planning, and I'll spare her."

I can't find my voice. I see the gun and the threat but I can't find my voice, can't stop staring at Blaine. And I certainly can't bear to look at Emma. Emma who I just handed over like she meant nothing.

"Three . . . two . . ."

"We wanted to know what the Compound was," I manage. The words come out hoarse and ragged from how much I've screamed. "I saw everything we were after downstairs."

Forged Me looks pleased. "Good, good. This is progress. And when is your team coming?"

"Gage would have killed them by now, and if not, they should have been here yesterday."

He lowers his weapon. "That was perfect, Gray. You see how this works? You give me what I want, and I don't have to shoot anybody. Remember that. It will make tomorrow's session go much smoother." He holsters his weapon and hauls Emma to her feet. "Take him back to his cell, Maldoon."

Harvey waits for them to leave. Then, rather than dragging me out, he opens a door that connects the two rooms.

"It'll be your only chance," he says, "if you want to say good-bye."

I step through the doorway in a trance. Blaine's just lying there and already the sobs are clawing their way up my throat. My hands are shaking, my legs unsteady. I sink to my knees beside my brother.

"I'm so sorry," I manage. "I love you and I'm sorry. I didn't mean it—what I said in Pine Ridge. I never mean half the things I say and I just—" I pull him to my chest. "I don't know why this happened," I choke out. "We put each other first. Always. And that's what I did. I put you first and now . . . and now . . ."

My throat's grown too tight and thin, my breathing completely erratic. I rock with Blaine in my arms and cry into his hair and keep mumbling his name over and over like he might hear me and wake up. Like he's just dreaming. Like I saw it all wrong.

Harvey steps into the room and says it's time to go. I tell him I'll go when I'm ready. He insists, and that's when I lose it. I bolt up, shove him. When he advances again, I grab a wooden stool by the lip of the seat, holding the legs out to fend him off. As Harvey backs away, I notice the blood. Blaine's blood. Coating my hands. Staining the front of my shirt. Splattered against the stool's wood grain from when . . .

I throw the stool at the glass window. It bounces off like a toy. I pick it up and try again. And again. And again. But the window won't break.

Still, I keep trying.

Even when it's pointless.

Even though I'm powerless.

Even though Blaine won't come back no matter how much I scream.

I give up eventually. Throat ragged, lungs heaving, I glance toward the doorway. Harvey is still standing with the guards, surveying me like I'm a rabid animal that needs to be put down.

They take me back to my cell.

Harvey slips something into my hand: a scrap of paper, folded so it's no larger than the pad of my thumb.

"For tomorrow," he whispers.

I slump to the floor, my head against the wall and my arms around my middle like I'm holding in my organs. Maybe I am. Maybe if I move I'll fall apart and never come back together.

I feel small and helpless and scared and alone.

Like a child.

Like a little boy.

Blaine saved me when I was nine.

It was late fall and we were at the lake so he could practice setting snares for rabbits. Xavier Piltess had spent most of the summer teaching him how to hunt, and because I still believed I was a year younger than Blaine, I could only day-dream about joining the lessons the following year. The bellflowers that usually carpeted the tall grass beyond the lake had transformed into brittle spokes with the changing temperatures. No purple petals remained. No green flushed their stalks. They were dirt brown and crunchy, like the leaves littering the forest floor.

"This is boring, Blaine. I wanna shoot your bow." It was lying behind him, the quiver stocked.

"You can catch things without wasting an arrow, you know," he said. "And it's important to practice both."

"Xavier said you can reuse arrows if your shot's good enough."

"When did you hear that?"

"When you guys came back yesterday. Xavier said not to worry about that shot you took that broke the shaft. Said when you get better you won't waste an arrow or an ounce of meat, that's how good you'll be."

Blaine kept his eyes on his work, trying to cover his embarrassment with a stern look.

"You're a nosy rat," he said.

"You're a boring slug."

"At least I know how to set a snare."

"I'll know next year, when Xavier teaches me." I toed Blaine's quiver, watching the arrows rock with the motion. "I hate waiting. It's not fair that you get to do everything first. I'm just as big as you." It was true. In size, we were shoulder to shoulder.

"Not in years. And stay away from my arrows."

I nudged them harder and the quiver spiraled away from me, spilling its contents as it rolled down the hillside.

"Hey!" Blaine jumped to his feet. "Pick those up."

"I'm not old enough to touch them, remember?"

Blaine folded his arms over his chest like he was our ma. "Gray, pick them up and quit acting like a baby."

"I hate you," I shouted. "You think you know everything." I kicked over the snare he'd been working on for good measure and fled. He chased me.

I didn't hold my lead long. Somewhere between the lake and the village, beneath the canopy of shedding trees, Blaine was practically breathing down my neck. He didn't have to pick the path—around a thicket, over rocks, beneath low-hanging branches—only follow me. I hopped a fallen tree, but having judged it poorly, my back leg caught on the trunk and sent me tumbling. I hit earth hard. The wind went out of my lungs and I felt a terrible heat in my chest, not far below my collarbone.

I coughed and gulped for air, but none came. My shirt grew damp. Blood, I realized.

"Gray!" Blaine crouched down beside me. "Oh," he said, taking in the wound, one hand on my shoulder. "Um . . . it's . . ."

The air had finally returned to my lungs and I risked a look at what was stinging my chest. I'd landed on an angry branch still attached to the tree trunk. Not just landed on, but impaled myself. I kicked my feet, trying to stand, and the pain reared through me. The branch was like a fishing hook, holding me against my will.

"Easy, Gray," Blaine said, like I was livestock he could tame with enough patience. "Easy."

I think with anyone else it would have been impossible to relax in that moment, but something about the way Blaine was looking at me told me he was going to make everything fine, that the worry was a weight I could pass to him. He would carry it for us both.

I looked up at the trees' limbs, bony fingers scraping a white sky, and tried to steady my breathing. Blaine sawed me free of the branch with his pocketknife. Then he pulled one of my arms around his neck and together we staggered out of the woods and into town, a small spike of wood still wedged in my chest.

Blaine took me directly to the Clinic. Carter ushered us in with anxious eyes but steady hands, and not much later I was bandaged and well, being told the branch hadn't been long enough to puncture my lung, but it had drawn plenty of blood. There would be a scar. And a tender recovery period.

"Why'd you help me like that?" I asked Blaine. He was beside me on an empty bed, our reclined positions mirrored. "Right after I said I hated you?"

"Because you didn't mean it."

"How'd you know?"

He sat up. Even back then Blaine was good at big brother looks. "If it had been flipped—me saying it to you—what would you have thought?"

I understood, but still felt like I had to make it obvious and undeniable. What if I'd been hurt worse? What if my lung *had* been hit and this conversation never happened?

"I don't hate you at all," I insisted. "Not the tiniest bit. Even if you *are* boring sometimes."

"Rat," he teased.

"Slug!"

And then we went back and forth, tossing every insult we could imagine at each other until we were shooed home and Ma became our audience instead of Carter.

As I bang my head against the cell wall, tears still streaming down my cheeks, it's this memory that haunts me. The puckered scar on my chest, and how Blaine saw me to the Clinic, and the indisputable truth that I could never truly hate him. I love him. I love him with the deepest parts of myself, and I'm horrified—ashamed—by my final words to him.

Screw you, I said in Pine Ridge.

I wish I could make it right. I wish I'd had the chance to speak the truth, even if he already knew it.

I don't sleep, but I cry.

Even after I am empty of tears, the ache remains, overwhelming and endless, like my bones are built of grief.

THIRTEEN

SOMETIME DURING THE NIGHT, I unfold the paper from Harvey. Like it matters. Like there's anything he could possibly say that will make things better.

Using the sliver of light seeping beneath my door, I can barely make out a list of names. I recognize two. Christie, the woman who swiped us through to the vaccine when we stole it months ago, and Sammy's father, who forged water ration cards in Taem.

There's a note from Harvey at the bottom: *All already deceased, so you can give them up without consequence. Destroy once read.*

Leaning against the door, I wonder if I should trust him. *We'll finish this later*, he said yesterday. I thought he meant my examination, but after his words to me in the production lab, the pain that registered on his face as though his thoughts were conflicting with his programmed orders . . . Was my mention of Clipper, paired with the music the boy had helped Harvey select, enough to jolt his senses?

I don't understand how it's possible. Not unless . . .

The Forged version of Emma could have been one of the first fives. Perhaps the *only* five at the time she joined our group. A test, a trial. Frank wouldn't have wanted to risk something going wrong with Harvey. Ironic in hindsight, because it's the fours that are flawed. If Harvey is an F-Gen4, he could be like Jackson—changing his motives, fighting his orders. Malfunctioning.

I clench the paper in my hand. I'm positive two of the people are safe to disclose. If Harvey *hasn't* cracked, if he *isn't* trying to help me, why would he give me even one name that might help me avoid torture?

I study the list until I've committed it to memory. Then I fold the paper back up and swallow it like a pill.

Harvey acts as though nothing has changed overnight. I'm back in his interrogation lab, strapped down to the chair, the tool tray waiting. It is only when Forged Me enters that there is any indication of new loyalties. Harvey grows very interested in double-checking my restraints. I hope for the both of us that he doesn't give something away.

Forged Me flips a switch and the mirrored wall flickers to life. Glass that only reflected the room during my previous visits is now alive with video of the entire Compound. I can make out the glowing aisles of the production lab, the busy docks of the shipment center. In another feed, Order members sit at workstations in a control room, punching buttons, jabbering into headsets, and examining surveillance feeds. No wonder I was caught so easily when I tried to escape.

"Looking sharp, Gray," he says, eying the Order uniform I'm still wearing from when I switched our outfits yesterday. He hasn't bothered to change either. It's a reminder, probably. A way to pull the image of Blaine's murder before my eyes without saying a word.

"A new day of questioning," he continues. "Today you will cooperate, or everything Harvey does to you"—he walks to the glass wall and taps a feed that shows Emma slouched in her cell—"will also be done to *her*. Understood?"

I can't look at him. If I do, I'll break down or start cursing him, and I don't want to give him the satisfaction of knowing that I'm in pain. And broken. And hate him with every fiber of my being.

He moves back to his chair and rolls up the sleeves of his shirt—my old shirt, one an Expat lent me when I first arrived in Pike. His left forearm is still without burn scars, and the fact that he hasn't been marked to match me yet is the only thing that keeps me sane. Otherwise, I feel like I'm staring at myself. It's like I held the very gun that killed Blaine.

"Let's start with the *Harbinger*," he says. "Where is it being printed?"

"I honestly don't know."

"And I honestly don't believe you. Maldoon?" He motions for Harvey, who selects a knife.

Even with the knowledge that what's done to me will be done to Emma, I wait until the blade is resting against my pinky—a threat of removal—before I give in. I want the moment I fold to look convincing.

"Wait," I gasp out. "I can't help with the paper, I swear it, but there's a Rebel spy in Taem who works for the Order. Christie something. She helped me get the vaccine in the fall."

"We already know about her," Forged Me answers. "And she's been dead for months. Cut his finger off, Maldoon."

The blade slices skin. My heart rate jumps.

"Flynn! Nathan Flynn. He forges water ration cards for Taem citizens. I heard some Rebels talking about him once."

"Dead, too. Executed years ago." He squints at me. "You know where his son is?"

"I didn't know he had a son."

"Samuel, according to our records."

"Never heard of him."

"Then none of this is useful to me." He motions for Harvey to continue and I realize that these names might not help me at all. Harvey's eyes look heavy behind his glasses. Even if his loyalties have changed, he has to continue in order to not raise suspicions. The knife again touches my pinky. He *will* cut off my finger if he has to.

I give another name. Forged Me says it's already known, so I give another. Again worthless.

"Are you toying with me?" he says, jumping from his seat and pushing Harvey aside. "Every single one of these names is old news. Give me something I don't know. Supporters in Bone Harbor. You say you don't know *where* the paper's printed, but what about *who*? Who's running it?"

"You asked for names and I'm giving them. I can't help that I don't have the exact ones you want."

He grabs the chair beneath the armrests and heaves upward. I flip back, and when my head strikes the ground my jaw clamps shut on my tongue. I taste blood.

The Forgery leans down so his nose is inches from mine, our eyes locked. Before he can speak whatever threat is surely waiting on his tongue, there is a knock on the lab door. The Forgery steps away and I'm left staring at the ceiling, my limbs still bound to the chair. I hear the door open.

"Isn't it obvious I'm busy?"

"You'll want to see this, sir," someone says. "Inspection team's here a few hours early and they found something down on dock 1B. A tracking device attached to the *Embassy*."

"Of course there's a tracking device," Forged Me snarls. "Tell them not to bother me unless—"

"Not one of our tracking devices, sir. Something else. Foreign. Slapped on to the hull like a hack job."

"Have Tambe see to it. He's above me."

"He's already down there, sir. And he asked for you specifically."

There's a groan from the Forgery, and then: "Maldoon! See if you can get anything useful out of him. I'll be back as soon as I can."

The door clicks shut and Harvey rights my chair but doesn't free me from the restraining belts. He walks out of view and then Mozart is sweeping through the room.

"So anyone listening won't overhear," he whispers as the melody builds.

"Who's listening?"

"Someone is always listening." He points at the mirrored wall. I catch Forged Me darting down a stairwell in one of the feeds. In another, a large rig is surrounded by frenzied workers. Dock 1B, I imagine.

"The image in the top row, two from the left, is just out-side this room," Harvey explains. In it, I can see two Order members standing guard in the hall. "I'm going to go on acting like I'm interrogating you—give a good yell every few minutes—but watch that screen. If you see someone approaching, let me know."

He pulls out the pliers and goes for one of my nails. Act-ing is easy. It's impossible to not flinch after what happened last time we were in this scenario. The pressure is far less intense when he pinches the pliers shut though. He doesn't pull back, but his hand seems to shake like he wants to.

"I'm sorry," he says. "About the interrogation and your brother and . . ." Harvey swallows. "I gave Frank Headquar-ters' coordinates, Gray. I had trouble remembering certain details when I woke up, so he had me go straight to work on the Forgeries. Code, genetics—that was second nature. But when Crevice Valley's location finally surfaced in late Janu-ary, I gladly revealed it. I thought the Rebels were the enemy. I was actually angry when Frank said he was waiting for the right moment to act. And now all those families and kids— Did anyone survive?"

"I'm not sure."

Harvey pinches the bridge of his nose like a headache's coming on.

"You truly want to help me now?" I ask. "After yesterday I thought—"

"Yesterday," he says, "changed everything. What you said about my work and how I hoped a victim of the Laicos Project might one day be thankful for it . . . I vaguely remembered saying that. Felt like it was years ago, but I knew the words were mine once you repeated them, even if some voice in the back of my head was telling me to ignore you. Then you mentioned Clipper."

He gives a pretend tug at my fingernail. I fake a scream.

"That boy is the closest thing I have to a son, and when you said his name, I could feel my chest cracking. Mozart was playing, filling the room with these glorious notes and it was like a spike of truth had drilled through my skull. Suddenly I remembered that the piece playing was the same exact piece Clipper helped me select in Crevice Valley prior to our mission, the piece Bree was going to use to stage the diversion. All our plans came surging back, all my work for the Rebels, the reason I joined them—it woke me up, Gray. I remember now, and I am so, so sorry."

And he looks it. There is pain written in the shape of his brows, regret in the creases surrounding his eyes.

"I want to help you," Harvey says, cringing through the words. "And do right by Clipper. That thought is like a spear between my eyes, but pain I can deal with. My goal was always to undo the work I started, to right wrongs. I bailed on Frank once, and I can do it again." He coughs, and takes a deep breath before continuing. "Whatever the real Harvey did, I can do, too."

"If you're thinking like the real Harvey, then you *are* the real Harvey," I tell him. Almost exactly what I said to Jackson once, as we sat in a dark, musty boiler room beneath Burg and struck an alliance.

Harvey manages a smile and it makes him look years younger.

"You said you had a plan?"

"An *idea* . . . a way to possibly stop the Forgeries."

"What about me and Emma? Is there even the slightest chance that we can get off this island?"

One side of Harvey's mouth pulls into a grimace. "I don't know. There's a guard at nearly every stairwell, usually a few more per hall. Doorways to the docks open only to key cards or wrist implants, and then there's the security booth that lets boats in and out of the channel itself."

"What about the limitless Forgeries? You made them, right?" His grimace intensifies. "Maybe we can sneak out with a shipment."

"It's a thought," he says, cringing as he considers it. When the pain seems to ebb a little, he adds, "Most shipments are heading to the capital and the other domed cities. A few are even going to exposed towns. Their numbers will increase the Order's presence tenfold, help silence people with wavering loyalties. In the end, I think Frank will march the Forgeries on AmWest. He's tiring of the Expats' antics, and he'll soon have the numbers to overwhelm them. And when he runs low, he can always build more. Because of this facility. Because of me."

I shake my head, trying to make sense of *why*. What is Frank really after? I remember a story September and Sammy told around a fire in December—about Frank's goal of avenging his family, whom he lost to AmWest bullets. Is this still about revenge? Somehow, it feels bigger.

A video feed on the mirrored wall cuts out unexpectedly, its picture replaced by static. I grab Harvey's arm, and he turns, following my gaze. The Order members in the control room continue to go about their work, not yet aware of the lost signal, but as we glance through the other visuals, we spot movement adjacent to the dead feed.

An Order member walks briskly through a hallway, a gun in hand. Two guards at the far end of the hall see him and nod in greeting, but the approaching Order member doesn't slow or acknowledge his comrades. He takes aim and shoots them dead. The shots are soundless on our end—just a *flash,*

flash at the end of the barrel—and then the shooter looks up, aiming directly into the camera, and fires.

The picture goes dead, but not before I see her face.

Her.

Because it's not an Order member.

It's Bree.

FOURTEEN

THE FIRST THING I THINK is that she is beautiful. It's a ridiculous thought in a moment like this, but it's what courses through me—awe at her, at everything about her. Second is the relief, overwhelming and fierce. I assumed her dead, had been trying to not even think of her because of it, and now she is here, as stubborn and brave as ever. She reappears in another feed, walking faster, with purpose and determination, almost possessed. Her gun trains up. Another shot, another dead camera.

She rounds a corner to find three Order members on guard. She shoots twice, two go down, and then her gun clicks, empty. She releases the magazine, which clatters to the floor. As the last man draws his handgun, she reloads her weapon and drops to the ground all in one motion. She shoots his kneecap. He falls, screaming, and after a better-aimed shot from Bree, he is completely still. She scrambles to her feet and is again on her way.

Something hot laces my finger.

"Ow! What the—"

A shallow cut.

"Well, you're not giving me anything useful!" Harvey shouts, holding the knife he's used to draw blood. "Quit staring at screens and answer my questions." He drops his voice to a whisper and adds, "She's heading for the holding cells, clearing a path right to Emma. This is your ticket out."

He brings the knife back to my finger, but doesn't apply pressure.

"What about you?" I ask.

"I need to grab something from the labs. I'll meet you at the docks if I can, but don't wait for me."

"But I don't even know how to—"

"Take the back stairwell. Two flights down you'll find the cells, another level down, the water."

He runs the knife over my knuckles—not hard enough to draw blood, but with enough pressure to make my whole body tense up. At the same time, he undoes the restraint on my left wrist with lightning speed.

"Dammit, that must have broken when he flipped you."

Harvey makes a brief show of trying to resecure it, then swears. "I need to get something to fix this."

He storms out, and as the door closes behind him, I recognize the brilliance of it. He'll still look loyal to anyone reviewing the video, but I'm left alone with an untethered hand and the means to free myself.

The feeds show someone waiting for Bree around the next turn. He must have heard the gunshots from her previous scuffle. She slows as she approaches the corner, back against the wall and elbow tucked to her side so the gun is held alongside her ear. In one graceful movement she pivots around the corner and extends her shooting arm. The Order member knocks it aside. Her bullet tears into the wall. He swings and his fist catches her chin. Bree flies off her feet and my pulse skyrockets.

"Come on . . ." I grapple with the restraint on my other arm, but I'm uncoordinated with my left hand and can't work the buckles fast enough.

Bree tries to scramble away but the man's boot finds her. He hauls her to her feet, slams her against the wall.

"Come on!" The strap slides free.

His hands are on her neck now, and he's lifting her up, pinning her to the wall.

I bend to work on my ankles.

She claws at his forearm. Struggles, kicks.

One strap left.

But Bree is fighting less adamantly, the fire leaving her eyes, and right when I'm certain it's over—that I'm about to watch another person I love die—a third figure steps into the frame.

His gun slams into the Order member's temple. The man drops like an anchor, and Bree crumples, too. She gasps, staggers to her feet. Her savior reaches for her, but she jerks away and spits a mouthful of blood onto the floor.

I can't hear her but I can read her lips. *I'm fine.*

Her savior sighs and turns to the camera.

Sammy, also dressed in Order gear. One shot and static overtakes the picture.

They're both alive. And they're here now, infiltrating on the day of inspection, mere hours early instead of two days as planned. It would explain why no alarm has been raised yet. The plan could be working—the key cards, the uniforms. Is the tracking device a decoy as well? Are most eyes elsewhere as they continue their "inspection"?

Then the real question hits me: *Do they even know I'm here?*

They must. If they were only after information, as the original mission entailed, they would never have fired so many shots. They'd have walked through the facility, taking mental notes, remembering details. Instead they're striking down anyone in their path and heading directly for the holding cells. The cells that I won't be in. Nor Blaine. Because Blaine's . . .

I swallow, unable to even think it.

The same silent alarm that flashed through the production lab when I first tried to escape kicks on, dousing the room in red. I look back at the control-room feed and find it frenzied, Order members shouting out instructions. On the docks, Forged Me looks up at the flashing lights, face livid. He turns his back on the rig and races into the facility.

Any cover Sammy and Bree had is gone.

I rip the final restraint off my leg and pull open the door of the interrogation room. The guards have left, drawn away by the alarm. I recall Harvey's directions, and run.

"Emma?" I sprint into the cell block, pausing only to quickly glance through each doorway. They are all open. And all empty.

"Emma!"

She's fled in the panic. That or Bree and Sammy have already been here.

Someone steps from the last cell. My Forged counterpart.

He looks frazzled. His plain shirt hangs crookedly on his frame, the neckline askew. The sleeves that were rolled up earlier have slid back down his arms. I wonder what this mess means for him. Frank is going to be furious.

"You said they were dead!" he spits, raising his gun. "That the team wouldn't be coming."

"I thought they were!"

"Well, they're going to end up that way! I will personally make sure—"

He cuts off at the sound of footsteps. Miraculously, even though it makes no sense for her to be returning to the cells when she's clearly already retrieved the only person in them, I hear Bree's voice.

"I'm double-checking, Sammy, and that's the end of it!"

The stairwell door slams.

Forged Me flinches and in that small drop of his focus, I throw my forearm into his, pushing the gun away. A shot goes off, straight into the floor, but I've seized the advantage. I push him backward, knock his arm against the wall. He drops the gun, and it's in *my* hand now. I have him pinned in place, the gun shoved so aggressively beneath his chin that he's looking up at the ceiling.

The doorway to the cell block is thrown open and Bree races in.

"Help me!" Forged Me begs. "Please. It's me. He's got me, the Forgery."

"Let him go," Bree says, her gun already aimed at me.

"Bree, he's lying,"

"Shoot him!" he urges. "Shoot him before he kills us both!"

Her eyes dart between us. "Step away from him." I don't move and her eyes narrow. "Don't test me. Step away right now!"

"Bree, it's *me*."

"Move back!" She looks fierce and empowered, completely in control. Her aim hasn't faltered once and I know what a good shot she is. If she decides to pull the trigger, she won't miss.

I take a few steps away from the Forgery, both my hands up. Forged Me stands a little taller.

"What is your biggest regret?" she asks us, and my heart lifts. This is it. Everything will be okay.

"What I said that night on the beach. How I told you I doubted us, said we weren't right."

"He . . . he tortured me for that answer," Forged Me stammers. "He made me tell him everything. Please, you have to trust me. It's me. It's Gray."

His acting is stellar: the desperation, the fear. I realize for the first time how convincing it all looks. He's unarmed and in the clothing Bree last saw *me* wearing. I'm still in the Order uniform. And now this—his lie that I've stolen the very answer that should save me.

I don't want it to be enough, but Bree's stare is murderous. "Put the gun on the floor—slowly—and slide it over."

"Bree, it's me. You have to believe that. I know everything about you. How you don't sleep well without the sound of waves, and have a birthmark on your hip, and are double-jointed. You're the best shot I know and stubborn as hell. Strong, too. So damn strong. You used to love herons, but now loons are your favorite, and you can call to them with your hands. I've seen you do it. And purple's your favorite color, right? You said so in the Tap Room once. Deep, dark, almost black purp—"

"He got all these answers from me!" the Forgery screams. "He's wearing the damn uniform. Shoot him while you still have a chance!"

"Shoot *him*. He's—"

"The gun!" she demands. "Slide it over now."

I consider firing at the Forgery, but my weapon is held in surrender, barrel pointed at the ceiling, whereas hers is already aimed at my chest. If I do anything other than what she demands, I'm pretty sure I'll end up dead.

I slide it over. She tucks it in the back of her pants.

"Now a few more steps," she says, motioning with the gun. "Then sit on your hands."

I shuffle backward—slowly, so she has no reason to fire—and lower myself to the floor.

When she's satisfied I'm no longer a risk, she approaches the Forgery. Her head is cocked to the side. She's still not positive. She's looking for the answer on his face, in his eyes. My gaze trails over Bree's waist. Her belt is loaded with ammunition but not a single flashlight. She doesn't stand a chance of identifying him by naked eye. Not with the flashing alarm, the chaotic pulses of red.

"Bree," Forged Me says, drawing a deep breath. "Thank you. I thought you'd . . . I didn't know if . . ."

She steps closer. Too close. He's going to get the gun from her waistband if she's not careful. Her hand goes fondly to his left wrist. She slides her hand beneath his shirt, reaching toward his elbow, pulling him nearer. He seems to forget everything else as she offers him her lips. My pulse is raging. I scramble to my feet, but just before their lips meet, a gunshot rips the air.

Forged Me collapses against the wall, an arm clutched around his stomach where Bree holds her gun. The gun I'd forgotten about as I watched her move to kiss him. The gun she fired right into his gut.

"You bastard," she says. "Did you honestly think I wouldn't know?"

She lets go of his arm and he slides to the floor in a heap, his breaths shallow and growing quicker.

Bree holds the gun I surrendered out to me, grip first.

"How could you tell?"

"His arm," she says. "There were no burn scars."

I touch my left forearm, glance back at her. Her lip is split from when the Order member hit her. I swear a bruise is already surfacing on her neck.

"Bree, I—"

"Not yet," she says, shaking the gun's grip at me. "Not until we're out of this."

It's like that moment I pulled her from the *Catherine* and knew exactly what she wanted to say, only reversed. At least for the two of us, and especially right now, words aren't necessary.

I take the gun from her and risk one last look at the dying Forgery as we flee the cell block.

FIFTEEN

ONE OF SEPTEMBER'S KEY CARDS gets us through the door at the bottom of the stairwell and into a warehouse. Darting through towering rows of crates and past frantic Order members, we keep our heads up and our posture confident. No one stops us. In uniform, we're just another pair of workers. Still, I worry about how long we have until the control room relays Bree's description to the Order members down here.

The cavernous warehouse opens onto the equally as cavernous shipping center. The water channel is in front of us, with long wharfs on either side, each sprouting docks like tree limbs. Enormous vessels are docked at the first few, making it impossible to see if the other docks house smaller boats, or no boats at all. Directly to the right, dock 1B is swarming with activity. It looks like the giant rig there was in the process of being loaded with cargo when the alarm went off. Now, half the crew is still trying to load it while the others run around, pointing between the boat and the warehouse, barking orders.

"Dammit, where is Farrester?" I hear one Order member shout.

"He's not answering. Either the com lines are down or . . ."

I can't make out any more as I tail Bree down the left wharf. We've passed two docks—1A and 2A—when something explodes behind us. I glance over my shoulder. Dock 1B is in shambles. A hole has blown through the hull of the boat secured beside it. Smoke billows. A shipment crate tumbles into the channel.

"Clipper's work," Bree shouts, breaking into a run.

"He's here?"

I'm guessing the supposed tracking device Bree's fake inspection team spotted on the boat was never a tracking device.

A speckling of bullets hits the wall behind us. We've finally been identified.

Bree lengthens her strides, and I do the same. About halfway up the wharf, she turns onto a dock and leaps into a waiting boat. It's small. Minuscule compared to the shipping rigs closer to the warehouse, but it has the Franconian emblem on the side and something about its shape tells me it will be fast. I jump on after Bree and it roars to life, tearing away from the dock.

"Wait! Emma!" I say, crouching down so I don't lose my footing. "And Harvey!"

"Harvey's alive?" Bree says.

"Like always, you're out of the loop, Nox," Sammy shouts. He's standing near the nose of the boat, hands gripping the wheel. "They're both below." He glances at me. "Blaine?"

All I can do is shake my head.

"Faster!" Clipper urges. I didn't even notice him when we jumped on, but he's in a seat beside Sammy, a bulky package in his left hand.

"This *is* fast!" Sammy shouts back.

At the mouth of the Compound, I can see the security station Harvey mentioned, a sturdy room with glass windows that butts against the water. From behind the windows, a guard is signaling for us to stop. The Gulf ahead is dark beneath the falling twilight, but we'll have trouble reaching it. A series of spiked metal poles rise a forearm's length from the Compound's channel. They are precisely spaced, ensuring no boat can slip through unless the blockade is lowered. Not even one as tiny as ours.

"Clipper?" Sammy says hesitantly.

"We should fit. May promised we'd fit."

Sammy doesn't slow. It looks tight. Too tight.

Several guards run from the security room and onto the surrounding exposed deck. They take aim.

The blockade is right before us now.

As they open fire, we duck. I swear a bullet nicks my ear, but the next moment we are flying between two of the pillars. A horrible screech sounds beneath our feet—the spikes tearing into the hull of the boat—but the next moment we are on the open water. I crane back toward the Compound, listening for the sound of a pursuing motor. All I hear is wind and our own motor, sounding wounded, drained. I look over the side of the boat, trying to survey the damage.

"I thought we were supposed to fit."

"It doesn't matter," Clipper says to me. "We're bailing soon anyway."

"Bree, get 'em up here for the jump," Sammy orders. She darts down the short half staircase to get Harvey and Emma.

"Jump?" I echo. "What shore do we plan to swim to?" As far as I can see, the only land in sight is the island we're fleeing, and our original plan had us traveling back to Pine Ridge in the disguised Order boat.

Sammy ignores my question and Clipper busies himself with securing his bulky package beneath his seat.

"Look, I get that the hull's breached," I shout over the

wind, "but we'll freeze to death in this water!" I remember the sting of the Gulf when the *Catherine* sank, how it made me seize up. The days have been getting a little warmer, but I doubt the water's changed much. We won't last long.

"They'll come after us if they haven't already," Sammy yells back. "So we jump, the boat blows up, and anyone trailing us sees the explosion and thinks we're goners."

Bree reappears with Harvey and Emma.

"Okay, that's the signal!" I have no clue what Clipper's referring to. "On three. One . . . two . . . three!"

We throw ourselves over the side of the boat. The impact is a viscous sting across my face, a claw at my side. I'm thrown about in the freezing water, gasping for air, momentarily uncertain which way is up. I resurface, my clothes heavy and my teeth already knocking. Not far away is the flaming shell of our boat. Smoke drifts up like a bonfire as the Gulf swallows it.

I swim, following Sammy. There's another boat just ahead, one strikingly similar to the *Catherine*. It's killed all its lights and I'm half-amazed we didn't crash right into it. A rope ladder comes over the side. I guess the team had a back-up plan all along.

We climb aboard and are greeting by a curvy woman who distributes more thick blankets than seems natural for a fishing vessel to have on hand.

"Dry as best you can," she says, "and then we'll go in and warm you properly."

Bree pulls a blanket snug over her shoulders. "Thanks, May. We owe you."

The woman beams and it makes her already plump cheeks get even plumper.

"And I don't get any thanks?" a guy behind her says. He's opposite of May in every way: tall and gangly, with skin that is leathering despite the youthful glimmer in his eyes.

May elbows him. "Carl, this isn't the time for sarcasm."

I look between the team and the two strangers they all seem to know. "I'm confused."

"Inside," May says, waving toward the wheelhouse. "Once everyone's warm and in dry clothes, we'll talk."

The team shuffles off, Clipper clinging to Harvey like a lost child, and my gaze drifts to Emma. There is so much I need to say, but I can't get my feet to move and that's probably for the best. She won't believe me. How could she after what happened at the Compound?

She glances my way, and her eyes feel like ice.

Tell her you're sorry about picking Blaine.

But I'm not. The situation was horrible. But I'm not sorry I tried to save my brother.

Then tell her you forgive her for Craw. Tell her you've been over it awhile now.

But I don't want to mislead her. My heart is elsewhere—tied up in another person—and I can't change that. Wouldn't want to even if I could.

At least tell her you still care about her. That you always will.

But she won't believe it. Not after what happened with Blaine and my Forgery and . . .

She's still staring at me.

Sammy is regarding her apprehensively, like she's a ghost that terrifies him, but he can't bring himself to look away.

It's such a mess, life. The way everything gets all jumbled and tangled and knotted. Why can't it be easy? Bree would say something like, *Because easy would be boring,* and she's probably right, but in this moment I'd love boring. I'd love straightforward and clear and tied up in a pretty bow. I'd love no surprises and happy endings and everyone getting what they wished. Right now, boring sounds pretty damn perfect.

Sammy pulls his gaze from Emma long enough to look my way, and I give him an encouraging nod. I don't know why he's seeking out permission. He doesn't need it.

"Hi," Sammy says to Emma. "I was a little preoccupied for introductions earlier—escaping and explosions and all—but I'm Sammy."

He offers his hand.

"Emma." She shakes it. "And thanks for before, with the cell."

"'Twas a small detour, and absolutely worthwhile if you ask me."

He flashes her a smile. She gives him a sympathetic one in return. Just like that, so *easily*, Sammy sets them on course.

I hope it continues to be easy for them. I hope it's easy and boring and downright effortless. They both deserve a break.

SIXTEEN

IT WENT LIKE THIS: THE team found the water crate Blaine and I dropped in Pine Ridge, and after following the trail, knew we'd been compromised. Back at the bookshop they theorized about how. Bree mentioned her evening with Gage at the pub—how he was fishing for details regarding the mission—and Badger put the rest together.

The team was ready when he arrived later that evening. Gage got just one shot off—which clipped Badger in the shoulder—before he was rendered weaponless. With some persuasion, he gave up the truth: Blaine and I had been taken to the Compound for questioning.

"Badger and Adam decided it was too much of a risk to come after you," Bree explains. Our team is in dry clothes now, crammed in the wheelhouse with May and Carl, who is steering us back to Pine Ridge. "They said our plan was solid enough to get us inside to poke around, to *look* and *observe*, but not to break anyone out. I told them it was a piss-poor excuse, that we had everything we needed to get to you guys and not doing so was cowardly."

"Charlie's sister," Sammy says, pointing at May, "arrived with the Order-disguised boat only to find the mission canceled. Course, Bree wouldn't give it up. Kept ranting about how it wasn't right, and we couldn't leave you. Hell, I thought the same." Sammy pats his chest like I might have doubted him. "I mean, we're practically blood at this point."

Clipper nods in agreement.

I feel this swelling in my chest. I know exactly what they mean. I know all too well, but if I try to put that in words, I'll choke up.

"So how *did* you change their minds?" Harvey asks.

"We didn't. Adam and Badger never approved of this." Bree gestures at the boat. "I organized it behind their backs. The inspection team was due to arrive late Friday evening, so I decided we should do what we were always planning—infiltrate. The key was to get to the Compound a few hours early."

"And we couldn't have done it without Carl and May," Sammy adds. "Their stand-in Order boat got us entry, and their trawler was waiting to pick us up once we fled."

"I'm grateful and all, but I'm still confused." I look toward Carl and May. "Adam didn't think this could be done, and he at least knew me and Blaine. Why would you two risk all this for strangers?"

"Just a gut instinct." May beams, her cheeks swelling up like fresh loaves of bread. "Every minute after I arrived at the bookshop Bree went on and on and it . . . I guess it reminded us of our situation, didn't it, hon?" She glances up at Carl, who nods. "I once staged quite a production to get Carl out of a bad spot and sometimes it's worth risks, regardless of the odds. Especially for people you love."

Bree looks mortified—she might even be blushing—but I'm hung up on May's words. My mind drifts to a letter I found in a deserted house in Bone Harbor a few months back. A love letter addressed to a man named Carl, begging him to come west, saying her brother Charlie—an Expat— would help stage a boat sinking to cover his trail.

"You two," I say, still staring between them. "Carl's from Bone Harbor."

May touches her chest. "How do you know that?"

"And Charlie, your brother . . . I thought he was a fisherman. That you both were."

"Our mother passed a few months back and Charlie and I are splitting our time between the sea and the shop now that she's no longer around." May asks again how I knew about Carl, and I quickly explain about the letter, how it was one of a few things that led the Rebels to reconsider AmWest's status in this mess.

It is so odd the way all these lives have overlapped. For some reason, it doesn't shock me as much as it could. Instead, I just feel incredibly blessed. That Carl cared enough for May to run away with her. That May was moved enough by what Bree kept repeating in Pine Ridge to consider helping with the rescue. That Adam brought us to Badger who worked in Charlie's shop where it all came together. Such an intricate web of relationships.

"We snuck out before Adam and Badger got up this morning," Bree explains. "Getting to the docks was easy enough with the boat and uniforms. Clipper set up the explosives—had a wetsuit and everything so he could get around unseen—and then after Sammy and I alerted the Order to the rogue 'tracking device,' we went in. Things didn't get messy until the alarm went off."

She doesn't know how much of it I saw in the interrogation room, and plows ahead with the story. I listen to her run through it—the guards, the way Sammy got her out of a bind, finding only Emma in the cells. I barely hear her. I'm caught up in her hand gestures and the way she speaks with such conviction. I want to tell her how it felt to see her on those screens. I want to tell her she is amazing.

"Bree refused to leave without you, so I took Emma to the boat," Sammy cuts in.

"I still don't understand why though," Emma mutters. "I'm a stranger."

"Um, Gray should probably explain that later," he says. I don't blame Sammy for not wanting to break the news to Emma. Who wants to tell someone that their Forgery tried to kill half the people on this boat? She gives me another icy look as he continues. "When I got to the boat, Harvey—who's supposed to be *dead*, mind you—was standing there with Clipper in his arms. The boy was hugging him like a teddy bear."

"I checked his eyes first!" Clipper says. "I knew what he was, but he seemed . . . I don't know. Something was different about him. And he said he'd been helping Gray." Clipper spins to face me. "That's true, right?"

"Yeah, Harvey heard some Mozart while I reminded him of his past life, and it jolted his loyalties. Now he's like Jackson, a malfunctioning Forgery."

"You say *malfunctioning* like it's a bad thing," Harvey says, but Bree looks unamused.

"So Blaine," Emma prompts hesitantly. "He's really . . . ? I mean I heard it, but I hoped . . ."

My brother . . .

Will they throw his body into the water and let the salt eat away at him? Will he settle somewhere on the Gulf floor like my father?

The room is suddenly suffocating.

Too afraid I'll spot pity on their faces, I leave without a backward glance.

It's cold on the deck, and I grip the icy railing just to feel its burn.

If I hadn't chased after Emma in Pine Ridge . . .

If I hadn't attacked my Forgery and tried to run . . .

Would Blaine still be alive?

I gaze out at the horizon, now a line of deep violet that blends with the night sky. If he were here, Blaine would tell me to not beat myself up. He'd probably even claim that this outcome was best, that he'd have wanted me to live if it could only be one of us. Because that was Blaine: putting everything in order, weighing lives like they were things you could barter with in a market.

The real irony is that for once I agree with him. I *can* weigh these two lives—mine and his—and I want it the other way. He has a daughter, a reason to keep going. He is—*was*—such a good person. To his core. To the very center of his being. It should have been him who lived. I wish I could have taken that bullet for him.

"Hey."

I flinch at the nearness of Bree's voice. She's standing a half dozen steps away, a blanket still over her shoulders, her face somber. It kills me, that look. It's like she can feel exactly what I'm feeling even though I didn't ask her to. Even though she shouldn't. Because I wish this on no one—the grief and guilt and horrible, aching emptiness.

She joins me at the railing and rests her forearms against it.

"My ma used to tell me that the dead never really leave us," she says. "She claimed they just changed form, went back to the earth, the sea, the sky. Sometimes I'd catch her whispering to the stars like my father was up there listening." Bree grips the rail and lets the weight of her body hang back, arms outstretched. The blanket nearly falls off her shoulders.

"I thought she was full of it. The dead are dead, right? All that fancy poetry is just a way for people to cover up the ache. But one night after a friend died, I tried talking to the stars, and I swear it helped. It didn't change the fact that he was gone, or how unfair it was, but I felt less alone. More grounded. Like I might actually be okay."

I'm trying to keep it together, but her words are too much. The stars seem exceptionally bright now, and when I look up at them I hear Blaine calling for me, over and over.

"Hey," Bree says again, her eyes searching mine. "It's okay."

And that's what breaks me, because it's not okay. It will never be okay: him, gone.

I slide to the deck and Bree's arms go around me, the blanket engulfing me at the same time. She has one hand in my hair, the other on my back. With my head against her chest I can hear her heartbeat, feel her draw an uneven breath. She pulls me nearer, tighter.

"It really will be okay," she whispers. "I promise."

Her breath is warm despite the cool March night and as she whispers this impossible promise into my hair, again and again, I realize how close we are. The small of her back is beneath my palm, the swell of her chest under my cheek. She smells like salt from the sea. Her neck is just inches from my mouth. I want to kiss her there, lean in and lose myself against her skin. She looks down at me and pauses, our lips just inches apart.

She won't tell me it's a mistake again. I know it by the longing in her eyes and the way her body quivers when my hand slides to her hip. Knowing it's my touch that causes her to react like this makes me want her more than ever. I start thinking about how else her body might move beneath my hands, how we might move together if—

I fly to my feet, let the cold wind wake me.

What is wrong with me? Blaine is dead—he's *dead!*—and I'm thinking with all the wrong parts of my body.

"Gray?"

"I can't." Even as I say the words all I can focus on is the way she felt beneath my hands. "I just . . ." I look at her, willing her to understand. "He's dead, Bree."

"Yes, and it's horrible. It's going to be horrible for a long, long time. Possibly forever. But that doesn't mean you have to suffer for every minute from here on."

"It's too soon."

"I'm not saying you should forget him, Gray, or that it will ever stop hurting. I'm saying you shouldn't force yourself to hurt any more than necessary, that's all."

"You don't know what this feels like, Bree. How it's eating me up. How feeling anything *but* the hurt seems like a disservice to him."

"No, I understand all too well. I've lost people I love, too."

Sure, a father she barely knew to his own Heist. A mother she's had years to come to terms with—just like my own. But nothing like *this*. Nothing recent and fresh and practically a part of her. She doesn't let people get close to her, so who could she possibly have lost that would cause her to feel what I feel right now?

"Punishing yourself—forcing yourself to hurt—isn't going to make things better." She reaches for me and I step backward. "Gray, I mean it."

"Why are you pressing this? You told me you couldn't

in Pine Ridge, that it was a mistake. And now that's all changed?" I can hear my voice rising, but it feels good, like I'm spitting out poison. "Now you want to throw the last two months of ignoring me out the window? How convenient. What perfect timing! Because guess who can't now, Bree? Me. I *can't*. You'll have to find someone else if you're that desperate. Heck, I'm sure Gage would be willing."

It's a cheap blow and I regret it the second it comes out of my mouth.

"Gage is dead. Badger shot him through the mouth."

"Not soon enough!" All I can see is how it's too little too late, how everything is broken beyond repair. "I told you I didn't trust him, but you still let him dig for info that night at the pub—let him flirt and buy drinks and ask questions, and Blaine might still be alive if—"

"Oh, don't you dare do that!" she snaps. "I know you're upset, and devastated, but no! Not that. It isn't fair. Do you realize everything we did—*I* did—to get back to you? I shot down over a dozen men for you. One of them couldn't have been much older than us. It's tearing me up, so don't go making me regret it."

"No one forced you to shoot them, Bree. Or to come after me."

"Ugh, you drive me crazy!" she shrieks. "Just because *you're* hurting doesn't mean you get a free pass to hurt everyone else, Gray. You keep doing that, and no one will be there when you actually need them. Not even me."

She pivots and is gone.

I stare after her, tongue-tied, trying to understand how I went from whimpering to raging in a matter of seconds. Earlier I wanted to tell her she was amazing, *is* amazing. Why didn't I say that instead of things I don't believe? She's all I have left, and I just pushed her away.

For the life of me, I don't know why I did it.

SEVENTEEN

THE RIDE TO PINE RIDGE takes much longer on May's trawler than it did in Gage's boat. The duration of the journey is compounded by the fact that we keep looking at our wake, waiting for the lights of a pursuing boat to appear.

I don't understand why they never do.

"They're probably too busy trying to save that precious ship Clipper blasted," Sammy offers. "Or maybe the security barrier's busted from when we hit it. Locked up, trapping them in."

"They have things that fly," I point out.

"You did blow up your boat," Carl says, one arm slung behind May's neck, the other on the wheel. "Might be they think you're all dead."

No one says anything after that. It seems a bit too lucky to me. We took Harvey, one of Frank's most valuable assets. How is it possible he doesn't care enough to be sweeping the Gulf for us? Is it because he already got what he needed from Harvey? The limitless Forgeries are well into production. And if so, then what about me? What was the point of bringing me all the way there only to let me slip free before getting any useful information? Maybe Frank's written it off as a lost cause now that my Forgery is dead and he has no double to paint with my scars.

I glance out the glass windows encircling the wheelhouse to where Harvey and Clipper stand on the exposed deck. Clipper hasn't stopped smiling since they went out there. I don't know what they're discussing, but I decide it doesn't matter because Clipper looks happier than I've seen him in months. He's telling a story with lots of hand gestures. Harvey watches over the rim of his glasses, intent and patient. His mouth forms a shocked *No*! in response to something Clipper says. The boy nods aggressively, still beaming, and Harvey shakes his head in admiration. He says something else and Clipper's face suddenly goes slack. Then he launches himself at Harvey and hugs him around the middle. The Forgery hugs him back. Like a father.

"We're almost there," Carl announces.

May bounces on the balls of her feet. "Help me on the deck,

Sammy?" And then to me: "Why don't you go round up the girls. I think they went to lie down for a few."

I have never wanted to struggle with ropes and buoys so much in my life.

I leave the bridge and take the stairs down to the crew quarters. The passage is eerily similar to the *Catherine*'s. The last time I walked down a hall like this looking for Bree, I didn't know if I'd find her alive.

Voices drift from one of the quarters ahead. They're not napping like May said, and so I'm not quite sure why I start walking as quietly as possible.

"I'm sure he wanted to save you both," Bree is saying, her voice unusually soft. Sympathetic. "Gray's heart is a lot bigger than he likes people to think."

"You've known him long?"

"Long enough."

There's a short pause and then Emma says, "I can't forgive him for it. I won't ever be able to look at him and *not* think about that moment."

I wish I'd been able to tell Bree about my Forgery, the choice he forced upon me. I should have leaned on her earlier, explained why it all hurt so damn much by talking my way through it instead of blaming her for something that isn't her fault.

"I understand completely, Emma, but at the same time, is

that fair? It was a horrible situation to be put in."

"Nothing in life is fair. A lot of it's luck and even then everyone gets screwed at least once."

Bree laughs. "I like you a heck of a lot better than your Forgery."

"*What?*"

"Never mind."

"No. You don't get to say *my Forgery* and then change the subject."

"I really think Gray should explain it to you, like Sammy said."

"Bree," Emma says, and her name sounds like a door slamming. "I'm not waiting any longer for an explanation. Frank had me tending to some of them in the hospital. I know exactly what they are, and exactly what they're capable of, so don't think you're doing me any favors by sparing me the truth. What did you mean when you said *my* Forgery?"

Bree exhales. "Gray thought it was you, the girl he brought back to Crevice Valley. She came west with us to Group A, served as our medic, waited for the perfect moment to betray our team. By the time we realized she was a Forgery, she'd leaked our information several times over."

"What? . . . I can't— Is she out there still?" Emma asks. "Please tell me no. Please tell me she's not—"

"She's dead," Bree says. "I shot her."

There's a muffled sob, and then relieved tears. I can hear Bree awkwardly trying to calm Emma, telling her not to cry, that it's over. My legs don't want to work, so I just stand there several paces from the room, completely useless. Which is likely what I'd be *in* the room, too. I've never been good in these sorts of moments.

"I could kill him," Emma says.

"Frank? No one here would argue that." Bree pauses a moment. "Look, I get it. I know how awful the Order is. It's impossible to face them and walk away without a scar—physical or otherwise. And yes, life isn't always fair, and a lot of it *is* luck, but if everyone gets screwed once like you claim, then the Order's turn is coming. We'll give them a violent shove in the right direction. Real soon. The team's been planning for so long I'm about ready to explode."

"Will you tell them I . . ."

"Had a minor meltdown as any sane person would when learning they had a vicious double? No. Not unless you want me to."

"Not particularly," Emma says.

"Then I won't. Seriously, I mean it. Why are you giving me that look?"

"Sammy told me you could be mean."

"Sammy said that?" The softness in Bree's voice is gone. "I'm gonna kick his sorry ass when we're back on land."

"See *that*," Emma says, and I imagine her pointing at Bree. "That sounds more like what he warned me of."

"I'm not mean," Bree insists. "I just don't think there's a point in taking crap from anyone. Too many people let themselves get walked all over and I decided years ago to say what I believe and not apologize for it. Some people call that mean. I think it's honest."

"But what if you're wrong about something? Do you apologize then?"

"Not always as soon as I should. But I do. After I work up the courage."

I feel like I'm listening to strangers become friends in the span of five minutes, and it's making me uncomfortable. Strangers should have walls up. They should be waiting for proof that the other is decent and trustworthy.

"Thanks for this." Emma draws a ragged breath. "I feel like I haven't just *talked* with someone in months. Actually, sometimes I feel like I haven't laughed in months either."

"Then maybe we should go find Sammy," Bree offers. "He's good for that. And besides, I owe him a piece of my *honest* mind."

I jolt to action, walking the remaining length of the hall noisily so they can hear me coming, and knock on the doorframe. "We're nearing shore," I say, hanging half my torso around the jamb. They're sitting on a bottom bunk together,

Emma with her knees pulled in toward her chest, Bree with one leg tucked beneath her and the other dangling over the side. Only Bree greets my gaze.

"Great. We'll be right up."

It's a dismissal; I'm not meant to wait for them.

Above deck I'm happy to help Sammy and May dock the boat. It's a straightforward task with a clear end goal and no surprises. The rig gets secured. The gear is unloaded. Everything makes sense.

The town is sleepy when we disembark. Smoke leaks lazily from chimneys and lights glow from behind only a few windowpanes.

"Be on guard," Carl warns.

"For?" Sammy draws his gun, though I'm skeptical it will even work after taking a swim in salt water.

"Nothing's waiting for us here, but that doesn't mean someone isn't waiting back *there*." Carl points in the general direction of the bookshop.

Harvey holds a hand out. "Give me a spare. I don't like being unarmed if we could be facing something."

This desire to carry a weapon is so unlike Harvey, but Sammy passes over an extra knife without comment. Harvey grunts, and his eyes drift toward Bree. She's standing on the edge of the wharf, facing the Gulf, and it's obvious she has plenty of firearms to spare. The rifle has returned to its place across her back, and two handguns are holstered at her hips. In the end, Harvey doesn't argue. He pulls Clipper a little closer and adjusts his grip on the knife.

As we start our walk to the shop, a loon call cuts through the night. I turn toward the water. Not a loon call. Bree. She's still standing on the lip of the wharf, her hands cupped at her lips. Her shoulders move as she draws another breath, and it is followed by a second cry, a whistle produced right from her hands.

I know she won't get an actual response—it's far too late for the birds to be out—but the song she's producing is so beautiful that I stand there anyway, mesmerized. It sounds like a good-bye, and I decide that, at least for me and Blaine, it is. I try to make my own, and not surprisingly, I fail.

I listen to Bree's calls and look up at the stars and talk to Blaine in the corners of my mind. I promise him I'll set things right. I'll get back to Kale, hug her for both of us, be as much of a father to her as I possibly can now that he's gone. I'll make sure his death isn't for naught.

With these promises, the ache in my abdomen becomes a fire, a fuel, a reason to keep going. I actually feel it happen. There's this small twist in my gut where the grief shrivels into a hardened pit of resolve. I feel so possessed in that moment, so at peace with my words to Blaine, that I realize I have no choice but to succeed. I'll make this right, or I'll die trying. And I'm completely okay with that.

Bree drops her arms to her sides, cutting a loon cry off abruptly. When she turns to face me, I feel like we're the only two people in the world.

"I'm so sorry about earlier," I say. "I didn't mean it."

"I know."

"You're the last person I want to push away, Bree. Ever. But I wasn't thinking straight and—"

"I *know*," she says tersely. "But thank you."

EIGHTEEN

"**WHAT IF YOU'D BEEN CAUGHT?**" Badger yells. "What if they'd traced the uniforms to Mercy? To *me*?"

We're back in Charlie's apartment above the bookshop, and this is our welcome.

"May?" Badger wheels on her. "So help me. I owe your ma for letting me run operations from the back room, but I don't owe *you*." Badger holds a finger an inch from her nose. "If you took that boat even when I told you not to, I swear I'll—"

"It was me," Bree says. "No one would have gone against your orders if I hadn't convinced them."

"You stupid, idiotic—"

The second Badger's hand pinches her chin, I knock him away.

"Don't touch her," I snap.

"I'll do whatever I damn well need to when my team ignores my orders."

He advances again and this time I throw my palms into his chest. He draws his gun and I draw mine and in the blink of an eye we are standing in the middle of the sitting room, staring at each other's barrels.

"She is the only reason I'm alive," I snap. "Her and this team."

"It very well could have played out differently."

"But it didn't, and you can't hold it against Bree—or any of them—for breaking me free and completing your damn mission in the process. Because that's what we did. I got all the info you were after and then some. We can figure out what to do with that together, or you can get the hell out."

Badger regards me over the sight of his gun, eyes narrowed.

"Gray, I'm sorry we didn't come for you," Adam says. "I really am. We couldn't risk it."

"It's done, Adam," I say. "The only thing we have control over is what happens next, and that's what I want to focus on."

Despite the late hour, we end up at the kitchen table, our differences temporarily discarded. I recount my time at the Compound. Every last detail, from the intel the Order was after and the interrogation I endured, to the production lab of limitless Forgeries and the way Harvey cracked and aided in my escape.

"It's worse than we thought," Adam says. "If Frank has those numbers, if he's already manning his cities with them, we won't stand a chance."

"Actually," Harvey says, "that's not entirely true." He upends his backpack on the table. A bunch of technical gear tumbles out, all secured in some sort of waterproof packaging.

"What's on the hard drives?" Clipper asks.

"Research, backup files, possibly your salvation." This must be the plan Harvey alluded to, and the gear he went to retrieve after leaving me partially unbound in the interrogation room. "I'll need access to a computer, and a bit of time to dig through everything, but I'm hopeful. This idea I have . . . It just might . . . Well, I'd rather confirm it will work before I give everyone false hope."

"Maybe Harvey can use your equipment?" Adam asks Badger.

"Sure."

"Just like that?" Bree says, snapping her fingers. "We walk him right into our inner circle and give him access to anything he wants?"

"Come on, Bree," Clipper says.

"I know you're happy about this, Clip, but he's still a

Forgery. One who was awfully quick to ditch his orders. It took Jackson forever to decide to help us, and Harvey turned like a switch was flipped."

I open my mouth to argue but no words come. Is *this* why the Order didn't follow us from the Compound? Do they *want* Harvey to be here with us? The possibility that I have brought a spy—one of the most brilliant men I know—directly into the Expats' inner circle makes me shiver.

"I untied Gray in the interrogation lab," Harvey says, glaring at Bree. "I told him how to get to the docks."

"And maybe you'll tell the Order how to find us next," she throws back.

"His tracker!" Adam says, jumping to his feet.

"I clipped him on the boat," Clipper says. "Emma, too. Had to do it the old-fashioned way—knife and feel—but those chips are at the bottom of the Gulf."

Harvey pulls the collar of his jacket aside to reveal bandages. I must have been on the deck when this happened. Throwing all my pain at Bree. Being horrible.

"See? He's clean," Clipper says to Bree. "I'll keep an eye on him. I'll shadow him every second in the labs. I promise."

"You make one suspicious move," Bree says, leaning toward Harvey across the table, "and I will tear your fingernail off like you did to Gray. Only I won't stop at one. You hear me, Harvey?" Then she leans into my shoulder and whispers, "We should keep an eye on him. Something's not right about this."

I nod, hoping she's wrong.

But she's not wrong often. And this doesn't bode well.

Beneath the blanket of night, we relocate from the bookshop to a hotel on the outskirts of town. Even though Badger took care of Gage and the few men helping him, Adam feels like the shop is no longer safe.

"I don't get it," I say to him as we walk. "We have Harvey. Why didn't they come after us?"

He shrugs. "They probably think he's dead—that we killed him and threw him overboard. That's where his tracker would have terminated."

"They're too smart to not dig for confirmation. Why aren't the docks crawling with Order members?"

"We've had a delicate treaty with the East for a while now. They might overstep their bounds on the water, but for the most part, they respect the borders."

"But *why* do they respect the borders? I feel like Frank could overrun us in a heartbeat."

"If you believe what you hear around campfires and after a couple drinks," Adam says, "Frank had a child with some lowly Union Central cook ages back. She was young, and so it was kept quiet, and they never married. When Frank's methods in AmEast became too much for the girl, she apparently took their kid and fled west. Some people think Frank's afraid to aggressively attack because he's still hoping for a reunion with his son, and doesn't want to compromise the boy's safety. Well, *man* by now, given all the years that have passed."

I rub the back of my neck. "I've never heard a thing about him having a son."

"You wouldn't have. These are AmWest tales. People go to all sorts of extremes to set their minds at ease, even if it means inventing stories."

"Do *you* think it's just a story?"

"Vik says the whole thing is laughable, and I agree."

We slow outside the hotel. I spot the Expat emblem carved at the base of the establishment's doorframe, ragged enough that most wouldn't give it a second glance. Adam exchanges a few words with the owner, three fingers splayed across his chest in greeting, and secures us rooms for the night. He takes a single for himself, and pairs the rest of us off.

I follow Sammy into the room we'll be sharing.

It is small, with a lone window looking onto a dingy alley, but the bed is spacious. A thinning quilt of Expat colors is spread across it. There's a faint scent of inactivity—dust and old air—suggesting the place doesn't get many visitors.

"I feel like I'm in a cave," Sammy says.

"With a bed?"

"I feel like I'm in a cozy but dimly lit cave."

I drop my bag near the window, too exhausted to give him a courtesy laugh.

"Hey, about Blaine . . ."

"If you're going to say you're sorry or it's awful or you can't imagine, please don't."

"I was going to offer to say a few words. And if you wanted, we could have a fire later. Sort of like we did after Burg."

I find myself pulling him into a hug before I consciously decide to do it. He's slightly taller than Blaine and thinner in build, and the moment I notice these subtle differences, my eyes begin to burn.

I break away, mumble my thanks.

"We'll make them pay," Sammy promises. "For this. For everything."

PART THREE

OF CODE

NINETEEN

IN THE MORNING, NOTHING HAS changed. We're still in a dreary hotel room. The sun has still risen. Blaine is still dead.

I hear the sound of a running shower first—Sammy— followed by the bustle of people moving through the alley outside the window. I pull on some fresh clothes and, though I desperately need to wash the salt and sorrow off my body, I make for the hall.

Harvey and Clipper don't answer my knocks, so I try Adam.

"He's talking to the owner," Bree says. She's standing in the doorway of her room, dressed in a clean tank that tucks into her belted and salt water—encrusted pants. Emma is behind her, a sweater pulled tightly around her torso. They wear identical scowls. It makes me wonder if Emma was always good at scowling and I'm only just realizing it.

"We're supposed to do chores or something this morning," Bree adds. "To pay for our rooms."

"You're kidding." If Adam thinks I'll be content to do chores—again, after everything—he's crazy.

"Did it sound like she was?" Emma snaps. "Do you think people say things without reason, Gray? Do things without motive?"

I pause, mouth open.

"I think I'll go check in with Adam," Bree says. She glances over her shoulder as she retreats down the hall, looking both apologetic and amused at once.

"You're a selfish bastard, you know that?" Emma continues.

"Excuse me?"

"What happened with Craw was *none* of your business. You showed up when it was convenient for you and then had the nerve to act like you were the only one wronged, like I was horrible for moving on with my life. I thought you were dead, Gray. You left me alone. For months. And even still, I was ready to put it all behind me once I knew you were alive. I told Craw it was over that very day you showed up at my door, and then I was left behind *again*. Somehow, I deserve to die for all that? For being human? You picked Blaine because he never *betrayed* you?"

"I picked Blaine because he was my brother."

"You picked him because you're too selfish to forgive me and too afraid to face the world without him! I won't ever forgive you for that."

"Good! I'll never forgive myself either. You think I wanted this, Emma? To have to choose? To lose someone?"

Her eyes have this quality to them I've never seen before: narrowed, vicious.

"It was easy, admit it. How could it be hard to toss aside the girl who didn't *wait* for you?"

"Stop it," I snarl. "I forgave you ages ago. You had a second chance with the first guy you ever felt things for in Claysoot and as far as you knew, I was dead. Like you said, the only thing you are guilty of is being human. It took me a while to understand that, but I meant every word when I apologized to you back in December."

"December?" Emma squints at me.

"She looked just like you, Emma. Everything was identical. Her voice and memories and the way she only smiled halfway. She was good with people, especially Aiden. That kid loved you. Sammy, too."

"Sammy?" She takes a step away from me. "He loved . . .

Is that why he's been . . . ?"

"The point is I'm over it, Emma. I told your Forgery the same thing, and I'm sorry you're only just hearing it now."

"You told her, and then she handed you to the Order? No wonder you picked Blaine."

"Don't do that," I say. "It was awful what happened on the Compound, but it had nothing to do with your Forgery, or Craw, or . . ." I sigh, defeated. "He was my brother, Emma. My twin."

"And I didn't outrank him. I get it," she says with a frown. "Good thing it wasn't Blaine and *her* in that room." She tilts her head in the direction Bree walked off. "That would have been a fun choice, huh?"

"That's not fair, Emma."

"Do you love her?" she asks. Her brows raise expectantly, and the thought of lying is exhausting. Emma is smart. She already sees the truth, or at least suspects it.

"Yeah," I say after a moment. "I do."

"Well, you thought you loved me once, too, so be careful."

I've never seen this side of Emma before, so vindictive. The previous night resurfaces—throwing my words at Bree, wanting her to hurt because I did—and I decide this isn't really Emma. It's Emma overloaded with grief, drowning in it.

Maybe she's right to never forgive me. Maybe we're beyond mending. I firmly believe that time can change anything, but even a distant friendship between us seems impossible right now, and that's so tragically depressing I can feel the ache like a sunburn on my skin.

"I miss him," I tell her. "I always will. But I *am* glad you're okay. I never wanted you hurt."

"Somehow, it's really hard for me to believe that."

She disappears into her room and slams the door.

It's an overcast morning, threatening storms by the taste of the air. I head for the bookshop, hoping to catch Harvey and Clipper at work. I'm still not sure what their plan is, but I know aiding them will be the best use of my time. Sammy was already hard at work coaxing Emma from her room when I bailed—not that I expected her to open the door for me—and Bree was bound to return with nothing but a list of chores.

The walk to the hotel seemed straightforward when Adam guided us last night, but as I try to backtrack under the weak morning sunlight, everything looks different. I'm about to scramble up a gutter and take the roofs toward shore when I spot a dark-suited figure crossing the alley ahead.

My heart rate spikes, and I dart behind the nearest

chimney, leaning into the building's facade. I wait a moment, then cautiously peer around the brick. No Order member. Just a man in a shabby jacket picking through an overflowing garbage can. I clench and unclench my fists. Everything with the Compound has me wound so tight that I see one Pine Ridge citizen wearing dark clothes and assume it's the enemy.

I shake my head and grab hold of a gutter. With the help of a windowsill and footholds in the adjacent chimney, I make my way to the roof. Then I hop a few narrow alleys, moving between buildings until I get my bearings. By the time I finally arrive at the bookshop it's drizzling.

Charlie is behind the counter, devouring another novel, and Badger is complaining about spies. He's now convinced that every single person working for him is one.

"Are Harvey and Clipper here?" I ask when Badger stops ranting long enough for me to get a word in.

"In the back." Charlie shakes a thumb over his shoulder, barely glancing up from his read. A gunshot from somewhere in the streets shocks us both. "What the—?"

I race for the nearest window, but Badger's already claimed it. I dart to the second and battle Charlie for a vantage point.

A bit farther up the street, a small group of children stands rigid with shock. Two men tower over them, dressed in dark uniforms, one with his weapon pointed toward the sky. There is no mistaking these men for civilians.

The Order member who fired the warning shot kicks the ball the children have been playing with. Their eyes follow it as it bounces down the street, but they don't dare move.

The Order member says something we can't hear.

The children stand a little taller.

Another demand is made, and when the children remain stoic, the nearest is backhanded. A man runs from a nearby building—maybe the child's father. He pulls the shaking boy to his feet, checks his face, then wheels on the Order members.

I want to tell him not to shout, but he already is. I want to warn him not to retaliate, but his fist is already flying.

A gun is drawn, a blast fired, and the man is on the ground.

The children stare. One starts to cry.

The sprinkling drizzle becomes a steady rain.

The Order member holds out a piece of paper and snarls a threat we can't make out. I know what's on that paper though. My face. Or Harvey's. Someone they want.

A trembling child raises a hand and points toward the bookshop.

We step away from the windows.

"Get them out," Badger says, and draws his handgun.

"But the streets . . . ," Charlie argues.

"The back exit. Then to May and Carl."

Charlie drags me into the back room, bolting the door behind us.

"What's going on?" Harvey asks. He's sitting at Badger's desk with Clipper, a series of notebooks spread out around the computer.

"The Order's in town," Charlie says. "We need to get you to the docks. May and Carl are pushing off for a few days of fishing, and you need to catch them before they do."

He clears a bunch of water crates from the center of the room to reveal a trapdoor.

"What about the others?" I ask. "Bree and Sammy and—"

"I'll try to get word to them, but you guys have to move while you still have the chance." Charlie yanks the trapdoor open. "Take the tunnel 'til it ends. The stairs there connect to Badger's house, which'll put you a block from the wharf."

"We can't just leave the rest of the team."

"You don't have a choice."

Back in the bookshop, the muffled ding of the entrance bell sounds. Harvey grimaces, surveying his options: the storefront or the trapdoor. For a split second I think Bree might be right, that he's going to march to that hidden door and throw it open, show the Order exactly where we're hiding. But he only grabs Clipper by the cheeks and plants a kiss on the boy's forehead.

"Go," he says, pushing him toward the trapdoor. "We'll be right behind you."

In the storefront, muffled arguing breaks out. Harvey shovels the notebooks and hard drives into his backpack.

We're in the dark tunnel and fleeing before we're able to hear how things unfold overhead.

TWENTY

BADGER'S HOUSE IS SPOTLESS: MINIMAL furniture, and even less personality. It's like he owns the place as a front and nothing more.

We survey our path to the docks from the second-floor windows. A few buildings obstruct the view, but from the commotion in town, it seems the Order is still congregating around the bookshop.

"Put this on." Harvey throws me a lump of cloth from Badger's dresser.

I shake it out. It's a dark hooded shirt. The hood is oversized, and when I pull it up, I feel completely shielded from the world. Harvey puts on one of Badger's hats in an effort to hide his own face.

When we're ready to make our move, Clipper sticks his head outside, scanning the streets. A quick nod and we're on our way, racing through the rain. It's now pouring so hard I can barely see more than a wingspan in front of me, but we make it to the wharf without incident. If there are Order crews keeping watch from their boat, they can't see any better than we can.

As soon as we're onboard, the boat lurches to life.

"Wait!" I cry to May. "The rest of the team."

I glance at the shore like I expect them to appear there, but all I see is a thick sheet of rain and a plume of smoke battling it. Right around where the bookshop stands. *Stood.*

"What are you staying out here for?" May snaps. "Head down. They'll be happy to see you."

"They'll . . . ?" My eyes trail to the nearest stairwell.

"In the crew quarters."

I take the steep stairs too quickly. They're slick with rain, and I tumble down the last few, catching myself on my hands and knees. In the narrow hallway, I call out for them.

Bree appears first, darting from one of the bunk rooms so quickly she has to pull herself to a stop by the jamb of the door.

"You idiot!" She shoves me in the chest with both hands. "Ducking out"—another shove—"and we had no clue where you were"—another—"and I thought . . . I thought . . ." She slumps against my chest and hugs me around the middle. "Damn, you scared me, Gray. You scared me so much."

"Sorry." I fold my arms around her.

Sammy steps into the hallway and Bree straightens, puts a formal distance between us.

"Nice of you to join us," he says.

"How'd you guys know to get to the boat?" I ask.

"Adam wasn't checking with the hotel owner about chores. A tip came in during the earlier morning hours—from one of Bleak's team—that the Order was in town. Couldn't have been more than five minutes after you left that Adam told us to pack."

"He thinks they're searching for you and Harvey," Bree adds. "I knew that Forgery would be nothing but trouble."

"We're heading for Bone Harbor," Sammy explains. "There will be no going back to Pine Ridge. Hiding will be impossible, and the Expats probably won't even make a stand against those Order members tossing town. Vik won't want to waste resources or lose supporters to a fight. We need them."

"For what exactly?"

"We'll have a tough time getting that info from Adam now."

I eye the crew quarters behind him. Emma stands in the doorway, but no one comes to join her.

"How?" I ask.

"He hung back at the hotel and promised to slow them

down, wanted to give us a head start," Sammy says. "If we'd known what he had planned . . ."

"He detonated something," Bree says. "Manually, from the inside, once the Order filed in. There's no way he survived the blast."

I wonder momentarily if the smoke I saw came from the hotel, not the bookshop. All those times I gave Adam a hard time about not being committed to this fight . . .

"And Charlie? Badger?"

"No word yet," Sammy responds. "Looks like it's our cozy little team again."

At a predetermined location on the Gulf, May's trawler meets a second. September waves to us through the rain, a small smile on her lips.

After securing the boats together—a near-impossible task in the choppy conditions—our crew climbs the railings and leaps over to September's ship. She introduces us to Daley, an AmEast fisherman who she claims is one of Badger's best clients. We're cutting across the water again before I have a chance to shout a good-bye to May and Carl, but maybe this is best. Good-byes lately have seemed so permanent. And this isn't good-bye. I hope not, at least. We'll just be walking different roads for a while.

Before we're in sight of shore, September ushers the team

belowdecks. She lifts a panel of flooring in the crew quarters to reveal a hidden storage compartment for smuggled goods. I imagine it's often filled with drinking water, but today, it holds spare fishing gear.

"You expect us to all fit in that matchbox?" Sammy says.

"Course not. Inspection crews know about this compartment. It's standard on a lot of ships." She hauls out the gear. "You're going below."

This is when we realize the floor gives way again, to a space no less cramped. We'll fit, but only if we all lie down, shoulder to shoulder, and are shut in like corpses.

"Come on," September urges. "I don't have time for fits of claustrophobia. I might have a few people in my pocket in Bone Harbor, but I can't escort you in plain sight."

"Will there be enough air?" Bree asks.

"It's ventilated," September assures her. "And it's not for too long."

"But *long* can be so subjective," Sammy muses.

"Just get in."

I go first. Bree follows. Then Sammy, Emma, Clipper, and Harvey, until we're lined up like game on a rack.

"Not a sound until I lift this door back up," September warns. "You have to wait out the inspection, and then for the port to clear. I'll get you when it's safe."

The panel comes down, trapping us in and leaving us blind.

"I'm in a coffin," Sammy says. "I've been buried alive."

"Shut up," Bree hisses.

The second panel is secured overhead with a muffled thud.

"Could be worse, I suppose. At least I'm sandwiched between two pretty girls."

Bree elbows him. "Shut your face, Sammy. You're wasting air."

"It's ventilated," he mutters, but he falls quiet after that.

We wait for what feels like forever. The rig eventually slows. I feel the ship scraping against a dock, hear the muffled shouts of the crew securing it. Footsteps follow overhead.

"I told you, already," September says. "We're clean."

"We'll be the judge of that," a gruff voice responds. Feet pound nearer, stopping right above us. Another stomp. "Hear that? This model's got a standard storage compartment, no? Garrett! Check this."

The first panel is ripped away. Gear is riffled through. I have never felt so helpless in my life. Beside me, Bree reaches for the gun at her waist. The space is so tight, she has to draw it with her left hand and awkwardly pass it to her right. She switches off the safety, presses the barrel to the wood above our noses.

"Just spare rope and netting, sir," the second inspector—Garrett—says. He sounds young.

"Fine. Close it up."

The gear is thrown against the board separating our compartment from the dummy one. The top slams shut. A bit of dust floods our space.

And Clipper sneezes.

We all go rigid.

"Damn dust," Garrett says, sniffling overhead. The floor creaks as he stands. "Well, aren't you gonna say bless you?"

"Kid, you better watch your mouth with me. Get out of here."

One set of boots leaves.

"This is the second time you've come into port on Daley's rig in the last week. You got a thing for married men?"

"Just like being on the water, sir," September answers.

A grunt. "I'm watching you."

He leaves. I breathe a bit easier. But then September leaves, too, the sound of her boots following the footsteps that have already faded.

Confinement like this makes you lose track of time. What feels like hours pass, and we are still in the dark. The compartment seems to grow smaller with each inhale. The walls are collapsing. The air getting dirty, heavy, thick. Bree is pressed firmly against my right side, wood against my other. My legs are cramping. My back aches.

"I'm regretting those jokes about coffins," Sammy says. When no one humors him, he adds, "Tough crowd."

"Sammy," Bree hisses, "I am miserable and cranky and uncomfortable. Do you really want to piss me off?"

Before he has a chance to answer, we hear footsteps returning. September. *Finally*.

The first panel is removed. The gear yanked up and cleared aside. Then, at long last, our ceiling is lifted away. I'm temporarily blinded. Everything seems large and my depth perception is off. When things make sense, I spot a face above us. Young and wide-eyed and frozen in fear as Bree brings her weapon to his forehead.

"The only reason I haven't pulled this trigger is because it will be loud," she says. It's then I notice his Order uniform.

"I'm Garrett," he says frantically. "I work with September."

"Sure you do."

"You think I couldn't see the second door? I'm no idiot. And I covered when one of you sneezed. I'm on your side."

"Where's September?"

"Distracting my boss so I can get you guys into town."

Bree's eyes narrow. "There are six of us and one of you. Do anything suspicious that might compromise our safety and it will be your last act." She lowers her weapon but keeps a finger near the trigger.

"Does she always show gratitude this way?" Garrett asks as he extends a hand to pull me to my feet.

"Pretty much."

Bree punches me in the arm. My limbs are too cramped to bother fighting back.

TWENTY-ONE

IT'S WEIRD TO BE BACK in Bone Harbor. I never thought I'd see this place again and I'm almost shocked to realize I missed the smell of it—the salt and wet wood and smoking chimneys.

Garrett leads us to a two-story house that looks as dreary as most homes in town. The west side of the building has aged twice as fast as the others. The paint peels from the Gulf's salty mist, and some of the boards are rotting, but inside, the place is dry and warm.

The first floor is shared by Garrett and his older siblings— one brother and one sister—who happen to be the same Expat-friendly citizens September mentioned working with when she visited us at the bookshop. She and Aiden rent out the upstairs floor.

"Did you want to see the basement?" Garrett asks the group after a round of introductions. "I heard you might need access to a computer while you're here."

Sammy lifts his shoulder, showing off his backpack. "I'm dropping this gear first."

"You, then?" Garrett says, nudging my arm. "I want to show you something."

Clipper offers to take my bag up for me, so I stay with Garrett. The main hallway is fully carpeted, but he grips a corner and strips back the material to reveal a trapdoor. I follow him down a rickety set of stairs and into a basement filled with computers, radio scanners, map-strewn walls, and enough crumpled wads of paper to fill several books.

"Bea's real picky about getting the stories right," he explains, kicking some of the paper aside. "Says people count on the *Harbinger* and we can't release anything but the finest. It would be irresponsible."

I eye a bulky contraption in the corner where most of the papers seem to congregate.

"You guys print it right here?"

He nods.

"But you work for the Order."

"I've had to do things I'm not proud of," Garrett admits. "I cover for folks as often as I can, but sometimes there's no alternative. If we want eyes on the most precious information, this is the way to do it. I have to be truly inside, and convincing.

"Bea started the *Harbinger* a few years back, before I even began this undercover stuff. She's always been the one with initiative. Our dad worked for the Order in Haven, and she fought with him every damn day because she didn't agree with his values. One day she took me and my brother and hopped a boat south without telling him. Dad'd probably call her a crazy conspiracy theorist if he saw what she was up to now. How she's got me working inspections to pick up stories, Greg listening to radio scanners and hacking into any Order database he can manage. That or beat the living crap out of her. Moral codes aside, it's probably good we ditched him. He wasn't right in the head."

Bea didn't look much older than September when we were introduced. She's probably been acting as a mother for more than half her life.

"Here." Garrett flattens out one of the crumpled pieces of paper. "This is what I wanted to show you."

My face fills the majority of the page. *Alive and Well Despite Order Rumors*, the headline reads.

"It's great, isn't it?"

I say nothing.

"The Order released some horrible photo of you the other day. Slumped against a wall. Stomach bleeding."

Of course they did. My Forged counterpart may be dead, but the corpse could still serve a purpose.

"You don't look like you took a bullet to the stomach," Garrett adds.

"That's because I didn't."

I could tell him about the Forgery, but it's too much—too heavy, too complex, too personal. The image of Blaine, slack and lifeless on the Compound floor, flashes through my mind.

"It's really good to meet you," Garrett says. "I've been . . . Well, it makes me braver. Each day I have to go down to the docks and search boats, never knowing when I'm going to find something I might want to hide, not sure if I'm going to have to turn someone in. It's easier to face that knowing you're doing the same thing. That you're my age. That you're fighting it all despite the odds."

"I'm not doing anything, Garrett. Your sister's really good at spinning things to fit her needs."

He glances at the wrinkled document.

"It's not true, then? That you stole a vaccine from beneath Frank's nose? That you outsmarted his troops in the Western

Territory and then crossed the border despite his best man being on your tail?"

"It's all true, but I didn't do it alone. I had help, and when I didn't, I had luck. I'm just a guy trying to get by. I'm nothing miraculous."

"People need to believe in miracles."

"But not lies."

He crumples the paper in his fist. "You repeat any of that to Bea and I'll punch your damn teeth in. People need this. *She* needs this. And so long as one person is still hopeful, nothing she prints is a lie."

He pushes the balled article into my chest as he leaves.

Upstairs, it's obvious September is treating her floor of the house as a temporary home. Bare walls. Mismatched chairs around a kitchen table. Little to no furniture beyond the mattresses in the bedrooms, and two sagging couches in the sitting area. Aiden's camped out there now, playing a game of Rock, Paper, Scissors with Emma as Rusty dozes at his feet.

"Again!" Aiden bobs a fist up and down, waiting for her to join in another round. He greeted her like a puppy when we arrived, bounding to her, hugging her around the legs. And she let him. Before I could even make eye contact with her, shake my head in a small cringe as if to say, *Don't tell him the truth*, she had already decided as much.

As I watch them sit on the couch together, her flattening her palm only to have Aiden snip it with his scissor fingers, I feel like I'm watching him play with her Forgery. Some pieces of Emma were in that thing. So many pieces. Especially her way with others, her temperament and caring nature, her desire to set everyone at ease. It's both amazing and profoundly terrifying.

"All right already. You've lost the last five rounds. It's my turn." Sammy grabs Emma around the middle, hauling her backward on the couch. She laughs. Aiden grins. The game continues. It continues like it never ended. I get a rush in my chest as I realize that it never has to. That if things go right—if we figure out a way to fix everything—moments like this might never have a reason to end.

September steps up behind me. "Stubborn as a cockroach, huh?" For a minute, I think she's talking about people, how they never give up, not even when every last odd seems stacked against them, but then she shakes a thumb at Harvey. He's digging through his bag, Clipper at his side.

"I told him he should eat first, get something in his stomach, but he insisted on heading right to work."

"You know Harvey. Setting goals and refusing to let up until they're accomplished."

"Passionate," she says, bobbing her head.

"Plus a touch of crazy."

September pulls her disheveled hair loose, smooths it back, and resecures it.

"Hey, thanks for everything earlier—the boat and inspection crew. What did you have to do to distract Garrett's boss?"

"He thinks I have a thing for married men. And he's, well, *married*."

My eyes widen.

"No, geez, Gray. I kissed the guy, but I didn't sleep with him. I've got my limits. I'm gonna have to wash my mouth out with soap later, though. I swear I can still taste the cigar he'd been smoking." She waves a thumb at the kitchen. "You hungry? I could go for dinner."

I feel like I'm always underestimating the women on our team.

After shoveling down some food, I take a shower. I am coated with days-old sweat, salt from my swim in the Gulf yesterday, and grime from the tunnel beneath the bookshop. To wash it all away feels like shedding a layer of skin.

Aiden and Rusty are asleep on the couch when I come out of the bathroom, but otherwise, the top floor is empty. I pull on my hooded shirt and head downstairs, where I find the team huddled in the sitting room with Garrett and his siblings. September is running some sort of debriefing meeting, but Harvey and Clipper are not in attendance. *Downstairs*, Bree mouths when she catches my eye.

I make my way to the basement. They look like father and son at the computers, both staring intently at the screens.

"Gray!" Clipper says, waving me over. "You won't believe this. It's amazing. It's—" He waves more frantically, and then grabs my wrist and tugs me toward the computer. The screen is filled with line after line of code. A forefinger against the screen, he says, "See?"

"Clip, you know I have no clue what I'm looking at."

"This is the core program that runs in all Forgeries," he explains. "It was on the stolen hard drives." Harvey gives me a queasy sort of smile, like he's moments away from being sick. "He's not feeling too well," Clipper adds in a hushed voice. "I think showing me all this is conflicting with his . . . internal orders."

"What's so special about having this code?" I ask.

"It's the building blocks of the Forgery," Clipper says. "It's what makes them loyal to Frank, what gives them purpose."

"And we can change it somehow?"

"Sure, we can rewrite this however we want but that doesn't do us any good. It's not like what we do here is tied to all the Forgeries already in existence. This is just a backup."

"What's important is this function," Harvey says, motioning to a section of the code. "I wrote it—well, the original me wrote it—ages ago, when I was working on the earliest versions of the Forgeries. This function is buried within a bunch of other functions, all of which make a Forgery loyal. It's been used in every model since the first.

"During my time at the Compound, as I worked on creating a limitless Forgery, or as the Order's been calling it, an F-GenX, this function always stood out as odd. It was sloppy. Nested in too many conditionals. It seemed almost unnecessary, but I never deleted it. I was worried removing it might break the Forgery's loyalty. And any time I tried to truly understand the function's purpose, the logic surrounding it would get all fuzzy, like I was trying to read the code without my glasses. But after Mozart brought all my memories back, I knew I had to take a second look at it. And this one little function . . ." He taps the screen again. "I know what it means now."

"It's like how Jackson's mind cleared once he broke," Clipper says. "Harvey couldn't understand this bit of code because his greater programming was telling him to ignore it, that it was nothing but lazy coding and he shouldn't overthink things. But now . . ."

"This is a fail-safe," Harvey says. "Frank didn't want one, but you should *always* have a way to pull the plug, no matter what you're building. I wrote this in secretly, hiding it in the code, and once I started doubting my work for Frank, I was glad I did."

"And this helps us how?" I ask, staring at the screen.

"The fail-safe function exists in every version of the Forgeries today, and it will run when they hear a certain audible phrase."

"Like a verbal order?"

"Not exactly. More like a very precise string of sounds," Harvey says. "Emit them in the right order, for the appropriate duration, and this function will be tripped, and the Forgeries' programming aborted."

"Which means they break down like you and Jackson?"

"No, when I wrote the fail-safe, it was with the intention of no loose ends, no room for second chances. This function will initiate an endless loop of conflicting orders, to the point that it will fry everything—the Forgeries' programming, their minds. It's sort of like inducing a massive stroke. Their brains will hemorrhage."

"So Harvey and I were thinking," Clipper says, "that if we played the right bit of audio somehow—say over the alarm system in Taem—every Forgery in that city would be disabled."

Disabled. That's a nicer word for it.

Is that how Frank justified his massacre of Burg's people when he feared them too volatile to benefit the Laicos Project? And does every Forgery truly deserve to be *disabled*? Jackson once helped us. Harvey is helping us now. Does this solution mean killing—*murdering*—thousands of innocent people?

I picture my own Forgery holding a gun to Blaine's head, and know the hard truth: Unless they malfunction, the Forgeries are the enemy, working against innocent people on Frank's behalf. We can't wait around hoping they cross paths with something that will cause their programming to flicker, not to mention that the Gen5s can't be tripped at all.

"You're sure this will work?" I ask.

"If the right audio is played, it should," Clipper says. "We've checked the function a couple dozen times."

"Well, shouldn't we tell the others? This is huge."

"There's just one problem," Harvey says. "I can't remember the audio combo. All I know is it's obscure, something random a Forgery wouldn't come across unless we meant to pull the plug."

"So how do we find it?"

"That brings us to what I do remember: I hid the answer in the code."

Harvey scrolls through it. I watch for a few minutes, and still the lines don't stop. It might as well be endless.

TWENTY-TWO

I SPEND THE NEXT FEW hours combing through what Clipper and Harvey refer to as the code's *comments*. They show me how to spot these—they are preceded by certain symbols—but the true giveaway is the fact that what follows is a legible, coherent sentence or two, rather than numbers and symbols and fragments of words. I work on one screen, Clipper and Harvey on another.

I'm not really sure what I'm looking for, but copying down suspicious comments into a notebook seems far more productive than being upstairs in a debriefing meeting.

While I work, Harvey and Clipper see to the code itself—the variables and functions and parameters, as they call them. I'm moving much faster through the endless lines than the two of them, but only because there are far fewer comments than code.

Much later, Harvey calls it a night. "If you're willing, we'd love some more help tomorrow," he says to me, and takes off his glasses to rub his eyes.

"Of course."

"Clip! You'll hurt your neck sleeping like that." The boy jerks upright. The shape of the keyboard is imprinted in his cheek. Harvey points at the couch against the far wall. "Go get a proper night's sleep, won't you?"

I duck upstairs, eager to do the same. Aiden's still asleep on the couch with Rusty, and besides their exhales, the floor is dead silent. I cut through the living room and into the small hall that leads to the bedrooms.

"Where'd you disappear to all night?" Bree is sitting just outside her room, her back against the wall and her legs stretched out in a V. I put a finger to my lips.

"Sammy's downstairs with the team still," she says. "And even if he wasn't, he sleeps like a deaf man. You could shout if you wanted."

Which would wake Aiden, who I was worried about disturbing from the beginning, but I don't bother pointing that out. She's in a mood. As though Bree's heard my thoughts, her face morphs into a scowl.

"You can't just disappear, Gray. You have to tell us where you're going."

"I was helping Harvey and Clipper, which you obviously knew since you told me where to find them."

She shakes her head. "I don't trust Harvey. It's not right."

"Look, Bree, I can't just sit around in meetings. If I'm not working toward avenging Blaine, then I'm wasting my time."

"The Expats and Rebels *do* have a plan. If you hadn't run downstairs, you'd have heard it firsthand from September. She relayed everything she knows from her discussions with Adam."

"Is this *plan* the one he and Vik have refused to share details about? Something involving coordinated strikes in various domed cities?"

"It's a bit more complicated than that. Bleak says hi, by the way."

"Bleak?"

"He joined via radio with Heidi to update us on the state of things in Pine Ridge. He asked how you were."

"If you talk to him tomorrow, tell him I'm—"

"Tell him yourself. I'm not a messenger."

She stands up. Clumsily. It's been a day since we fled the Compound, the perfect amount of time for muscles to stiffen and aches to set in. Bree rubs her neck and I catch sight of the bruises roping it. I can make out the exact points where that Order member's fingers tried to cut off her air.

"It's fine," she says, aware of my gaze.

"No, it's not. Seeing you like this will *never* be fine." I touch her chin and try to angle it so I can inspect the second bruise along her jaw. She knocks my arm aside.

"I've taken hits before you were around to worry about them."

"Will you quit being tough for one second and hear what I'm saying?"

She glares at me.

"I'm serious, Bree. If you're allowed to worry when I disappear for a few hours, why am I not allowed to hate seeing you like this? Do you think I don't care? You think I *want* to spot bruises on you? Especially when I'm the only reason you have them? All I want is for you . . . for us . . ."

I falter.

How is it I've lived most of my life without her? She walked into my world—no, dragged me into hers—that day in the forest beyond Crevice Valley, and it was like a new start. Ever since that moment, I've been slowly waking up.

I've lost my father and my twin. The only family I have left is a niece so far away she feels irretrievable. But I look at Bree now and know I can face anything. She makes me want to stand taller. Just being in her presence makes me want to be more. And even as she leans away from me, everything in her body language closed off and guarded, I want her nearer. I want her and it's still too soon.

"Are you going to stare at me all night, or was there something else?" She's still scowling, arms crossed.

I open my mouth, close it, open it again.

"Bree, I'm in love with you."

She takes a step away, like the words somehow slapped her. "What?"

"You heard me."

Her eyes narrow. "Even though I gave you the chance to say this a dozen times over, and you always ignored it? Even though we fight all the time?"

"You said that fire was good."

She rolls her eyes and looks away.

"The fights are never enough to make me not want you, Bree. Is it easy? No. Do I sometimes want to wipe the smug look off your face and tell you to shove it? Yes. Do you drive me absolutely crazy? All the time. But I know I'm no easier to deal with, and I'd rather be angry with you than with someone else. I'd rather argue occasionally than be content every day. You are the only person who challenges me one moment and steadies me the next, and you're not afraid to stand up to me. Ever. You know what I need—often before I do—and you're always willing to be it."

She's finally looking at me again. Staring, actually.

"I've been horrible. I pushed you away. I said things I didn't mean. I probably don't deserve you, but you need to know how sorry I am. And how I feel. How I want to be what you need, too. I can't promise to always be good at it, but I swear I will try my hardest. Now and every single day for as long as you let me."

She shakes her head, exhaling sharply. "Why do you have to do that?"

"Do what?"

She pushes me in the chest. "That! Say everything I want to hear when I made up my mind to forget you." She pushes me again, looking like she might cry. "Dammit, Gray, you're making it impossible for me to hate you."

"And that's a problem?"

She smiles and chokes back a sob. A single tear trails down her cheek. I brush it away with my thumb.

"Don't tell them I cried."

"Bree, you are the strongest person I know. Tears won't change that."

There is a quiet moment when her eyes search mine, and then she lunges at me. Our mouths collide. We kiss once, twice. Deeper, faster, more urgent. I pick her up and she wraps her legs around my waist. Her arms lock behind my neck. She is so tiny in my grasp, but her presence is enormous, surrounding me, drowning me, making me drunk. I stagger a little. We crash into the wall, her back taking most of the impact, and she gasps.

"Are you okay? I didn't mean—"

She kisses me quiet, more teeth than lips because she's smiling so wide. Then she pulls back, breathless. "When I say I want you, I mean *all* of you. So don't do it again: Don't hold in the hurt or hide the truth or say things you don't mean. Be honest with me, always, or this is the last second chance you'll get."

And then we're kissing again, even as I carry her into my room and shut out the world.

I lower her onto the bed. Her lips are no longer enough, the clothing between us suddenly thick like armor. I pull off my shirt, tug hers overhead. We shed layer after layer until we're nothing but skin against the sheets, against each other. Her hair is splayed out on the pillow, brilliant and pale. I take in every inch of her. Really, truly look at her. Maybe for the first time ever.

With a hand clasped behind my neck, Bree pulls me nearer.

"You're sure?" I ask against her lips. "Couldn't we . . ."

"I've been taking something Jules gave me since Pike. It's fine."

"Positive?"

"Yes."

"But what if—"

"Gray? Quit talking."

We move closer. And closer. Everything slows. Everything but my pulse. Bree buries her hands in my hair when we're one.

And I stop thinking.

TWENTY-THREE

BRIANNA NOX IS IN MY bed when I wake up.

She looks like she fought a war during the night. Her hair surrounds her head in a tangled halo. Her mouth hangs open. It's comical how widely stretched her limbs are, like she was sprinting somewhere and then dropped dead mid-stride. But she's wearing my hooded shirt, and while it's on inside out and the cuffs swallow her hands whole, I have never seen anything better. She could wear nothing but that shirt from this day on and I'd be happy.

I kiss her forehead, and she starts awake so violently she nearly head butts me.

"Where—?" Her eyes dart to the bed sheets, soaked in early morning light; the shirt she wears; then finally, me.

"Hey," she says, smiling so shamelessly my chest aches. "Is anyone else up yet? Should I—"

"No."

Bree raises an eyebrow. "Why do I get the feeling you're trying to keep me in your bed?"

"Maybe because this is a first and I want to prolong it. You're too good at sneaking out on me."

"Stealthier than you and always will be."

She stretches—toes and arms in opposite directions, back rising off the mattress—and I can no longer keep my hands to myself. She fights me halfheartedly, but with a yank, I have her pinned beneath me. I kiss her neck and she laughs, then her chin and she hums, her lips and she's quiet. Not just quiet, but completely still.

"What's wrong?"

She examines me with a heavy sort of gaze, and the fear hits me. She regrets it. Last night, us. She wishes she'd said no.

"Bree?"

She stares at my chest.

"Please say something."

"I don't want this to change things," she says, tracing the line of my collarbone with her forefinger. She has no idea how hard this makes it for me to focus.

"I've never needed anyone, Gray. That sounds awful, but

it's true. I've been alone for most of my life. I've taken care of myself. When I met you, you reminded me of someone I was once too willing to change for, and then when I realized I liked you, it scared me. Because we truly *were* a good fit. I didn't have to change around you. Not in the slightest. We were strong individually, and even stronger together, and that was terrifying, because it made me want you more. And if I wanted someone else, did that mean I was reliant on him? Did it mean I'd lost my independence? I want to be me. I only ever want to be me."

"Bree, there's *us*, but it's not possible without you *and* me. Two independent pieces. And reliance? I think life would be really lonely if we had to face everything on our own."

She flattens a palm against my chest. "Just promise you won't treat me differently now. I want us to be the same."

"I told you last night that I was done being a jerk."

"That's not what I mean." She bites her bottom lip. Exhales. "Look, if I argue with you and you don't agree with me, please don't fold just because of *this*." She motions between us. "Or if I'm doing something stupid, don't hold back from calling me out on it because you're afraid of hurting my feelings. Don't treat me like I'm suddenly delicate."

"That was my plan all along: sleep with you so I could hold the reins, turn our relationship into something completely opposite of what I love about it."

She punches my shoulder. "I'm serious! It's really hard for me to talk about this stuff, and then you have to go and turn it into a joke." She winds up again, but I grab her wrists and pin them against the mattress.

"Okay, okay. So it was a lame joke. But it's ridiculous; ninety-five percent of why I love you is everything you just said: how this works two ways, how we're there for each other but don't define each other. I get it. Really."

She stops wrestling to free herself, and I let go of her arms.

"What's the other five percent?"

"The way you look in my shirt."

She rolls her eyes. "In that case, I'm taking it off immediately."

"I'll like that even better."

I dodge another punch, and end up alongside her, staring at the ceiling.

"So who'd you change for?"

"This guy from Saltwater. I was hopelessly in love with him and he didn't even see me."

"I didn't see you at first either, Bree. Sometimes people are stupid."

"But I walked away when I didn't think you appreciated me. I didn't do that with Lock. His ma took me in when mine died. We grew up under the same roof, and I think he thought of me as a sibling of sorts, a best friend. I let him have everything—and I mean *everything*—thinking that it would change things, that he'd look at me differently, love me the way I loved him. Truth is, if someone doesn't see you before sex, they definitely don't see you any more after."

She runs a hand over the mattress between us, smoothing out wrinkles in the sheet.

"Lock tried to make a run for it before his eighteenth birthday, and washed up dead on the beach. With the exception of his younger brother, Heath, I was alone and completely lost, just weeks from my sixteenth birthday and a Snatching I wasn't certain was coming. I promised myself then to be all I ever needed. If I opened up to someone again, it would be because the feelings were mutual and it would benefit us both, not just him."

"Do you regret it? Lock?"

"No. It's not one of my fondest memories, but it made me who I am now. I'm stronger because of it. How could I regret something like that?"

"I regret a lot of things. Like my final words to Blaine, and all those people we left behind in Burg, and the way I treated you."

"I could have been more upfront. I could have told you exactly why I never spent a night, but instead I made you guess."

"I should have seen."

"Maybe." She rubs the hem of the blanket with her thumb. Outside our room, a door is closed forcefully. The shower turns on. Bree climbs from the bed despite my objections.

"I should probably go see what September has planned for today. Am I right to assume you're going to keep helping Harvey regardless of how much I distrust him?"

I nod.

"Glad to know you're still not afraid to tick me off."

She retrieves her clothes and changes with her back to me. Moments later she's in her typical boots and cargo pants, top tucked in at the waistband so my eyes can't help but fall there. She bunches up my shirt and throws it at me.

"When you're ready to talk about Blaine, let me know. And it's okay if the answer is never—maybe it's something you have to deal with on your own, maybe I overstepped the other day on the boat—but I'm here if you need me."

"Bree," I say as she pulls open the door. "I really do love you."

She smirks. "You're such a sap."

The door clicks shut, only to reopen a heartbeat later. Holding on to the frame, she leans into the room.

"I love you, too," she says. "I'm pretty sure you already know that, but I was worried *sap* might not have translated properly, and wanted to clarify."

"How very thoughtful of you." Bree smiles at me a long moment, and when she finally turns to leave, I toss back, "Sap."

I have a horrible experience while showering. One moment I'm invincible, drunk off the memories of last night, buzzing from Bree's words this morning, and the next I'm crouched and hugging my knees as the water rains down on me, muffling sobs into my fists.

How can I be so happy when my brother is dead? How can I be devastated when Bree's forgiven me? I find my feet and force myself upright. I slap my cheeks. Turn the water cold just to jolt the life back into my veins.

Get downstairs, I tell myself. *Go back to work. This will all be easier when the fight's finished.*

When I step back into the bedroom, Sammy is sitting on the bed, his arms folded over his chest.

"Why was the door locked when I came up last night?"

"Yeah . . . Sorry about that. Where'd you crash, a couch?"

"September and Aiden took the couches so the team could have beds. Remember?" I don't, since I was downstairs when the team decided how to split up rooms for the duration of our stay. "My only option was Emma's," he clarifies.

"So you stayed with her? That couldn't have been too terrible for you."

"She made me sleep on the floor, Gray," he says very seriously. "And she swore that if I even *tried* to get in the bed, she would knee me so hard between the legs that I'd never be able to produce children."

I smile. "Yeah, that sounds like her."

"Give me a heads-up next time, okay? I need to mentally prepare myself for floorboards when I have my mind set on a mattress."

"It just sort of happened. It wasn't planned."

"But it did"—he raises his eyebrows suggestively—*"happen?"* I shrug, and Sammy breaks into the biggest grin I have ever seen grace his features. Then he claps my shoulder like I've done something heroic. "Think she'll be any less uptight now?"

"That's exactly the kind of thing you should never say to her. Not unless you want to lose a limb."

"Obviously. I'm not suicidal."

TWENTY-FOUR

IN THE KITCHEN, THE WEST-FACING window frames a square of the Gulf like an oversized painting. I pause to watch the docks come to life.

"Did you eat?"

Emma.

She's in the mouth of the kitchen, hair wet from a shower. She tosses a biscuit at me, and in the time it takes to catch the small meal, she's joined me at the window. We stand there in silence, watching the gulls ride the wind along the shoreline.

"I don't even know what I'm fighting for anymore," she says. "I climbed the Wall for answers about the Heist, which we have, and you, who I've lost and can't look at the same even if I hadn't. So what now? What's the point?"

"The point?" I stare at her out of the corner of my vision. "Emma, this is where we change everything. Claysoot, your mother, Kale. Don't you want to get them out?"

"They're safest where they are. It's this world they should fear. Frank. Forgeries. A complete lack of freedom."

"All the more reason to remove him from power." She gives me a look that reeks of doubt. I don't know—or like—this person she's becoming. So pessimistic, so beaten. "And they aren't free, Emma. They're slaves."

"To what?"

"The Heist. The Council. All those stupid rules they've created just to last another generation. We both hated the slatings. I don't want Kale to have to deal with that when she's older. I want her to be able to make her own choices. Remember the birds?"

She glares. "Do *you*?"

Of course. I might feel differently about her now, but the birds, that idea she planted in my mind of permanent pairs, is something I'll never forget. Emma changed me. She changed me for the better.

A group of gulls soars past, heading for the white-specked shoreline. One lands on the section of roof right outside our window and starts pecking at the shingles as though he can drill his way into the first-floor rooms. I cup my hands at my mouth and though I expect nothing, I blow into my palms. The most feeble whistle cuts between us.

"Did you hear that?!"

I adjust my hands, try again. This time it's unmistakable. Not as pure and crisp as the cries Bree can produce, but audible.

"Ha!" I push the window open and stick my torso through. Clinging to the top of the frame, I pull my feet after. The gulls are screeching and the water is lapping and the world smells like salt and hope and possibilities. We're going to be okay. All of us. The Rebels, the Expats, our steadily shrinking team. My eyes stream from the fierce morning wind, but I stand on the shingled roof, my hands in position, whistling again and again to the loons that are nowhere to be found.

"Well, I'm glad one of us is happy with the way everything's panned out," Emma mutters.

I turn around, but she's already gone. It's Aiden in the window frame now, one hand tangled in Rusty's copper coat. He refuses to move for me.

"Why'd you lie about Emma?" he asks.

"It's complicated."

"I'm not letting you in until you tell me."

I want to be honest with the kid, but the whole of it will

give him nightmares and leave me weak in the process. He puts a hand on the glass pane, threatening to lock me out.

"Aiden . . ."

He looks up at me. The wind whips through my shirt.

"Sometimes people lie because they're trying to protect you. They're trying to help."

"But you made me think she was dead. All that did was hurt."

"I'm sorry about that," I say. "Really. I just didn't think we'd see her again."

He taps on the pane, sucks on his bottom lip. Then: "Will you play a game with me?"

"Yes. Absolutely."

He steps aside and lets me slip back into the house. I wish all negotiations were so simple.

After a few rounds of Rock, Paper, Scissors with Aiden, I head downstairs. Harvey and Clipper have rewritten portions of the code and pinned them up on the far wall. Select letters and symbols are circled, lines connecting them like cobweb strands.

"Did you guys get any sleep?" I ask.

"Barely," Clipper says through a yawn. "But it was worth it."

"You found something?"

"Think so." He taps one of the pinned-up comment blocks, and I step closer to read.

/* Master logic and Most Operations vary depending on Forgery's Zoning (test group origins, location assignments, etc.). Corresponding Algorithms should Run accordingly, though some errors Triggered in early model Forgeries. Backtrack(Ø) catches and resets Forgery logic per K492 in these instances. */

"The Forgeries have specific zoning?"

"That part's not important," Harvey says. "But *backtrack*"— he taps the word with a forefinger—"is the fail-safe function. It's embedded in the conditionals I was talking about last night. If it's initiated, that's the end of them."

"Okay, so how do we initiate it?"

"We're still trying to figure that out. K492 is referenced only once in the entire program: here. In this comment." Harvey tilts his head to the side. "What are you trying to tell me?" he asks the code.

"I thought the capitalization was weird," Clipper says. "The way there's random letters capitalized in the middle of sentences." He points to another scrap of paper pinned on the wall where he's listed them out.

MMOFZCARTFBFK

Harvey taps a pencil against the desk. Clipper and I stare at the letters.

"It's too quiet in here," Harvey grunts. "I need music. I can't work without music."

And right then, the letters jump at me. I've never seen the name written out before, so I could be completely wrong, but after Harvey broke through his programming from the same thing, it seems too much to be mere coincidence. I leap to my feet and grab the marker from Clipper.

"Forget the third sentence. Just look at the first two." I cross out letters from the last sentence.

MMOFZCARTF

"We're trying to eliminate the Forgeries, right? So if you remove them . . ." I strike both Fs.

MMOZCART

". . . and remove the properly capitalized letters at the start of each sentence."

MOZART

"Holy. Shit," Clipper says.

Harvey slaps the back of his skull. "Watch your language."

"I saw it as soon as you mentioned music," I explain. "That *is* how it's spelled, right?"

Harvey nods.

"So what song?"

"K492: *The Marriage of Figaro*. I don't know how I didn't see it earlier."

"I don't get it," Clipper cuts in. "If this is right, the fail-safe won't work."

"Why not?" I ask.

"You guys already played this once in Taem. When you went after the vaccine, this piece—the overture—was used to stage a diversion, and it didn't wipe out any Forgeries then. Plus, it helped wake Harvey up at the Compound, not shut him down." Clipper twists toward the scientist. "Maybe the fail-safe requires a different act?"

Harvey shakes his head, a lively smile creeping over his lips.

"No, I remember now, but gosh did I do a good job trying to hide it from prying eyes." Harvey pins a fresh piece of paper on the wall and snatches the marker from me. He rewrites *Backtrack(Ø)*, then points at the zero.

"I think I purposely meant for the zero to be misleading. It looks like a natural parameter—a number would be passed through when the function ran—but I was only trying to remind myself that *Ø* means *Overture*, and *backtrack* is both the function to undo the Forgeries *and* the method in which to play the piece."

None of this is making sense to me, but Clipper's eyes light up. "Play the overture *backward*."

"Right you are, genius." Harvey ruffles the boy's hair.

"So this is it?" I ask. "Play this piece of music backward and it will off every last Forgery?"

"That's the gist of it."

"Is there any way to test it?"

Harvey rubs the back of his neck. "Not unless you have a collection of classic operas lying around. Plus, there's a good chance I won't survive a trial. We might only get one shot at this."

"But you're already operating outside your programming."

"I don't think you're comprehending my idea of a fail-safe, Gray. When the time comes, it won't matter whether I'm a free-thinking Forgery or Frank's most loyal man. There's no avoiding this shutdown sequence. It's integrated into every model."

Clipper, suddenly understanding the true weight of Harvey's words, shakes his head. "Maybe there's another way. Maybe—"

"No, Clayton, this is it. Besides, how are you supposed to successfully fill my shoes if I'm still around?"

"I don't *want* to fill your shoes. I didn't want you gone before, and I definitely don't want it now!" Another swear follows.

"What did I tell you about that language?"

"You're not my father, Harvey," Clipper snaps, and shoves his way out of the room.

The trapdoor slams and Harvey turns to me. "He'll come around." Then he smiles. Like Clipper's blowup was over something trite. Why is this man always so content to sacrifice himself for others? Does he have no survival instincts, no drive for self-preservation?

"So," he says, "how about we bring the rest of the group up to speed?"

TWENTY-FIVE

AFTER WE'VE ALL GATHERED IN the kitchen on the first floor, Harvey explains how the fail-safe is hidden within the Forgery's base code.

"Gray said you guys have a plan of your own—"

"Although he has none of the details since he avoided last night's meeting," Bree interjects.

"—and we think if we coordinate our efforts with yours, odds for success will skyrocket."

September's eyebrows are pulled down, making her already angled features appear even sharper. "Explain how this works again. I understand the audio will trigger the termination, but how do we get every Forgery to hear it?"

"Clipper?" Harvey says, giving the boy the floor. "It was your idea after all."

Clipper glares at Harvey, arms crossed, looking angry enough to tear someone apart with his bare hands.

"I guess I can tell—"

"We override AmEast's alarm systems," Clipper spits out, "and replace the standard sirens with the overture. Any domed city is bound to trip the alarm when a staged attack occurs, and then we'd be broadcasting the overture across speakers in every government building, public square . . . pretty much the whole of the cities."

"Please tell me we can override the system from here," Sammy says, but the tone of his voice suggests he knows this won't be possible.

"I can prepare from here," Harvey explains. "I'll write a virus that will trick the alarm system into playing our audio, but it has to be uploaded to Taem's network manually, and then sent to the other domed cities as well."

"Manually meaning *in person*? From Taem?" Sammy's face is growing paler by the second.

Harvey nods.

"This won't help with Forgeries stationed beyond the domed cities," September points out.

"True," I say. "But most of them are in the cities, and given what I learned in the Compound, they're shipping more out as we speak. This could eliminate the majority of the forces in one fell swoop, giving us a huge advantage. And rounding up any surviving Forgeries later shouldn't be too hard."

"We've got undercover forces already preparing in most domed cities," September says. "And I've been prepping people here in Bone Harbor. Bleak's ready to spring on the Order folk in Pine Ridge soon as we give the word, and Heidi's heading for the borders."

"Am I the only one who thinks this plan is absolutely ridiculous?" Bree straightens in her chair. "We can't do a test run, because we don't have a copy of the overture. But we're still going to get back to the most secure city in AmEast without being seen, while Gray's face is strung up all over the country and Harvey is probably the Order's most-wanted resource. And then, what? Ask to have a go at their alarm system? Take a few minutes alone in the labs?"

"We've done something like this before," I say. "When we stole the vaccine in the fall, there were nearly as many risks."

Bree turns to Harvey. "Let me guess. The only person who can manually upload this virus is you, right? Because it's complicated. And will need some fancy, superhard coding work at the last minute."

Harvey looks wounded. "It would be easiest for me, yes. Clipper could probably handle it, but if we only get one shot at this, I think I should be the one at the wheel."

"Of course you do," she sneers. "Of course."

"How do we even get back there?" Sammy cuts in.

"The same way we did last time," Harvey explains. "It's Gray's face on the wanted posters now. I'll escort him into Order custody and—"

Bree is out of her seat in a flash. She throws an elbow into Harvey's jaw, then wrenches his arm behind his back.

"You think anyone here is going to buy that?"

"Bree!" I yell.

"I've dislocated your shoulder before, Harvey," she says, adjusting her hold on his arm. "I can do it again."

"Dammit, Bree!" I have to use so much force to pull her off, I know she'll end up with a bruise on her bicep from my grip.

"You believe this?" she says, turning on me.

"It's the best opportunity we have."

"It's the worst! There's no guarantee they'll bring you to Taem when they pick you up. You could end up back at the Compound or dead in a ditch. And even if you *do* get dragged to Taem, how convenient that Harvey is the only one who can execute this plan. Maybe the overture won't do a damn thing. Maybe it will make the Forgeries stronger. Maybe he'll put a bullet in you on Frank's behalf and then march into Union Central a hero."

Harvey wipes at the corner of his now-bleeding lip.

"He's been helping us, Bree," Clipper says. He looks almost annoyed that he's forced to defend Harvey so soon after their argument. "He's good."

"And I've been alone downstairs with him," I add. "If Harvey had it out for me, he could have slit my throat several times by now. Plus, if this *does* work, you realize what it means, right? Harvey will die helping us do this. He won't survive the overture."

Eyes narrowed, Bree wheels on September and Sammy. "What about everything Adam and Vik were planning with Ryder before we lost contact? Our conversations with Heidi and Bleak last night? We just throw it aside?"

"The way I see it, this can only improve our chances," September says. "We do it in conjunction with the existing plans. Plus, I finally heard from Vik this morning. I was waiting to tell everyone, but Elijah reported from Crevice Valley. They were hit. Hard. Nearly everyone's dead except for the few who made it into the underground fallout shelters. Ryder's alive. We're still waiting on a list of survivors, but based on what Elijah relayed, it sounds like no more than a hundred made it."

Clipper sinks to the floor, his hand on his bracelet.

"The Rebels at Crevice Valley were supposed to be part of the organized strike," September continues. "This blow . . .

it crushes our numbers in the East. We need an edge there now more than ever."

Bree has not stopped shaking her head. "And Vik's okay with this plan?"

"I'll reach out to him," September says, "but I'm telling you now he'll be on board. The Expats and the Rebels will act come the planned date, and this, if we pull it off, only tips the odds further in our favor."

"It's too much of a risk," Bree insists.

"No one who played it safe ever accomplished anything."

Bree turns to me. "Gray?"

She wants me to agree with her. She wants me to say it's foolish and a long shot and dangerous. And it is. But it's also the edge we need, just as September said, and I want to see the look on Frank's face when he watches his Forgeries crumple. I want to be there when his last defenses no longer surround him so that I can look him in the eye and end his life for Blaine. For all of them.

Bree scowls at my silence.

"You don't have to be a part of the team that heads east," September says to her. "You can stay here with me, help with the fight in Bone Harbor. It will be safer along the Gulf than in Taem."

"You think that's what this is about? Me wanting to stay where it's *safest*?" She snatches her firearm off the table and thrusts it into her waistband. "You're all idiots."

I grab her arm. "Bree . . ."

"I know I told you to not feel bad about disagreeing with me. But I still expected you to use your brain."

She wrenches herself loose and storms out.

The rest of us plan late into the evening.

It's exactly a week until Sunder Day, an AmEast holiday commemorating the anniversary of the West's official secession and the end of the war. A Sunder Rally will be thrown in Taem. Spirits will be up. Guards will be down. This is when we will attack. It is also, I learn, the date Adam, Vik, and Ryder were always working toward.

Every day now is precious.

Harvey will start work on the virus for the alarms first thing in the morning, and a day or two before the Rally, we'll let ourselves be spotted. Or rather, Harvey will turn me in. We won't have the virus on us though, not when it's likely we'll be searched. Sammy and Clipper will take it to Taem by car as soon as possible, then wait to make a transfer drop.

"What if Vik doesn't like our plan?" Clipper worries aloud.

"He will," I say. "And if for some odd reason he doesn't, we move forward anyway. Go rogue. No one's around to stop us, and we're doing this. *I'm* doing this. We've done enough waiting for a lifetime."

"I'll update Vik first thing tomorrow," September assures Clipper. "Until then, how about we toast our new plans?"

A bottle of liquor is pulled out. Glasses are filled. I keep expecting Bree to wander into the kitchen and join us, even if only reluctantly, but when a second round is poured, it's obvious she's holding firm. What hits next is the paralyzing idea of carrying out these plans without her. I set my drink on the table and excuse myself.

TWENTY-SIX

BREE'S DOOR SWINGS OPEN WHEN I push on it. She's sitting on the edge of her bed, elbows against her knees and gun clasped in her hands. It's pointed at the far wall, but her forehead rests against the barrel.

"Hey!" I say, darting in and pulling the weapon away from her. "Dammit, Bree."

She looks up at me, eyes red. Her gaze trails to the gun and then back to me. She makes a small *pshh* noise, and says, "I was just thinking."

"Are you drunk?" She keeps staring straight-ahead, like she can see through my torso. "Are you?"

"I'm upset!" she cries, leaping to her feet. "Is that not allowed? Does something have to alter my mental state before I'm allowed to get emotional?"

"Just answer the question."

She glares. "No. I'm not drunk."

She was crying then. I'm not used to seeing her like this, exhausted, eyes bloodshot from tears. Before she can turn away from me, I grab her arm.

"Why are we fighting?"

"Because he's going to ruin us—*you*—and you can't see it!" she says. "We have absolutely no proof that Harvey won't turn on us."

"Jackson helped us once."

"Jackson did what would benefit him. Always. He saved you from Titus because he knew he'd die, too, if he didn't, or be stuck beneath Burg. He let you climb the Wall because he thought the pursuing Forgeries wouldn't hurt him. He thought he'd be able to run right back to Frank, that his family was there to take him home." She shakes her head. "Don't you see, Gray? There are Forgeries and there are people, but nothing in between. Jackson was always looking out for himself."

But Bree didn't hear Jackson's confessions to me beneath Burg. She didn't hear him talk about things he shouldn't have been able to remember, or admit that he loved his younger brother—an emotion impossible for a programmed Forgery. He didn't stay behind in Burg because he thought it would save him. He stayed behind because he knew it would save us.

And I would bet my life that Harvey is the same. Bree wasn't there to watch his face come alive with awareness at the Compound, to see him undo my bindings in the interrogation room and let me walk free. He wants nothing more than to help us.

"The Sunder Rally's in a week," I tell her. "Sammy and Clipper are leaving for Taem soon—to be our backup inside."

Her face pales.

"I want you with them. In that car. Having my back."

"I do have your back, Gray. I'm telling you right now that I don't trust Harvey."

"But *I* trust him. Is my opinion worth nothing?"

"If it wasn't your life on the line, maybe it would be different."

"Blaine's life was on the line once, too. So was my father's. And Bo's and Xavier's and so many more. I made a promise the night we got back to Pine Ridge that I would avenge Blaine or die trying. That's all I'm living for now. To make things right."

"And what about the people you still have, Gray? Me and Sammy and Clipper. Are we not worth living for?"

"I can't walk away from Blaine. I have to do this."

"But he's gone, Gray." The heaviness in her voice reaches

her eyes. "The only people you'll be walking away from if you do this are the ones you have left."

When I don't say anything she lets out an audible growl and rips back her bedsheets.

"You can leave now. I'm kind of tired."

"Bree . . ." I put a hand on her shoulder and she shrugs me off.

"Bree, I need you with me on this," I try again. "Please don't stay here with September. *Please*."

She studies me, her expression torn. "When did I ever say I was staying?"

"But you just . . . and everything you said downstairs . . ."

"Is still true," she finishes. "I think the plan's stupid. I'm terrified it will backfire. And I'm furious that even with me admitting all that, you're still going to run with it. But I don't have a choice, Gray. When did I *ever* have a choice?"

I search her eyes, confused.

Bree pulls her shoulders into a defeated shrug. "The only thing I'll regret more than handing you over to certain death is not being there to try to stop it. And if I can't stop it, I want to be with you until the end."

"That sounds self-destructive, especially for you."

"Loving someone is self-destructive." I must look skeptical because she adds, "Seriously. Love makes people irrational. I mean, the way I feel about you—sometimes it scares me, Gray. I stormed the Compound for you, struck down men, shot your double right in the stomach without a second's hesitation, and I'd do it all again. I'd do anything not to lose you, and that's dangerous."

"I'd do the same."

"Which makes us dumb."

"Not if we keep our heads. We've gotten through everything before. We can get through this, too."

"I hope you're right," she says. "I really do. Because every time I tell myself the same thing, it feels like a giant lie."

I can't sleep. In part due to nerves—there are no shortage of unknowns lying ahead—and also because I can't shake the look of fear on Bree's face, her unwavering opposition to the plan. Still, for the first time in months, I feel as though I am doing the right thing. I am exactly where I need to be, walking the only road left to be traveled. This sort of possessed nature reminds me of when I climbed the Claysoot Wall. My heart's already somewhere ahead of me, and now it's only a matter of letting my feet catch up.

"Anxious?" Sammy asks as I roll over again.

"Yeah. You?"

"Sure, but you're keeping me up more than the nerves are, flopping around like a dying fish."

The image makes me smile. Not that he can see it in the dark.

"She's not really staying behind, is she?"

"No. She'll come."

Sammy exhales. "Thank God. Did you have to beg?"

"Luckily, no, because it probably wouldn't have helped. Didn't you watch me beg for her forgiveness the last two months?"

He laughs lightly, then adds, "Shit, man. Why is it that anything worth having is always a second away from being taken from you?"

"Just life keeping you nimble, I guess."

In the distance I can hear the muffled crash of waves—surging onto the shore, pulling back, crashing again.

"Hey, Sammy? What'd you do after your father was executed?"

"Broke every dish in the house, screamed until my throat was hoarse, and burned the photos I had of him because his smile was driving me crazy."

"But after that? After the anger and the grief?"

"There is no after. I still feel it. Every single day. That's why I ditched Taem and took to the forest. I didn't care if it put a target on my back for the rest of my life. I was going to make sure I made my father proud, carried out his work in my own way. And I never thought I'd say this, but the end might finally be in sight." Another small pause. "Why?"

"I just want to be sure I'm doing the right thing. Even if people I trust are telling me the opposite."

"All I know is if you ignore what you feel in your gut, you'll regret it forever."

Exactly my thinking. I angle my head so I can see him. It's too dark to make out much beyond the outline of his face, upturned and focused on the ceiling.

"I'm glad this mess brought us together."

"Together?" He side eyes me. "I thought you were all about Bree. You don't want to cuddle, do you?"

"Night, Sammy."

"What, I can't joke and lighten the mood? It was getting too serious in here."

I smile in the dark. He can't see it, but he senses my mood just as Blaine would and adds, "Keep flopping and I'll tear your gills out."

It's the best threat I've heard in ages.

TWENTY-SEVEN

VIK IS IN FULL SUPPORT of our plans. In fact, he even has a few suggestions that strengthen the odds in our favor, and he agrees to pass the information along to the necessary people back east.

I spend the better part of the day getting Bree up to speed while Harvey and Clipper slave away in the basement. The boy is gathering damning Order information that can be leaked just before the coordinated strike—hopefully it will encourage additional civilians to join the Rebels. Harvey labors over his code, writing the virus needed to infect Taem's alarm system. When it's finished, it will just be a matter of getting into Union Central, uploading it to the system, and referencing an archived version of the overture that Harvey promises will exist. Frank may have outlawed certain arts for the general public, but he saved the best of the best. An indulgence allowed only for himself and a few select Order members—like Harvey, when he still worked in Union Central's labs.

The following evening, he waves a thumb drive at me and says we're ready.

September has a car waiting in an alley on the southern edge of town, one window purposely broken, the paint stripped down to make it appear as if it's been rusting there for years. She claims she had to trade an arm and a leg for the vehicle, but she still has four limbs, and like a very slow child, I'm the last one to understand the figure of speech.

"Extra gas is in the back," she says, tossing the keys to Sammy. "Don't even ask me what a pain it was to secure."

"So the fuel was easy to get?"

"Dammit, Sammy." But she smiles.

"You have the files?" Harvey asks Clipper.

"For the tenth time, yes. Do you want to see?"

"No, no. Every time you open the bag I worry the drive will fall out and then I have to ask again."

"We'll keep our eyes peeled from the Taem safe house," Sammy says to me and Harvey. "Soon as we catch wind that you guys have arrived, we'll make our move."

"Sewers. Can't wait." This from Clipper.

They were the least conspicuous option though, the only road that will lead to me no matter where I end up being held.

"Enough chatter," September says, waving the trio to action.

I offer Clipper my palm, but he opts for a parting hug over a handshake. He's taller than Bree these days, the top of his head even with my nose.

"Stay on your toes out there, genius," I tell him.

He moves on to Harvey, and I spot Bree standing in the bedroom hallway. With a gun on her hip. And a jacket zipped high beneath her chin. And a full pack weighing down her shoulders.

My chest clenches. I wanted her to be a part of this, I did, but now that she's loaded up and ready to go, I'm suddenly terrified that this will be the last time I ever see her.

I surge forward and pull her into a hug, try to memorize the feel of her in my arms.

"Bree!" Sammy calls from the living room.

"I'll see you real soon," I tell her, and press a kiss to her forehead. "Trust your instincts and everything will be fine."

"My instincts are saying to stop right now. To not let you out of my sight. To make sure the Order doesn't take you again."

"But they'll be taking me *to* you. You'll be waiting."

Her lips purse, her brow fills with lines. "I love you," she manages.

"Same."

One more kiss, quick, and she steps around me. When I turn, Sammy is standing at the mouth of the hallway.

"Take care of her," I say.

"You know she doesn't need it," he answers.

"And you know exactly what I really mean."

"That I do."

When I turned twelve, Xavier promised to make me an adult-sized bow. It was a month before his Heist and he said it was his gift to me. I was the best shot he'd ever trained and he wanted me to remember him after he was gone, be reminded that I couldn't even fire an arrow straight before receiving his guidance.

It took him a few days to find a fitting piece of maple, and another to strip it of bark, cut string notches, and shape the grip with wrapped leather. But it was the last step—stringing the bow—that seemed to take far longer than the hour Xavier worked on it. When you're anxious for something, waiting becomes its own form of torture.

It's been two days since the team left for Taem, and it's felt like two years.

Bea printed her most recent issue of the *Harbinger*

yesterday, in which she insisted on reporting that I'm back east and planning something, despite my objections. It led to another search on the Order's part, and they were unbiased in their efforts. Despite Garrett's position, the house was stormed. Harvey, Emma, and I sat huddled in the basement, afraid an exhale might give us away. The place was tossed, but the Order was too busy tipping furniture and pulling bookcases away from the walls to examine the wall-to-wall carpet beneath their feet. They never found the trapdoor.

Tonight, under the cover of a cloudy sky, Bea disappears with her brothers for one of September's underground meetings. Even Emma tags along, but it's deemed unsafe for me to leave the house. When I'm spotted tomorrow, it will be on purpose. Until then, we're not taking unnecessary risks. Understandable, but the house is starting to feel like a prison. After a final round of Rock, Paper, Scissors with Aiden, I leave him in Rusty's company and visit Harvey.

"We're heading home tomorrow night," he says when I enter the basement. "You ready?"

"Taem's not my home, Harvey."

I pull up a chair and watch him for a while. He's been spending every waking hour staring at a screen since the team left, and I have no clue what he's even looking at anymore. The virus is set and done, in Clipper's hands and somewhere much farther east.

"What have you been doing down here? I thought your work was done."

"It is. I'm just reading."

"Why?"

He squints, leans closer to the screen. "It's fascinating."

I run my thumb along the edge of the wooden desk, flinching when it catches on a splinter. Harvey's eyes move back and forth behind his glasses, occasionally narrowing, sometimes glinting. Like the code is a thing he respects, a person he's in awe of.

"Are you absolutely positive this is going to work?"

"No," he says plainly.

"What?" I sit bolt upright. "In the meetings you said—"

"It *should* work. I really think it will. But I also thought the Forgeries would keep people safe and that Frank would use them for good. At least initially." He takes his glasses off and turns to me. This is a thing Harvey does. When the glasses come off it means a speech and deep thinking. Unless he rubs his eyes, which means he's in desperate need of sleep.

"Science is a powerful thing, Gray, a wonderful thing," he says. Deep thinking it is. "But when it is used to serve one man, rather than the masses, that's when it fails. It becomes personal. Technological advancement should benefit many and benefit them equally. If one person rises to the top, if he or she benefits substantially more than everyone else, well, that's a step in the wrong direction.

"I *think* the fail-safe will work, I really do, but I don't know for sure. Just as I didn't know how to make an F-GenX until it was finished and functioning. If I knew things for certain, we wouldn't be in this mess."

He sounds so much like the *real* Harvey, so passionate and rational. The last time I saw that man, he was a projection in the night that lit up Taem's dome.

"How'd you die, Harvey? Do you remember?"

"I have memories of sitting in Frank's office with you," he says. "Then medics visiting me in a guarded room to fix my shoulder. They injected me with something and it all goes cloudy after that. The next memory I have is opening my eyes to the sound of Mozart. As for the moments in between . . ." He bites his bottom lip, sits back in the chair. "I'm not sure how he—how I—died. Taem papers reported I took a bullet when fighting broke out in the square."

I remember something Bo said about Harvey getting hit by cross fire that day. I truly hope it was that fast.

"We never should have left you."

"I was dead."

"We should have checked."

"And maybe we wouldn't be here right now if you had. Maybe you'd be dead, too. Or maybe the vaccine wouldn't have made it back to the Rebels. Life is too complex to go examining all the *if*s. Worry about the here and now, and the fork you're approaching. Focus on *those* decisions."

He puts his glasses back on, turns to the screen. I examine his profile.

"Bree still doesn't believe you're you," I say.

Eying me over the rim of his glasses, he says, "Guess I'll just have to prove her wrong."

TWENTY-EIGHT

EVEN THOUGH THE NEXT DAY passes at a torturous pace, night finally, inevitably falls.

"Remember, you are truly cut off until you make contact with Sammy," September says. "Garrett can relay anything that might go down in the transfer, but it's a dead zone between here and Taem."

I'm well aware of this, but let September have her moment. It sets her at ease, all this orchestrating of plans. I pull on my jacket and backpack. Harvey has my gun, which, if everything unfolds as planned, will make sense once the Order takes us into custody.

The round of good-byes is quick, nothing but curt handshakes. Not even Emma lingers over her words.

"See you sometime," she says to me. Aiden leans against her hip, one hand in Rusty's mangy mane.

"Let's hope so," I respond. She gives me a half smile, but it seems forced.

A moment later, I'm stepping into the crisp evening with Harvey. It is nothing short of marvelous to breathe in fresh air again. To feel the wind on my face. I am not made for indoors.

My stomach is twisting as we make our way to the port. Tethered boats sway on the choppy water, the starry sky reflecting off the vastness of the Gulf.

We meet Garrett at the docks as planned. The stiff cuff of his Order uniform scratches at my wrist when we shake.

"Time to make all Bea's *lies* mean something," he whispers. "You guys ready?"

I nod. "Ready as we'll ever be."

"Okay then."

I close my eyes because I know I won't be able to take it otherwise. Garrett clocks me good. Twice. The second sends me staggering backward.

"Go on then," he says to Harvey. "Call them."

Harvey points my gun at the night sky and lets off a shot. It's deafening in the stillness.

"Over here!" Garrett shouts, bringing me to the salt-slicked docks. He presses a knee to my back and I let him gather my hands there as well. "I've got— Holy hell! I said over *here*! Hurry up!"

Another two Order members come running, peeling from darkened streets where they were stationed.

Hands find my back. I'm flipped. Tugged to my feet. A pointed nose examines me. "Is this who I think it is?" I recognize his voice. Garrett's boss. The inspector September distracted. He's younger than I expect.

"Sure looks like him," Garrett says.

"It is," Harvey affirms.

"Who the hell are you?"

"Harvey Maldoon. Gray held me hostage since he escaped our facilities a week back. I barely got the jump on him tonight."

"Make the call," the inspector says to someone behind him. Then he turns to me. "Got business in Bone Harbor? Think you can sneak into my port in the dead of night?"

"I *did* sneak in. If I hadn't lost hold of my gun, you'd still have no clue I was here."

He knees me in the stomach. As I hang buckled over, sucking in air, Harvey tells the Order member to go easy, which results in the scientist's loyalty being questioned.

"You clearly have no clue who you're talking to," Harvey says. "Frank is going to be elated if you bring this boy in unharmed. Even more thrilled when I come with him."

"And me," comes a voice from inland. "He'll be glad to have me back, too."

I glance up and my chest seizes. Emma. Jogging down to the docks like she owns all of Bone Harbor.

"I told you to run," Harvey snaps, improvising expertly fast. "Why would you—?" He turns back to the Order member. "She was with us, another of Gray's hostages. When I overpowered him, I told her to bolt; I didn't know how long I'd be able to hold him."

"I work in Taem's hospitals," Emma says to the guard. "I was one of the best set of hands in that place. I just want to go home."

Home? To Taem? What is she playing at? She was set to stay here in Bone Harbor, watch over Aiden, help September come Sunder Day.

The inspector leans backward, yelling into the darkness. "What's the word on that call?"

"They're sending a rig immediately. Secure him."

"Allow me," Harvey says.

I know it's part of an act, but as he strikes me with the handgun, I can't help but question everything. His smile—so malicious, so willing to play this part. His cool reaction to Emma's joining, and his lines so swiftly delivered they almost seemed rehearsed. I cringe as he winds up again.

The world goes blurry, then cuts off entirely as a bag comes down over my head.

I'm jostled, shoved.

I listen while Emma gives her name, and the Order welcomes her back into its ranks. The roar of an approaching helicopter drowns out the world.

As I'm forced toward it, the panic hits. Deep in my chest and then surging upward, like a sickness I need to eject, like a burn scorching from the inside out.

This is wrong. Emma shouldn't be here. There's no reason for it. Not unless she somehow persuaded Harvey to let her join. Or maybe she's trying to accomplish something—revenge, justice. Have I become her biggest enemy?

Is that ridiculous, to think it all comes back to that? To believe that Emma—sweet, gentle, loving Emma—could be driven to act this way out of hate and bitterness?

I writhe against the ropes.

Bree, Sammy, Clipper.

I need them. I need them and I sent them away.

An extra set of hands pushes at the back of my spine, forcing me forward. Then I'm hoisted up, shoved. I land on my side, strike my head against a hard surface.

Next comes the roar of an engine, the nauseating feeling of the world dropping away beneath me.

At least one part of the plan is still unfolding as arranged. We're flying. Hopefully east. I don't know what I'll do if we're not.

When I come to, it takes me a moment to remember being shoved into the vehicle, the fall that caused me to strike my head. I have no recollection of what followed, how I got to wherever I now am. Or how much time has passed since the flight.

They gave me something, I'd wager—to knock me out and blur my senses.

I sit up in the darkness, and feel a restraint pull against my neck. My fingers find rope. Coarse. Brittle. Once I know it's there, the scratch of it against my skin is so discomforting I wonder how I'd ignored it previously. The rope continues upward, much farther than my hands can reach. I've been collared like a dog.

Lights clap on. I'm in a stark, unadorned room, on a platform raised several feet from the ground and smaller than an average mattress. It's a miracle I didn't fall off the thing while asleep.

I hear a door open behind me, and when I twist, Frank is entering the room. Hopefully this means I'm in Taem.

"You're like a fly, Gray," he says in that silky voice he commands, so smooth it made me once trust him. "A pesky nuisance that keeps buzzing around, creating just enough trouble to royally tick me off."

Frank walks around the platform, bringing his fingers together in a mellow wave. Pinky to pinky. Ring finger to ring finger. His eyes are piercing—murderous—as they lock with mine.

"Gray, something's been troubling me. There are roaches crawling around the outskirts of my cities. They are greedy and ungrateful. All they do is consume. They eat and take and they grow their colony. They think there's a better way because they don't realize that they are pests, that they will destroy any chance of security and safety with their ways. They are trying to invade my domed paradises that keep *out* the evils of the world.

"I thought you might help me deter them, but to be perfectly honest, you no longer seem worth the effort. The intel you've given up is mediocre at best, and the longer I let you scurry around, the stronger these pests seem to grow. You're fueling them. Dangerous, don't you think? To let people believe in something that won't actually help them?"

I grunt.

"What can you offer them, truly, besides a silly newspaper and the wild impracticality of blind hope? They've latched on to this idea that *I'm* the roach, the evil that needs to be removed, but I built them these hives. *I* kept them safe when the world was rotting. *I* gave them water when everyone else was parched. No, I think I know how to deal with them now, how to stamp out this growing infestation."

He pauses, lacing all but his pointer fingers together, which he brings to his lips.

"You are expendable, Gray. In fact, I think watching your life bleed out during the Sunder Rally might be the best way for me to show just how little power these Rebels have, how they've invested all their energies in a losing battle."

He plans to execute me, then. Publicly. Perhaps broadcasted to all his domed cities. Fine. That will give Harvey the perfect opportunity to do his work.

"Unless . . ." Frank moves very near the platform, so close that I can make out the wrinkles surrounding his eyes. I could probably kick him if I were brave enough to risk trying. "Unless you are finally willing to cooperate. Unless you have some information I might be able to use to my advantage."

"Like Headquarters' location?" I bluff.

"Oh, no. I already took care of that." He runs a forefinger along the edge of my platform and glances up at me. "What is being planned? Some sort of strike, correct? Your people have your spies, and I have mine. I know something is in the works. Details, or your life."

"These threats mean nothing to me," I say. "Not when

anything I say will be used against people—to punish them, imprison them, destroy them. That's all this has been: you on a power trip, thinking your way is the best way—the *only* way—and forcing it on everyone."

"You think this is still about governing?" He laughs. "My father was always trying to fix the country, the men in power before him tried to do the same. But the truth is that the government isn't broken. People are. I'm fixing people, Gray. I'm making a world where people are grateful and fair, where they follow rules and laws, where order trumps all.

"I crafted Forgeries to fight AmWest, to keep them at bay; and now I will use them to secure a new social order for all of AmEast. *Laicos. Social.* This has always been about people, Gray. I birthed five societies when the project started. They've birthed the most loyal, dedicated soldiers imaginable. The best type of citizens. *Worthy* citizens."

"You're crazy," I manage. It's a lame response, but I can't come up with anything else.

"People who don't want order are the crazy ones. You are the outlier. Your people are the terrorists. You threaten our way of life, you try to tear down the world we've created. My people thank me, Gray. I've given them everything—safety, security, protection from the West—and the Forgeries can uphold that. They will be the new Order, one that never fails or tires or thins. They will carry on what I've crafted long after I'm gone. Although perhaps I'll never be gone either."

He smiles at this and my stomach clenches.

If the fail-safe doesn't work, it won't matter how many papers Bea prints with my face on them, or how many Rebel supporters go around whispering her clever slogans. The Forgeries are limitless, and people are only so many. They will be run into the ground.

"Tell me what you roaches are planning," Frank says, "or it's your own execution."

"I'll be dead either way, so I think I'll avoid betraying my team as my final act."

He steps away from my platform, a half smile on his lips. "Roaches have wings, Gray, but they're not the best fliers."

The platform lurches beneath me and slowly begins to lower. I scramble to my feet, look up toward the ceiling. The rope is still slack.

"You killed Marco in a similar manner, did you not? Such a stellar soldier, Marco. Perhaps one of the best humans I had working beneath me. Felt like a Forgery sometimes given how loyal he was."

My platform keeps sinking. Slowly. Painfully slowly. I pull on the rope as hard as I can, hoping in vain that it will snap.

"You can hang now, or you can tell me the Rebels' plans and die a martyr for them later. Harvey can even do the honors. It will be just like last year, only reversed."

He rubs his hands together expectantly.

The floor sinks farther. I feel the rope tighten above me and rise onto my toes. Next comes the pressure against my windpipe, cutting off my air.

"A strike on the Compound," I choke out, our agreed cover. "Trying to destroy the Forgeries I discovered when you held me there."

"When?"

"During the Sunder Rally."

My toes are barely touching the floor anymore. My throat is screaming.

"Interesting," is all Frank says, and he keeps watching. As my toes lift off the floor. As I claw at the rope beneath my neck. As I gag.

This is an awful way to die. For the smallest moment I pity Marco for what I did to him. I feel my lungs shudder, heave, beg.

I hear footsteps, someone else entering the room. Harvey walks behind Frank and leans forward to speak into his ear.

"Sir," he says, "I really think we should make a spectacle of it. It will pack more punch."

They both regard me calmly. I kick as though I can swim through air.

Frank frowns, but signals to someone. The rope is cut and I drop like a stone. Pain rockets through my knees and back when I hit the platform.

"See you at the Rally," Frank says.

I'm on all fours—retching and gasping—but I can hear his smile in the bright tone of his voice. When I look up to confirm it, he's gone.

A door slams.

The lights bang off.

Darkness again.

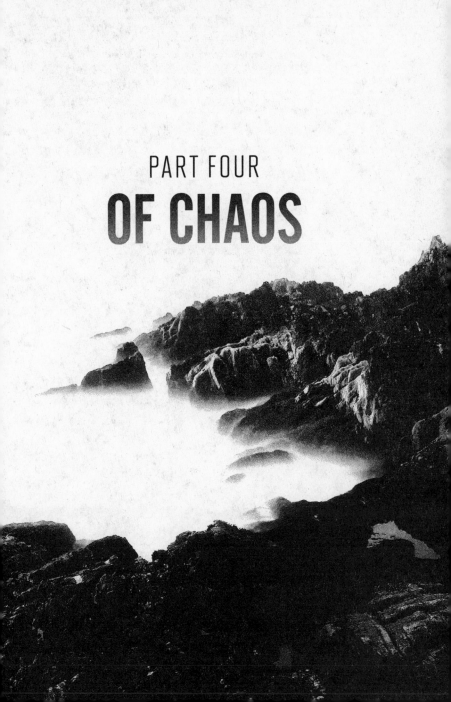

PART FOUR
OF CHAOS

TWENTY-NINE

I SIT AT THE FOOT of the platform, legs stretched out before me. My right ankle hurts from when I lowered myself over the edge and dropped to the floor. It was a longer fall than I predicted, but in the darkness, I'd tried anyway. Now, with nothing but my thoughts to entertain me as the evening unfolds, my fears are multiplying.

I should have come east in the car with Sammy, Bree, and Clipper. Why did I think the best option was Harvey walking me directly into the enemy's claws?

You needed to be sure Harvey could earn Frank's trust, the rational part of my brain whispers. *You needed him to be welcomed back into the Order's inner circle.*

And yes, since I left the Compound with Harvey in tow, supposedly my hostage, it only makes sense for Harvey to reappear with me as his. But then a few more minutes pass and my pulse begins pounding all over again. I'm in a locked room, completely helpless, and awaiting my own execution. If the team can't get to me, I know they'll act when I'm transferred to the Sunder Rally. We broke down all the various rescue possibilities in Bone Harbor. But still . . . What if something goes wrong? Something can *always* go wrong. The execution could happen here. I might never be moved and my death could be broadcast nationwide during the Rally from this very cell.

Calm down, I say to myself, knocking my head against the platform again. *Calm. Down.*

It takes a very, very long time for me to fall asleep.

I wake to someone jerking my arms behind my back, where they are then secured in cuffs tight enough to break my skin if I struggle. I'm tugged to my feet, blindfolded, and then shoved into a car. I can't see a thing, but the sound of the door slamming, followed by the rumbling engine, is unmistakable.

"Take the back way," a guard at my side says.

The vehicle pitches over a rough patch of road and picks up speed. Either the windows of the vehicle are blacked out or it's still predawn, because I can't sense a single ray of sun as we accelerate.

The guards ramble about ordinary things as we drive: their pay, wanting more time off, that wedding last weekend when so-and-so got lucky. One of them mentions a sick daughter at home. They sound so . . . *normal*. If I didn't know better, I'd assume I was in a car of Rebels.

"This is the turn."

The vehicle slows, rounds a corner. Again picks up speed.

"Hang on. Is that bridge out? Why are . . ."

We brake aggressively.

I hear the explosion before I feel it: a deafening roar, followed by a rumbling beneath the car's wheels.

"This left! Turn here!"

I'm thrown against the door, banging my right shoulder. Another explosion. Debris of some sort rains down on the roof.

"Back! Back! Before we're boxed in."

The car surges, driving in reverse. My stomach twists. Pops echo outside the car. I hear what sounds like heavy rain against the windows, but we're still moving.

A third rumble. Screeching brakes. We turn fast. Too fast. I feel the right side of the vehicle lose traction with the ground. The sensation of tipping lasts only a moment because soon there's no sense of up or down at all. I hit what

I assume is the roof of the car, then I'm thrown back in the other direction. The vehicle lurches to a standstill, but the popping gunfire continues outside.

My head is throbbing and the entire right side of my body aches. Blood trickles down my brow and is absorbed by the blindfold. I try to shrug it off, but when I strain against my bound wrists, the cuffs only seem to get tighter.

"Pete!" the guard pinned beneath me shouts. He shoves me off and I feel him lean toward what would be the front of the car. "Pete?" He gags. "Oh God. Oh . . ."

He grabs my elbow and tugs. We're moving up, but it would be toward the right-side doors if we hadn't rolled. He won't stop yelling about pain in his leg, but it seems like he's faring better than Pete.

I hear him struggle with the door, curse about his injuries, struggle some more.

"Help me with this," he growls.

"Take off my blindfold."

"Forget it."

"Do you want to die in here?"

He swears again, then pulls the blindfold free.

The car is a disaster. What would be the left side is flush with the ground, but by the buckled state of the roof and doors, I'd say we rolled more than once before coming to a stop. The driver—Pete—has split his skull open on the steering wheel. The second man up front isn't moving either.

Beyond the cracked windshield is a fading twilight sky. All I can make out is thick smoke and the shadowy outlines of a few buildings. We could be anywhere—Taem or Haven or even some town I've never heard of. Visibility's too poor to determine if there's a dome overhead.

The world reeks of fire and fuel. I've never forgotten that sharp smell—not since Sammy used diesel from the *Catherine*'s engine room to help me light my arrows on fire last December. The smoke is thick outside, a few licks of fire behind it. Those flames can *not* meet us. Not if what I'm smelling is our vehicle leaking all its fuel.

I throw my weight against the door with the guard, but it doesn't budge. The fire creeps closer, tearing up the road. More gunfire echoes from somewhere beyond the spider-web of cracks on the windshield.

While the guard holds the latch, I throw my weight into the door again. Nothing. Again. Still jammed.

Something rocks our vehicle. Some*one*.

I see the legs of the figure climbing onto the car, crawling toward our window. He pulls on the door. I throw my weight into it, and this time, it gives. The door doesn't swing open so much as it is heaved, a heavy grate being moved against its will. An arm reaches in, dressed in dark leather. We grab each other's wrists. I know who I'm holding without seeing her face. I would know the shape of her anywhere.

She hoists me out, then fires twice into the vehicle. I spend an exhale feeling bad for the guard, and then Bree is tugging me down a narrow alley as the flames make their way into the car. I follow her black form—black pants, black hat, black leather jacket that clings to her frame like a second skin. She's wearing a mask to protect against the smoke and runs through thick billows of it like I'm wearing the same.

The fight continues back in the street, gunfire against gunfire, smoke pluming in the wake of flames. We duck into a building. Bree leads the way up a flight of stairs, through a window and into a neighboring building, down several stairs and into a basement. It's deserted, but an angry alarm blares, red light flashing. The place has been evacuated—by Bree somehow, or maybe because of the fighting outside.

This has all been planned. Meticulously. And she must have had help. There's too much gunfire for it to be just Sammy and Clipper. They must have contacted other Rebel supporters in Taem after arriving at the safe house.

Bree spins to face me, palms out, and I barrel into them. She tears off her mask, then the hat.

"Your biggest regret," she demands.

"Saying I doubted us." I don't know why she's asking this,

not when my one and only double died at her hands at the Compound.

She keeps pressure on my chest and pulls out a flashlight. "And the person I told you about after our first night together." I blink, temporarily blinded. She gathers a fistful of my shirt and pushes me backward. "What was his name?"

"Lock?"

She lowers the flashlight and I realize I should have been suspicious of her, too. I know it's her now that she's mentioned our conversation about Lock—a private moment, a recent one—and the scar above her eyebrow only confirms it further, but how foolish of me. How dumb and trusting and naively stupid to immediately believe the first Bree I saw outside of Bone Harbor was my Bree.

"Do you want to check mine?" She holds out the flashlight like she's heard my thoughts. Then she shakes her head and pockets it. "Actually, no time. Loons. Herons then, loons now. We good?"

"We're good."

Bree grabs a small axe from a wall lined with tools and points at a table. "Hands here." With my back to the table, I lift my hands onto the surface, and stretch them as far apart as the cuffs allow.

"Don't mi—"

"I won't. Just hold still."

I feel the air move as she brings the axe down, followed by a vibration that stings at my wrists and travels to my shoulder socket.

"One more," she promises.

A *whoosh*, the clink of the restraint splitting, and my arms swing free. Each wrist is still cuffed in metal, but they're no longer tethered together.

She throws the axe aside. "Sammy's waiting."

"How many people did this take?"

"Does it matter? It worked."

"But—"

"I think someone's following us, Gray. Explanations later."

I didn't hear or see anyone, but if she says someone's on our tail, I believe it. We race through the massive basement, which is filled with machinery as large as the ceiling allows. At various intervals we pass medical kits mounted into the wall, emergency breakers to cut power to machines, fire alarms. This must be a factory, and by the look of the equipment we run past, we're on the production level.

"Where's the safe house?" I yell as we run.

"Not close."

"So how the hell are we going to get there?"

"Sewers."

Of course.

She takes a sharp turn, leading to a flight of stairs. "Up this, out the window, then a half block to the entrance." She even dares a smile over her shoulder before taking the stairs two at a time.

The gunfire is getting louder again, almost as though we've circled back toward the fighting. I can see the window at the top of the stairs. The sky has nearly lost all its color.

Bree hits the landing, shoves the window open.

"Wait," she says as I put my hands on the sill. She turns back toward the stairwell, gun poised. A few seconds tick by and she frowns. "He was right on our tail. I heard him."

I don't know how. I can barely hear her over the blaring alarm system, and she's screaming right into my ear.

"We must have lost him."

"Don't." She grabs my arm and hauls me away from the window. "Something's off." Her forehead furrows. She reaches behind her back and pulls a spare gun from her waistband. "We check together. You take ground level, I'll check above."

"A trap?" I ask, accepting the weapon.

"I'm not sure. Something though . . ."

We flank the window. She counts, her voice a whisper, and on three, we both pivot, angling outside. The ground is clear, no one in sight. At my side Bree yelps, and ducks back into the building. I hear her gun clatter to the floor. Right then I know it is indeed a trap, but not on the streets. No, this is worse. I move slowly, knowing what I'm going to see before my eyes actually take it in.

Bree is in the hands of an Order member. He has her held against his chest like a shield, a knife kissing the smooth skin of her neck. In his other hand is a gun, aimed directly at me.

"Put your weapon down," he orders, and I can't see a single reason not to comply.

THIRTY

"DON'T DO IT, GRAY," BREE says. "Don't do anything he tells you to."

"You really shouldn't test me," the Order member says. "After all, you know I have it in me to follow through." He shifts so that he is no longer fully sheltered behind Bree. I can see only half his face, but my stomach drops. I'm looking in a mirror.

"You were dead. She shot you."

"I was *dying*," my Forgery corrects. "But stomach wounds are a slow, painful way to go, and it bought me time. Enough to be flown to Taem and receive expert medical care. So thank you for that. Now, put your gun down."

With half his face still hidden behind Bree, I barely have

a shot. *Barely.* I've never been good with handguns. Not like Bree. And if I hit her . . .

I tuck my elbow in, letting the gun train toward the ceiling. "Dammit, Gray!"

"That's a good boy. Now put it on the floor."

"Don't," she says. "I'm begging you not to."

But what am I supposed to do? What can I possibly do?

"Shoot him. Take any shot you've got," she urges.

"So noisy." The Forgery brings his blade to her lips and hushes her. She falls silent, but he continues to apply pressure, to the point that she gasps. The knife slips into her mouth and I can see it like a blister rising, pressing against her cheek from the inside. My blood thins at the sight of it, then slows at the words spilling from my Forgery. He makes his threats as though they are a song he enjoys singing: Bree has a dirty mouth . . . She used it as a weapon against him and he should take it from her . . . She's a dog who needs a muzzle but perhaps she'd be safer without a set of lips at all.

Her eyes lock on mine and she rolls them. This is so like her to judge me even now, to criticize my hesitation. Like I have a mountain of options at my disposal. There is nothing to shoot, no part of the Forgery I can hit without also hitting her.

Bree slides her feet into a broader stance and rolls her eyes again. An exaggerated motion. And I understand.

She is going to roll.

Before I can reason with her, she stomps down on the Forgery's foot. He howls. Then she bends, throwing her hips into his gut and rolling him clear off his feet and over her back. He smacks the floor, and my bullet finds him next. Twice. So there can be no mistake. I pick up Bree's dropped weapon and double-check the Forgery. He's gone. Gone for good.

But when I glance up, I realize worse damage has been done.

Bree is bleeding. Everywhere. There is so much blood I can't tell where her mouth ends and the injury begins.

I rush to her, cup her face. His knife fought its way free. When she bent over to throw him off balance, she did so even with the knife pressed against the inside of her cheek, even when that motion required her to fight against the very edge of the blade.

The corner of her lip doesn't end where it used to.

She's not screaming in pain—not yet at least—but she's sputtering as blood pools in her mouth, catching the overflow in her hands.

I tug her away from the window and down the hallway. The medical kits were abundant on the lower level, but here it feels like forever until I find one. I yank it from its brackets and pull Bree into a nearby bathroom. I drop our guns and riffle through the kit. I pull out bandages and press them against the wound.

Bree swears awkwardly through her ruined mouth. "Is it bad?" she asks.

"Yes," I say, because I know she doesn't want a lie. "But you'll be fine."

I find a surgical needle, medical thread. I can stitch, and I can fix her. Not that she's broken. She has never, *ever* been capable of being broken. Not even at the hands of that worthless lump of flesh cooling down the hall—some horrible shadow of myself.

Bree sits on the edge of the sink as I try to clean away the excess blood, but the bandage catches the ragged flesh of her cheek. And that's when the tears come.

She's caught sight of herself in the mirror.

I'll admit it's nasty. It's one of the worst, most unnatural things I've ever seen, a smile that stretches into her cheek. She swears again. The tears fall. I tell her I can make it better even though I'm not positive I can.

I clean the wound with a solution I find in the kit. She screams, her hands digging into my forearms.

"You're okay. You're going to be fine."

She digs her nails deeper into my skin.

Next come the stitches. The needle snags as I force it into her cheek. It takes all my self-restraint to calm my shaking hand, to continue drawing her cheek together, to look at her perfect face and know I'm going to scar her. That this, even the good I'm trying to do now, is another wound she'll wear for the rest of her life.

I've sewn to the corner of her mouth before it dawns on me that I don't know how to close off the stitches. I wish Emma was here to make this right. Her work would be cleaner, less intrusive. But she's not, and so I do as best I can. I tie off my work, snip the excess string with a flimsy pair of scissors I find in the kit. The moment I finish, I kiss Bree. Right on that wrecked mouth, as far away from the fresh stitches as possible. She tastes like blood and I hate that it makes me cringe.

I throw the dirty bandages and utensils in the sink and dress the injury. It's bulky and awkward, the way the gauze is taped over the lower half of her cheek. She's shaking, I realize. Her entire body is convulsing.

"What is it? Pain? Do you need something?"

The front of her leather jacket is shiny with blood, and a few dried streaks trail down her chin and neck. Something defeated is written on her features, a sort of doubt and hope-lessness I've sensed in her only once before—when we were trapped beneath Burg and she cried against my chest in a pitch-black holding cell.

"Hey."

She won't pull her gaze away from the mirror.

"Bree!" I grab her wrist and her face snaps to mine. "I love you so damn much," I tell her.

Her bottom lip quivers, and her eyes work over me, lingering on my hairline. She fishes a wipe from the med kit and pulls me nearer. I stand between Bree's knees, my thighs against the cool sink she sits on, while she tends to my forehead. I'd forgotten about my own injury, the blood I felt trickle behind the blindfold as the vehicle rolled. She cleans the wound, fighting against the shaking of her own fingers, and then applies a small bandage. No stitches needed, I guess.

The alarm keeps blaring, dulled slightly by the door that separates us from the hallway. The fighting seems incredibly distant right now.

Bree looks at me. No, not just at me, but into me. It makes me feel weak and capable in the same breath. Then, as though something has jolted her out of a dream, she jumps from the sink and snatches up her gun.

"The sewers. We're late and Sammy's going to think the worst."

It's only when she's resorted to her typical demeanor—channeling strength and sureness—that the shock crashes down on me. My legs go slack. I brace myself against the wall, my opposite hand shaking as I clench the gun.

I can't lose anyone else. I can't.

"Gray," she says. "I need you with me."

I swallow. With both hands on her gun, Bree trains it up and steps into the hall. Because she asked me to, and because there's no one I'd rather follow, I make myself move.

THIRTY-ONE

I HOP FROM THE LADDER and my feet hit the water with a splat.

It smells fouler than death down here. Like mold and waste and stale liquid.

"Watch your mouth, the bandage."

"Relax, Gray. I'm not about to stick my face in this filth."

Her words might be slow and clumsy, but the Forgery's knife certainly didn't injure her sarcastic tongue.

The tunnel is barely wide enough for two people to walk abreast, and the only light source comes from street-level grates every hundred paces or so. As we walk farther into the sewers, the murky water grows deeper. Thankfully there's a raised walkway at the next intersection. The new cross tunnel is twice as large, with a ladder leading to an elevated area running parallel to the water flow. I try not to think that my hands are holding rungs Bree's filthy boots just trekked waste against as I climb after her. Overhead, an occasional vehicle rumbles past on the streets.

"Do you think they'll track us?" I ask.

"They'll try. Especially once they get a reading on where that Forgery last transmitted." A backward glance. "You should see the signs in town. Frank's promoting the heck out of the Sunder Rally, asking everyone across the country to tune in. He's even offering extra water ration cards to families as a way to ensure they'll attend in person.

"The Rally's going to open with executions—a bunch of unlucky bastards getting the axe publicly—and then he's unveiling the Forgeries. He's not calling them that, of course. It's painted like he's going to introduce everyone to a new task force, additional law enforcement to protect and serve each community, even the domeless ones."

"I was supposed to be a part of those executions," I tell her.

"I know. All of Taem does. You're the biggest selling point. Frank's been dismissing the news the *Harbinger* printed—the truth behind water resources, the deaths in Stonewall, the battle at Burg. He claims all that blood is on your hands, that the Rebels and AmWest are terrorists and you're pulling the strings."

My mind drifts back to what Isaac once stated on the Gulf:

Revolutionaries and terrorists are one and the same. We are the minority, threatening the norm. But it's right, what we are doing. Isn't it?

Bree glances over her shoulder. "What happened to your neck?"

I didn't pause long enough in the bathroom to examine myself in the mirror, but I imagine I have rope burns from my near hanging. Maybe bruises, too.

Bree scowls as I tell her the story, then follows it with her own. The drive east with Sammy and Clipper was uneventful. Rebel sources confirmed I was being held at an interrogation center on the outskirts of the city. As planned, Harvey leaked the time I was to be moved to Union Central, plus the route the car would be taking. The Rebels coordinated their attack, detonating roadblocks at predetermined intersections to turn around the armored car and lead it to a dead end of their choosing. Street teams held the incoming Order forces at bay as Bree and Sammy moved in for me.

"Where's Sammy now?"

"At the safe house," Bree says. "Unless something went wrong."

She pauses as we reach another junction, then swings her legs over the edge of the walkway and scrambles down the ladder. Back into the waste. She points at an offshoot about the size of the tunnel we used to first access the sewers.

I sigh, and follow.

The safe house is no more than a block from where we emerge aboveground.

Sammy and Clipper are waiting for us, along with Elijah. The place belongs to his cousin, who we're introduced to upon arrival. Elijah has been staying here for the last few nights. Ryder is in town, too, at a different location. *Preparing*, Elijah explains.

If I never hear the words *preparing* and *planning* and *waiting* again, it will be too soon.

We are shown to the basement where we'll stay for the night, and it's not pretty. A few cots are set up between dusty crates and storage boxes. A lone window just inches shy of the ceiling might offer some light come morning, but right now the cluttered room is dingy and gray. There is moisture in the air. I feel like I'm back in the sewers.

"You think this is a show or something?" Bree snaps.

Clipper averts his eyes from her bandaged cheek, suddenly very interested in his boot tips.

"What happened?" Sammy asks.

"A knife," she answers.

"A knife?"

"Did you go deaf since I last saw you?"

Sammy's eyes flick my way, and I give him a tiny head-shake. Bree has absolutely no desire to talk about what happened in that factory. I know it as surely as if she said it to me. Maybe someday she'll be able to go into detail, but for now—just as I've buried the tragedy of Blaine in my core— she only wants to move forward.

As Bree picks the locks of my cuffed wrists with a bent bit of metal, Sammy rattles off details Elijah shared with him before we made it to the house.

Frank is moving forward with his plans as though nothing has changed. Sunder Day is tomorrow and he is still pretending that I'm in his custody. "The illusion of order precipitates order itself," he's been saying to his closest advisors. At least that's what Harvey's relayed.

"Has anyone heard from Emma?" I ask.

"Yes, my clairvoyant connection to her has been quite strong lately," Sammy says. Then, more seriously: "We haven't been in touch with September yet, but Elijah said something about trying tonight. So maybe soon?"

Meaning Harvey leaked my transport information to the team, but never mentioned how Emma joined us in Bone Harbor. I feel the left lock click and the metal cuff swings open. I roll my freed wrist, but the knot of discomfort in my stomach only intensifies. Bree grabs my other arm, and as she goes to work on the lock, I share my fears about Emma's motives.

Sammy shakes his head. "She wouldn't cross us like that. I know her."

"You knew her Forgery," Bree points out, "and that thing was ruthless."

"But why?" Sammy continues. "What can she truly gain from this?"

"Could she—?" Bree cuts off and swears. "Maybe she's still a Forgery."

"She's not," I insist. "I checked her eyes. And you killed her one model."

"Maybe you saw what you wanted because of who she is, what she means to you. Maybe—"

"Dammit, Bree, I'm not that blind. This is her."

Sammy rubs his knuckles with a thumb. "Then what the hell is she after?"

"I have no idea. She must know something we don't."

"Sounds like one hell of a secret," Bree says.

Sammy rambles off a few theories, none of which make much sense, but he's already been betrayed by Emma's Forgery, and I don't think he has it in him to withstand it again. He loves her, even after everything, and he wants her to be a person worthy of that.

The second cuff clicks open, and I massage my wrist.

"I'm still dropping the files tomorrow, right?" Clipper says.

"Absolutely," I answer.

This doesn't change a thing. Clipper needs to deliver the virus-bearing thumb drive, and the Order recruiting event tomorrow—part of Rally activities and open to any citizen thirteen and up—is the perfect opportunity. It will get him inside Union Central, in plain sight, without raising any suspicions. Harvey will retrieve it from the predetermined drop point and go immediately to work. All while the rest of us get into position downtown.

The Rebels and Expats will make a stand—in Taem, in other domed cities, in exposed and underprivileged towns. Harvey's virus will see to the Forgeries once the alarm is tripped. And the three of us—me, Sammy, Bree? We'll be camped out with Frank in our sights, waiting. First clean shot any of us have, we take.

"I don't know, guys," Bree says. "It's possible Harvey and Emma are working together. Maybe it's not the smartest idea to have Clipper deliver the drive. The Expat-Rebel strikes will still happen, and we can still be looking to take that shot at Frank. But we don't *have* to tweak the alarms. Especially when there's no proof the fail-safe won't work in the Forgeries' favor."

"I'm going in," Clipper insists. "Harvey's good. I've seen it."

"The same way Gray saw that Emma is?" she counters.

"Sometimes I think you're too proud to ever admit you might be wrong."

"Clip, you can rub this in my face if I am. Actually, I hope it comes to that. Because I've got a bad feeling."

"So we just give up because you've got a *feeling*?"

"No, we make the decision as a team."

"Team!" he erupts. "*Team?* You're the only person who's still bent on hating Harvey. The *team* decided what to do days ago, so join or back down."

"Elijah's right upstairs," Sammy says. "We could have him weigh in."

"Nothing changes," I say firmly. "The fail-safe could give us an incredible advantage, and we're not backing down just because Emma's got us on edge. I don't care what Elijah has to say about it."

"Then I hope someone has maps," Bree mutters. "We should review tomorrow's route."

Beneath the city's dome, Rebels prepare for the coordinated strike. The same should be happening in Haven and Lode and Radix. Gears are already in motion. The fail-safe will be the unexpected component. A surprise cog.

Taem itself is growing restless. Elijah reports that fights

are breaking out on the streets. Shops are being looted. A water conservatory was tipped as citizens overwhelmed guards in an effort to score a few extra gallons for their families. He says a few of these acts are our people, already at work stirring the pot. As for the others? They're natural, cropping up among ordinary citizens. Sunder Day is meant to remind them of their freedom from the West, the day their lives became safe again, but this year, it's doing the opposite. Before the Continental Quake and the War, there was always enough food, water ration cards didn't exist, and the Order didn't patrol streets all hours of the day. But Bea's paper is the spark that started a wildfire. Stories that began in Bone Harbor crept east. *You aren't alone in wanting something better*, those pages promised. And people are finally believing it.

Still annoyed with Bree, Clipper heads to bed early, and the rest of us pore over city maps and sewer lines late into the night. The Rally couldn't be happening in a more central location. We have plenty of options to get there, but the sewers will be safest. Bree points out where we can split up, and we decide on a rendezvous point for later. By the time we settle into our cots, sleep does not come easily.

I close my eyes and try to conjure Blaine behind my lids. It shouldn't be difficult, and yet I can't picture him properly. A few features are off, foggy. I've forgotten the exact shade of his eyes and the angle his mouth would take when he'd shoot me a disapproving look. He's already becoming a ghost, a memory, and yet the pain is as sharp as the day I lost him.

In the darkness a cot creaks.

I feel Bree beside me, lifting my sheet, sliding into my arms.

"What's wrong?" I whisper.

She presses her face into my chest. I kiss the top of her head. The cot is not quite big enough for two, but that hardly seems like something to complain about.

"Nothing," she responds. "Everything's perfect now."

We fall asleep like that—together. We'll face tomorrow the same way. And if I have her—if we have each other—I know there is nothing we can't face.

THIRTY-TWO

CLIPPER IS ALREADY GONE WHEN we wake. Bree bolts upstairs and peers out the windows with the hope she can still catch him.

"I wanted to tell him good luck," she says, letting the curtain fall back into place. She glances over her shoulder at me, and her conflicted expression reeks of regret.

"Knowing Clipper, I doubt he's still angry with you," I say. "Don't worry about it."

She nods repeatedly, but I feel like she's struggling to convince herself it's true.

Elijah left sometime during the night to set up his post, but his cousin sees us off. He gives us extra scarves and hats to keep our faces shielded, and we head out as civilians file to the Rally downtown. We make it to the sewers without incident, and ditch our extra layers in the safety of the tunnels. Sammy breaks off first. Another block underground, and it's Bree's turn. My hand finds her wrist as she turns to leave.

"Are you okay? How's your cheek?"

"Stitches itch, but I'm fine," she says.

"Bree, I want you to know that—"

"No good-byes," she demands. "I'll see you in a bit."

She kisses my cheek and is gone, her boots slapping against the water and waste. I watch her climb the ladder to the street. She doesn't look back, not even as she pulls herself aboveground and out of sight.

It all feels too familiar, this sort of parting before the impossible. Last time she kissed my cheek and ran into Taem's belly we left the city with her in my arms, unconscious and bleeding from a bullet wound to the shoulder. I put a fist to my forehead.

Nerves. Damn nerves.

When I was young, I was daring and bold and stupid. I jumped from high tree limbs. I loosened arrows too close to town. I wholeheartedly believed that I was invincible. But I see the truth now: I'm human. Frighteningly, fleetingly human. Like Blaine who is gone because of a bit of metal no larger than my pinky.

I count to ten and then make myself move. At the next junction, I hang a left. Exactly as planned, a ladder waits.

I grab a rung and climb.

My post is a top-floor office overlooking Taem's public square from the southeast corner. Through the window, I can see the crowds beginning to gather, citizens and Order members alike. The raised platform I stood on last fall has been reconstructed since the fire, and its new beams look smooth as ice compared to the aged building at its rear.

I'll have a decent shot. Maybe. It all depends on where Frank ends up standing. Stupid Rally security. If Order members weren't posted on the roofs, in addition to the streets, this would all be a lot easier.

I lock the door even though the building is empty and climb onto the desk. I push away the ceiling panel directly above the computer. Reaching blindly, my fingers find the rifle Bree and Sammy planted when they arrived in Taem a few days earlier. Long barrel, attached scope, one magazine. A year ago I'd never heard of a gun, and now, while I still tend to mix up model names, I can list off basic anatomy. It's a skill I'm not sure I'm glad to have acquired.

I crouch alongside the window and peer through the slats of the blinds. The wall behind the platform is alive with visuals of other domed cities. Similar squares. Steadily growing crowds. A group of Order members struggle to raise a canopy-like tent over Taem's platform. Just what I need. Another obstacle to fire around.

I open the window, set up my shot in accordance with where I think Frank will sit onstage. Then comes the waiting.

I wish we were wired—me and Sammy and Bree. The silence gives me too much time to think about all the things that can go wrong. Did Clipper make the drop? Has Harvey uploaded the virus to override the alarm system? How many of the people filing into the square are on our side? When they burst into action, will others join, or will the Order silence them in a flash? And what about Emma? Emma, Emma, Emma.

Sometime around midday, the official festivities begin. The stage swarms to life, filling with high-ranking Order members and political officials. And of course, Frank.

I peer through the scope and mutter a curse.

Harvey is shielding Frank like a bodyguard. From the northwest corner of the square, Sammy won't have a shot at all, not with the video-illuminated wall at the back of the stage and the canopy raised overhead. And Bree—at the other southern corner of the square—likely has the same shot I do: one that requires shooting through Harvey to get to Frank.

I can almost picture her reaching for the trigger anyway. *Two in one*, she'd say.

But what if he hasn't gotten to upload the virus yet? I wait, breath held.

A shot is never fired.

Good, she's thinking the same as me.

We'll just have to be patient. Harvey will move eventually. He knows we're here waiting, and he'll drop his act at the right moment.

A series of speeches are made, some given by Frank's officials on the stage, others broadcasted onto the wall behind the platform as the Order speaks from various domed cities. The war is recounted, the freedom won from the raging West, the need to keep the figurative walls between the two countries strong and high. Claims that AmEast has never been stronger, that the Order has secured a new future for its people. Out of ash and destruction, Frank made it possible to once again feel safe.

There are no executions. Frank would never admit it, but I bet he opted for motivational speeches over executions because of the growing tensions beneath his dome. He doesn't need more martyrs.

When he finally stands and approaches the microphone, the crowd falls eerily silent. Harvey still shadows him on one side, a second advisor on the other. I wish I were on the roof, wish I could just get up and relocate to a position where I'd have a clear shot. This damn window and its limited width.

Frank thanks the people for their patience as he hunts down more water for the masses, announces his gratitude that they have let him lead for so long.

"It has not been an easy job, but we grow stronger each day," he says. "As does the Franconian Order. Our numbers have increased exponentially, and these new soldiers will serve you, the people of AmEast, tirelessly."

At his words, an influx of Order members appear at the edges of the square. Some look identical. Forgeries.

On the wall behind Frank, additional forces can be seen filing into the streets that surround the square. The video feed flutters between Taem's streets and those of other domed cities. In each, the number of F-GenX models is overwhelming, the civilians encircled like livestock in a corral.

"Many of you are aware of the growing threats we face— AmWest's inability to realize the war is over, our own people led astray by terrorist propaganda and untenable lies. I assure you now that I will not let these people jeopardize our future—*your* future. I will continue to fight for AmEast. I accepted this role hesitantly years ago, and today I happily embrace it."

"And what of all the people you have struck down to main- tain your perch?" a voice says. "Those who dared to question if you were the right man to *embrace* your role?"

The crowd parts around the instigator like he breathes death. He's speaking into a cone-shaped device that amplifies his words, and when he momentarily lowers it, recognition flickers over Frank's face.

"Ryder, old friend. What gutter did you crawl out of to attend these festivities?"

"Why, I crawled from the woods, Dimitri, from my ruined home. Although you already know this, seeing as you dropped the bombs on us. On me and anyone bold enough to admit we didn't think your rule was the best Taem—or AmEast, for that matter—could do."

"Careful what you say here, Ryder."

On the adjacent rooftop, I can make out a few Order members taking a knee along the building's edge.

"Do I sound too much like the *traitorous* West?" Ryder turns to address the crowd, raising his voice. "If a few hundred of us here think like the West, maybe the West isn't that horrible. And if thousands of us think like the West, perhaps we are the majority. Perhaps it is Frank and his Order who are outnumbered."

Frank raises a hand. The gunmen on the roofs ready their weapons.

"What are you going to do, Frank? Shoot me? Shoot all of us?" At Ryder's comment, the undercover Rebels move forward, threading through the crowd like a herd moving among trees. They surround Ryder, forming a barrier of bodies and pushing everyone else to the outskirts of the square. These outlying civilians look between Ryder's army and the Order, uncertain who to stand with.

"That's what you do to those who oppose you, is it not?" Ryder continues. "Execute them? Hunt them down? Eliminate them before they can find anyone else sharing their views?"

At this, the wall behind Frank roars to life with new footage: Rebels picking their way out of the rubble of a collapsed Crevice Valley. Bone Harbor homes being torn apart during search-and-seizure efforts. The hotel we stayed at in Pine Ridge billowing with smoke and Order members combing the streets. And then I see Burg, too, as it was when Frank first tried to terminate the Laicos Project there, and then Burg again, under snow and explosions. The latter is captured from the view of an aircraft, Adam's men swooping in to give us a chance for escape.

Photos flash between the clips. My father. Clipper's mother. Xavier tossing a dart and Bo mid customary tapping. I even catch a glimpse of Blaine and me sitting in Crevice Valley's hospital when he was still recovering from his coma. There are other faces I don't recognize, but I'm positive their lives all ended too soon.

I knew Clipper was compiling this footage, but nothing

could have prepared me for seeing it back-to-back, one image after another. It's like a blow to the chest.

The video compilation flies by faster: arrests, fires, water-rationing lines, one-off executions in dark side streets. Boat inspections and boat sinkings.

All at the Order's hands.

"You claim AmWest is our enemy," Ryder yells. "You claim to keep us *safe*, but we have safety with one another." He turns to the crowd. "AmWest has managed without an Order and without water rationing. They have helped some of our own when we were in need, and they are willing to stand with us now, right here. On Sunder Day. It is time for a new split in the East: the people from the Order. We don't need the shelter and security Frank promises. We need to stand together now, before it's too late. Before we really are outnumbered. These new forces in the square, these soldiers he passes off as recent recruits, are only the beginning. Go on, Clip!" Ryder yells to the sky. "Show them."

The visuals change again.

A poorly lit, expansive room I once stood in dumbfounded. Row after row of Forgeries. Glowing. Growing.

"If you think the Order is overbearing now, just wait until their numbers are endless," Ryder says.

Move, Harvey, I mutter to myself. From my angle, he's still blocking all but Frank's shoulder. *Move.*

"This is the AmWest threat he shows you," Frank says, his tone as calm and sure as ever. "Do not be fooled. Ryder is the one who has hidden all these years while I fought for you."

The visuals update, showing additional feeds from the Compound. The production level, but also the warehouse, the docks, the Franconian emblem on the crates and boats, and uniformed men walking the hallways.

The people on the outskirts of the crowd murmur, whisper.

"You've heard the rumors," Ryder says. "Some of you might have even read about them in an underground paper. There *is* a resistance. There is a boy as wronged as you; a fugitive standing for freedom." Bea's paper lights up the screen. My face. Her captions. Her lies that are becoming truths right this moment. "He is here, among us. He is just one person, but he will fight if you do, and together, we are many."

The whispers grow to a chorus. As the Forgeries press in on the outskirts of the crowd, weapons ready, the first aggressive contact begins: a shove, an elbow, a thrust.

"So I speak not just to you, citizens of Taem, but to all the domed sister cities, and to the people cut off from shelter years ago and still scraping by every day," Ryder continues.

Frank's head whips to the screen. The panicked words of an advisor are picked up by the microphone. "This is broad-casting everywhere? Cut it. Cease transmission."

"Will you stand with me, with the East *and* the West?"

Ryder urges, arms outstretched.

"Does no one have a shot?" Frank says, a hand at his ear. He's speaking to the Order but like his advisor, he's too near the mic.

"Let us Rally," Ryder finishes. "Let us Sunder our ties with the Order."

"For the love of God— Take it!" Frank shouts. "Anyone. Take the shot!"

A blast.

Ryder crumples.

Someone screams.

And the fighting erupts.

THIRTY-THREE

THE CROWD SURGES TO ACTION and almost as quickly, the Forgeries push in. Order members on the roof fire tear gas into the square. From windows, additional shots ring out, more of Ryder's people springing to life from their posts.

I bring my eye back to the scope. Harvey is ushering Frank toward an armored car just off the side of the platform.

I reach for the trigger.

Come on, Harvey.

He bends.

A little more.

Just enough.

Before I can pull the trigger, a bullet clips Harvey in the arm, missing Frank altogether. There is shouting, more

Order members swooping in. Frank is hurried into the car. Eyes snap up to where the shot came from: Bree's post. They point. Something is shouted.

Swearing, I tear my sight away from the scope. These buildings are going to be searched. I need to move.

The fighting is deafening now. Popping gunfire and exploding blasts and screams. Too many screams. The alarm is finally tripped, but it's the standard one, an emotionless, looping drone. Does this mean Harvey couldn't get ours uploaded, or that he *chose* to not bother with it?

No time to dwell on it.

I leave the rifle and flee the way I entered: the elevator shaft until the first floor, then an air duct to the basement and back to the sewers.

Around the very first corner, I collide with Bree. We both fall into the shallow filth. She scrambles to her feet and immediately takes the lead.

"Why did you take that shot?" I ask as I run after her.

"I thought I had him."

"But now Harvey's hit and if he didn't get to the virus yet . . . if he's hurt and can't—"

"I messed up, okay? I'm sorry! Will you pick up the pace?"

I bite off a retort. As we race through the water, we take turns I don't remember from the way in. Actually, I have no idea where we are, but I know one thing: We should have joined up with Sammy by now.

"Bree, what about Sammy?"

She doesn't slow.

I grab her arm. "Hey!"

She turns, and this section of the sewers is so poorly lit, I can't make out anything but the whites of her eyes. Beneath my fingers, I can feel the cuff of her shirt.

"Where's your jacket?"

"I had to shed it."

"Why?"

"Will you quit it with the interrogation? We have to get to the rendezvous point."

She tries to break away and I don't let her. "We said we'd meet in the sewers. Where Sammy first split off."

This shirt. The familiar material. How she's leading me somewhere.

It's not right.

My heart plummets.

I know what's happening, but I don't want to admit it, because it means having to reach for my handgun, the spare on my hip, and what if she beats me to the shot? Hers is already drawn. She's had it out the whole time.

Something explodes on the streets, and a flash of light

makes its way into the sewers through the drainage grates. It illuminates her for a second, from the neck to the waist. She's wearing an Order uniform.

"Why are you wearing that?"

"Gray, you're scaring me," she says.

"Why are you wearing that uniform!"

"To blend in. I got the jump on this young Order kid around my size. Shot him and took his top."

"Where?"

"Where what?"

"Where did you get the jump on him?"

"In the square."

My hand goes to her neck, and I shove her into the wall. She drops her gun on impact.

"Shit, what is wrong with you?" She thrashes in my grip.

"You wouldn't have had time—to fire the shot that hit Harvey. To also be in the square. To still get to the sewers the same time I did."

I draw my gun with my right hand, keep her pinned against the wall with my left.

"Gray, it's me, dammit! I fired the shot, and ran into an Order member on the half-block stretch back to the sewers. I swear it's the truth. I *swear*!"

"You just said you crossed the kid in the square."

"I meant the street! How can I think straight when you've got a gun on me?"

It sounds just like her. Feels just like her. I don't have this in me. I can't put a gun to her face and pull the trigger. What if I'm wrong?

I reach for her cheek, desperate to feel a bandage, to find proof that she is *my* Bree. Before my fingers can graze her face in the darkness, a voice freezes me solid.

"Gray?"

It's her, but distant. Somewhere else in the sewers.

I shout her name.

"Don't move." Her response echoes, bouncing off the tunnel walls. "I'm coming to you."

It's her. The *real* her. Unless the girl rushing to meet me is a Forgery, and the one I'm about to shoot is Bree. Using my momentary break in concentration to her advantage, the girl in my hands knees me in the gut. My grip slips. She scrambles away on all fours.

"What's your favorite bird?" I say, wheeling on her. "Answer immediately or you're dead."

She pauses, straightens. Something glints in her hand. The gun. She found it.

"She's coming, Gray. That thing. Please, we have to—"

"Answer the question."

"Herons," she says.

"Herons?"

"Yes, herons. Always."

Another blast on the streets, another flash of light. This time I see a flicker of her face—Bree. Beautiful. Scowling. And not a single flaw on her skin. She looks like the girl I met months ago in Crevice Valley.

I exhale and squeeze the trigger.

Footsteps pound up the tunnel behind me. "What the heck are you doing all the way out here? We need to grab Sammy." She has a flashlight. The beam falls on the crumpled body. I turn away and nearly lose what little food is in my stomach.

"Shit," Bree says, staring at the corpse. "Gray . . . ?"

She touches my shoulder, and my hands again act on their own. Her neck. Her neck in my hands. Doubles. Limitless numbers at his disposal. I can't trust her. Can't trust anyone.

"Loons," she says. She doesn't struggle in my grasp, just lets the flashlight trail up at the ceiling and answers calm as anything. It's enough light for me to see her bandaged cheek, the scar above her eye. "Herons then. Loons now."

I release her immediately. My hands shake.

"I'm so sorry."

"Don't be." She touches her holstered gun. "And you?"

"Saying we wouldn't work."

She doesn't draw it. No need for flashlights now, for checking scars or eyes or anything else. I gather her in my arms. Pull her into my chest. Her leather jacket is cool against my skin.

"There's no time for this," she says, and I know she's right.

We backtrack, and I try to ignore the visuals replaying in my mind. How it looked just like her. How I put a bullet in the mirror image of the person I love more than anything in this world. It makes my breath short. And I'd been ready to choke her—*my* Bree.

"You hit Harvey," I say, to distract from the madness raging in my head.

"I thought I had a shot and I took it. I was off by a fraction of an inch. Rehashing it won't change anything."

We round a corner and nearly collide with Sammy.

"Where have you guys been?" he shouts. Bree shoves her forearm to his windpipe and knocks him against the wall. "Shit, Nox! What the hell?"

She checks his eyes, lets him go. "We have to keep moving."

"What about the plan, the alarm?" he asks. "Where's the shutdown sequence?"

Bree shakes her head. "Maybe Harvey really *is* working

with Emma. They're the only two we can't account for right now."

A clatter to our right makes us turn. A canister, lobbed into the sewers, starts leaking gas. Almost immediately my eyes are burning.

Bree yanks the collar of her leather jacket over her mouth and nose. "This way," she says.

We flee.

Only to greet more gas.

Backtracking, we return to the junction and take the only open route left.

"They're trying to smoke us out," Sammy says.

"They're leading us where they want," I correct, which, not surprisingly, is back toward the dead Forgery. To wherever she was trying to bring me originally. My stomach coils. We pass Bree's double, take a few more turns. Ahead, gas looms. Behind, the same. We have one remaining option: the ladder leading aboveground to our right.

"Shoot," Bree says, skidding to a halt. "I know where this leads. We're only blocks from Union Central."

"How is that possibly a bad thing?" Sammy says. "Everyone's down at the square."

"*We* should be in that square," I say, the guilt creeping over me. This was our plan, and none of it is working. People are dying because of it. We might end up dying. I can barely breathe anymore, and my eyes feel on fire.

"Just climb," Sammy urges. "I have absolutely no desire to die in this filth."

We scramble up the ladder, push aside the grate. It dumps us in a narrow alley, directly in front of a set of wheels. The vehicle is a standard Order model—like the ones that ambushed the *Catherine* a few months back—but the driver is not. It's Clipper. He yells at us to get in and we don't argue. As soon as Bree slams the door, we're flying.

"How did you find us?" I ask.

"Harvey." Clipper's driving is rough and twitchy. About as horrible as mine. "The Order thought the shooter was moving by the sewers, and they wanted to guide him toward Union Central. Harvey told me where to get you."

The gas must have been a last resort, thrown in by the Order after the signal from Bree's Forgery stopped trans-mitting.

I twist around. Through the rear window, I watch another few Order vehicles skid to a stop and surround the sewer access point. The drivers glance in our direction right when we turn a corner. They could assume our vehicle is filled only with other Order members. Then again, I feel like we're bound to run out of luck eventually.

"You should see the feeds, guys," Clipper says. "Everyone's rioting. Not just in Taem, but the other domed cities, too."

"But the alarms," Bree says as the vehicle swerves around another corner and onto the main road. It's eerily deserted. Union Central looms ahead, looking stoic behind its majestic gate.

"They'll update," Clipper promises. "It takes a few minutes."

"Harvey never mentioned a delay."

"That's because—"

A cobweb blooms over the windshield and Clipper slumps forward. The weight of his arm yanks the wheel left and we collide with a building. My head hits the seat in front of me. Smoke billows from the front of the vehicle.

"Clipper!" Bree shrieks. She leaps from the car and pulls open the front door. "Clip. Dammit! Help me, guys. Help me!"

Sammy is clutching his middle and drawing shallow breaths. He's not bleeding—not that I can see—but he seems incapable of moving. I crawl over him and am in time to help catch Clipper's weight as Bree pulls him from the front. There's a gurgle of blood at the boy's lips, a surge of it on his chest.

"Shit, shit, shit," Bree mutters.

"Clipper, you hang in there." I put a palm against his chest. The blood doesn't slow. "You stay with us."

I glance up at the bullet hole in the windshield. The angle, the aim . . . There's a gunman in one of the nearby buildings right now. Probably with us still in his sights.

I take Clipper's hand in mine. He tries to tell us something, but coughs instead. Bree screams words my ears don't register.

Clipper looks young. He looks so young.

"We're going to make this okay, Clipper. You're going to be fine."

But already, his grip on my hand is slipping.

Damn, he looks like a kid.

Cars screech to a halt behind us. Order members spill into the streets. I yank the twine bracelet off Clipper's wrist.

The boy's head is slack against his chest as we're dragged away. He looks directly at me, but there is no light in his eyes.

THIRTY-FOUR

BREE CLENCHES HER JAW AS the car speeds up the street. The bandage on her cheek is dark and wet, stitches pulled from her screaming.

I feel the coarse weave of Clipper's bracelet with the pad of my thumb.

Thirteen.

I was just coming into my own as a hunter at that age. I spent my evenings terrorizing Maude by pulling the Council Bell and my days flirting with Emma. I goaded Blaine whenever possible but silently wanted him to think the world of me. Anything was possible. Even in a world where life ended at eighteen, I thought I could do anything.

All the things Clipper could have done, all the things he

might have been . . . They've been taken from him. Stolen. Stripped right out of his hands.

He was a kid. A damn kid. Still growing. Looking a little different each day.

Thirteen.

The rage in my chest threatens to take over.

I reach for Bree, thread my fingers through hers. She squeezes back.

It's just enough to keep me from shattering.

In Union Central, the alarm flashes red, its cry as standard and plain as ever.

We are dragged not to a holding cell, but to the enclosed and vacant training field. The oblong stretch of grass is surrounded by screens, each filled with chaos. In the downtown square, flames dance from building windows and smoke trails domeward. Where people have fallen, their bodies are trampled by those still fighting. The forces wearing dark uniforms outnumber the rest. Additional vehicles are driving into the square. From every angle, the Forgeries look endless.

Though I don't recognize all the locations, I see similar uproars on other screens. Haven, perhaps. Radix, Lode.

We are outnumbered. Outsmarted. Outmatched. Without the fail-safe, the people are doomed to be overrun.

The Forgery guiding me pushes between my shoulder blades, urging me to walk faster. We are brought to a line painted on the grass and told to kneel.

"I can't . . . breathe," Sammy gasps, "let alone . . . kneel."

He is kicked in the back of the knees. Bree and I submit without a fight.

From an observation deck, Frank and Harvey watch the whole thing. The scientist's shoulder is bandaged from Bree's misfired shot, and when he sees us kneeling and beaten, his mouth twitches. Into a smile? A grimace? I can't tell.

"Traitor," Bree snarls.

I'm about to admit that she was right all along, that Harvey was never working with us. His plan existed to pull all the Rebels and Expats from hiding, to draw us out for the slaughter. But then . . .

The alarm changes.

The blaring cuts off and morphs into a staccato mess. It is not a song but a cacophony. The notes seem to surge and soften in all the wrong places, to pulse and spasm. Frank clasps his hands over his ears. The Forgeries do the same. I would, too, if they hadn't bound my hands together upon exiting the car. The noise is nothing but a deafening, convulsive fit.

"What the hell is wrong with it?" Frank yells.

"Not sure, sir." Harvey tilts his head as he listens, like he's admiring the madness of it all. "I'll go check."

He slips inside. Frank returns his attention to the Forgeries on the field and draws a finger across his neck.

I feel the muzzle of a gun press to the back of my head. In the corner of my vision I see Bree tensing as well.

My last thoughts are funny. I've been in this situation before and I could think only of the present, of the things I would miss, of questions left unanswered. That's not the case this time. I know Sammy and Bree are coming with me, so I don't linger on them. I know Clipper will be waiting wherever we go. And Blaine, too.

For a fraction of a moment I am undeniably content. If everyone I love and care about isn't in this world, why the heck am I fighting to stay in it? But the thought brings up a memory: Emma and me at a window in September's apartment. She sounded just as resigned, as hopeless.

So when I hear the safety flick off, I'm thinking about her. About her choices. Her still mysterious goals.

Even after everything, I hope she finds some level of happiness. I can't imagine it will be easy to cope with the guilt once she's facing this world friendless.

The alarm fades, then spasms back to life, looping as planned.

Behind me, the Forgery barks out a cough. I feel the

muzzle drag across my skull, then break contact altogether. The coughing fit grows worse, and when I turn, the Forgery is writhing on the ground. They all are—the two that had Bree and Sammy at gunpoint, and the other two standing guard. I snatch up a dropped gun, and spin. My hands are still bound, but I can aim well enough. My finger can pull a trigger. But when the balcony comes into my sight, Frank's eyes are rolling back in his head. He staggers a moment, hand on the doorframe, and then collapses just like his Forgeries.

Like he *is* a Forgery. Or was.

I can't tear my eyes away from the place where he fell. Did I ever meet the real man? Was it a Forgery down in the square just earlier, addressing the public while the real Frank cowered in safety?

I twist, taking in the screens that surround the field. The Forgeries are dropping everywhere. In Taem's public square, in the streets, beneath other domes. It's like watching a tall grass blow in the breeze, a visible wave crashing.

Harvey staggers through a ground-level door and onto the field. He looks breathless. Shocked, but very much alive.

"You're fine! It didn't . . . Clipper's going to be—"

I bite off my words, but Harvey looks us over—Bree's bleeding cheek, the bracelet still clasped in my hand, Sammy slouched in the grass—and knows.

"That kid," he says, fighting back tears. "God, I loved that kid."

This is the second Forgery I've heard make a declaration of love. Something that should be impossible. How fine is the line between human and not? Have we done something both necessary and wrong with the fail-safe?

Bree offers Harvey her palm. "I'm sorry I doubted you. That probably doesn't feel like much now that you've proven yourself, but I still need to say it."

As they shake, panic flashes over his face. He doubles over, landing on his knees.

"Harvey?" I rush to his side.

He coughs, spattering the grass with blood, then rolls onto his back. It's happening. Was the fail-safe delayed for him because he'd broken through his own programming already? Because his sacrifice made him more human than Forgery? He dissolves into a coughing fit and I realize I'll never know the answer. The only thing I know for certain is there is no stopping this, no way to help him, and it brings me to my knees.

Harvey's back arches. Bree and I each grab one of his hands and try to hold him still as he flails. The screams coming out of him are so much worse than anything the other Forgeries went through.

Bree glances at the gun in the grass, then at me.

"Do you want a bullet?" I ask Harvey. "It would be quick."

He shakes his head in a spasming rock. "Just you two."

So we hold his hands, even when he squeezes ours to the point that our skin goes white beneath his grip. He begs for it to be over, cries shamelessly, and then, as quickly as it began, he shudders and is still. Blood trickles from the corner of his mouth.

Bree feels for a pulse along his neck and frowns.

An Order member bursts onto the field. "Weapons down! Step away from him."

"He's dead," Bree says.

"Weapons *down*!"

Emma follows the guard. She's wearing a medical smock over her dress, and her right hand clenches a handgun.

"Which one first?" the Order member asks her.

She brings her gun to his temple. "Neither."

"But you said . . . I thought . . ."

With her spare hand, Emma pulls a syringe from the pocket of her smock. The needle is buried in the soft flesh of the guard's neck before he even registers the threat. He frowns, and then his face goes entirely slack a second before he collapses.

Emma turns to us and frees our bound hands. "Crap," she says, her eyes falling on Sammy. "He looks even worse in person than he did on the cameras. Here." She shoves a small piece of blood-covered metal into my palm. "His office," she says. "Use the wrist chip to get there. Then the bookshelf. There's a false room."

I notice the bloody bandage on Emma's arm. She cut her wrist implant out. She cut into her own arm to retrieve this chip.

"Whose office?" I ask, completely baffled.

"Frank's," she urges. "I figured it out a while ago, before they planted me in Pine Ridge to wait for you. He'd visit me in the hospitals a lot. *I was gifted*, he said. *Had talent like Harvey.* Sometimes his eyes were perfectly human. Other times they weren't right, like the Forgeries'. I got good at spotting the difference in the glare of operating lights."

Bree's eyes drift back to where Frank's crumpled form sits, and she swears.

"I'm sorry I didn't tell you," Emma continues. "I wanted Frank to trust me, which meant making sure none of you did. I was going to do it myself, two days ago when we got back, but I was worried if I killed him first, the Gen5 would suspect everything; and if I killed the Forgery first, I *knew* Frank would. One of them was always watching. So I waited."

"And now?" I ask.

Emma drops beside Sammy and pulls one of his arms behind her neck. "And now Sammy needs medical attention, so you two will have to do it for me."

THIRTY-FIVE

EMMA'S CHIP GETS US INSIDE and up the necessary stairwells. When Bree and I burst onto Frank's floor, the few workers present step out of our way without a fight. Something is changing. It's as if they know Frank's grip is almost exhausted. They are deciding whose graces they want to be in when the smoke clears.

His office is locked, and this is the one door that doesn't register Emma's chip. I throw my shoulder into the door as I twist the knob. Slam my palm against it. "Come on!" Not now. We can't hit a dead end here.

"Gray!" Bree shoves me aside and aims where the teeth of the latch are hidden within the wood. She fires once, twice, and the locking mechanism gives.

The office is empty.

We walk in with our guns up, scanning the room. Papers lay scattered across the floor. A desk drawer hangs open as though files were grabbed in a hurry.

"Got it," Bree says. She's found the section of shelving Emma mentioned, although I can't imagine how Emma discovered it. Maybe she visited Frank's office and found it already open, or caught someone in the act of coming or going.

Bree pushes, and the section recedes, then slides behind the rest of the shelves to reveal a second office. The floor is slate gray and dull, and a narrow corridor branches off to the left. A series of surveillance screens hang on the walls, currently showing the square downtown. Without the Forgeries, the fighting is more evenly matched. There are no cushioned chairs in this office, no elaborate drapes or grand glass windows. The only decorative touch is a picture frame propped up beside the lone computer. The woman in the photo looks uncannily familiar, though I can't remember ever meeting her.

A gunshot deafens me in the tight quarters.

I duck, hands cradling my head. A second blast—or maybe it's the same bullet—strikes a screen, which crackles and goes dead. Frank darts from behind a large filing cabinet and races down the hallway. I send a bullet after him. It hits his leg. He staggers around a corner, firing blindly back. It is by sheer luck that the bullets hit the wall and not me.

I round the corner only to see him turning another.

"Damn, this place is big. Bree?" I turn. She's not behind me. "Bree!"

As I backtrack, my lungs seem to shrink. I all but fall into the secondary office. She's on the floor, leaning against the wall.

I drop to my knees and scramble to her.

"Are you hit?" My hands are on her, checking her face, her torso.

"Just grazed," she says, wincing as my hands move to her arms. "Right there."

I pull back. It's then that I notice the tear on the upper arm of her jacket, the blood. And the fact that her tank is shorter than it used to be. A pale rag, torn from the hem of her shirt, is in her opposite hand. She was trying to secure the material over the wound, slow the bleeding.

"Go," she says. "I'll be right on your heels."

"We stay together."

"Gray . . ."

"No. Just stop." I snatch the rag from her and tie it around her bicep. "Good?"

"Good."

I help her to her feet—she cringes—and we take off down

the corridor. It forks and branches often. Frank must be able to access half of Union Central through these hallways.

We turn or stay straight as he did. The path is made obvious by the blood from his leg—smeared against walls he paused to lean on, splattered against the floor where it fell as he ran.

Another turn and we're facing a narrow stairwell. I ascend half the flight and look over my shoulder. Bree's leaning against the wall, shivering.

"I'll be right behind you," she promises. "Go. Please?"

I slow, take a step toward her.

"Go!"

My feet carry me up the rest of the stairs. I shoulder my way through a door, and it bangs open into blinding light. I'm on the roof. A helicopter is backlit by the sun, the blades already alive. My bangs whip into my eyes as rooftop rubble swirls at my feet. Squinting against the wind, I see motion in the front of the rig. I fire and the pilot goes still. Another Order member leaps from the rear, and my bullet finds him before his feet hit the roof. No more movement.

"Frank!"

I'm not climbing into that helicopter. He's going to come to me. In the open. Where I can see him and fire a shot easily.

"Quick to run now that your Forgeries are dead and no one's willing to stand and protect you, huh?"

Still nothing.

"There's no way out except through me."

With his hands held in surrender, Frank steps from the helicopter and onto the roof. "Gray," he says. "The unHeisted boy. Here to put a bullet in me?"

"Believe me, you deserve worse."

"For trying to protect people? They need to be told how to think, what to do. Just look at them." He waves in the vague direction of the square. "They are tearing one another apart. People can't be trusted with their own two hands, let alone their minds."

"Enough!"

"Are you going to shoot me, then? Is that how the fugitive for freedom frees his people? By killing the one person who's kept them safe?"

"Yes."

I pull the trigger.

The hammer strikes.

But no bullet flies.

Is it jammed? No, I'm out. This is the Forgery's gun from the training field. I didn't know how many rounds I was carrying, hadn't been counting as I fired.

My head whips back to Frank, and he's already in the process of drawing his weapon. I dive, tackling him to the ground. He's slow, and I easily dodge the punch he throws.

It's the dust and rubble that he tosses in my face that costs me my advantage. Blinking, eyes burning, I stagger away. My hip hits the lip of the roof, the wall that separates me from a deadly drop. Frank's hands are on the front of my shirt. He pushes me backward.

I can feel the hook of gravity, how I'll topple to my death if he applies much more pressure. I will my feet to dig into the roof. My hands grapple for something, anything, to keep me on *this* side of the ledge. The only things they find are Frank's fists clenching the front of my shirt.

And then, without warning, Frank pauses.

I blink away the last bits of dirt to see what's made him loosen his grip.

Emma.

Emma no more than three paces away with a gun aimed at Frank's heart.

Her form isn't great, but she's close enough to not miss. I think. Her gun hand is shaking, and the corners of her eyes wrinkle as she takes aim. She might not have it in her to pull the trigger. Emma's a fighter when it comes to *saving* lives—stitching cuts and setting bones and tending to illness. Saving, not killing. She couldn't even kill that Order member below. All she did was drug him.

I look toward the stairwell, desperate to find Bree there. The door bangs in the wind.

"Let go of him," Emma says. Far quicker than I expect him to, Frank caves. I stumble away, rubbing at my burning eyes.

"Now sit on the wall."

He complies.

Emma moves nearer. One step. Two.

"Doll, you can't be angry with me," Frank says. "Not after all I've done for you."

"Don't call me that."

"Please," he says, hands held in surrender. "I'll leave, I'll do whatever you want, but please show mercy. All I've ever wanted is to fix people. I'm not the villain you've made me."

"You've oppressed everyone who turned to you for guidance. You've murdered people for having their own opinions."

"You're looking at it wrong. You and Gray and all these brainless Rebel romantics think the answer is letting people run wild," he says. "But structure and rules yield order. Too much freedom makes people bored and greedy. They tear one another apart. Everyone would see that if they stopped fighting me long enough to listen. All I do is protect people. My whole life has been spent keeping people calm and safe and—"

"Living in fear," I say. "Afraid to speak their minds."

"People cannot be trusted!" A vein bulges on his forehead.

"Not with anything breakable and certainly not with the future."

"Stop it!" Emma shouts. "Not another word." The gun shakes again in her grip and Frank sees it.

"Put the gun down, doll. You don't know what you're doing."

"*I'm* making the demands now."

He laughs, and she loosens a bullet into his foot like she's Bree. Like she doesn't have a thing to fear and will pull any trigger necessary. The same possessed determination I've seen on Bree's face now graces Emma's profile. It's the look of a person about to do the unthinkable. Maybe no one is above killing.

Frank swears in pain, jerking to grab his foot, but when Emma brings the weapon's barrel back to his heart, he goes bone still. A bead of sweat drips from his brow and strikes the dust-covered rooftop.

"Promise all my people can walk free," Emma says. "Everyone in Claysoot and any other test group. The Laicos Project is over."

"Done."

She presses the muzzle to his forehead. "Swear you'll let your citizens elect a new ruler. Anyone the majority favors."

"You have my word."

"They will try you however they see fit, and if by some

miracle they let you walk, you'll disappear. Permanently."

"Seems only just."

"Good." She lowers the gun. "Then this new world has no room, or need, for a person like you." She grabs him by the ankles and lifts.

It happens both immediately and in slow motion. For what feels like hours he hangs on the brink of death—momentum not yet claiming him—and then he's toppling. His arms flail out. Shock blows over his face. And he's gone.

I dart to the low wall, peer over.

Dimitri Octavius Frank is dead, a broken heap at the foot of his headquarters. The blood around his head is as dark as his uniform.

Emma sinks to the ground and unravels. She pushes the gun away. Her shoulders shake. She's crying—not audibly, just tears.

"Don't touch me," she says as I move nearer.

"Emma . . . you just—"

"*Don't.*"

With her feet tucked beneath her and the determination gone from her face, she looks years younger.

"Thank you," I say.

Emma wipes her cheeks with the back of her hand. I should do something, not just stand here watching her cry, but she told me to keep my distance. I feel completely use-less. She stares at the gun sitting an arm's length from her knees, and because I worry she'll stop talking altogether if I don't keep her at it, I make my mouth work.

"How'd you find us?"

"Left Sammy in the hospital wing with some nurses. I found the door open in Frank's office, then followed the blood trail."

The blood trail.

"Bree!" My eyes dart to the stairs.

"Gray, wait." I take one look at Emma's face and know what she's going to say, know exactly how bad it's going to be when I enter the stairwell. I race away. Across the roof. To the door.

I drop to my knees at the sight of her.

She's slouched just two steps from the top, her good hand tucked inside her leather jacket and beneath her injured arm, like she's holding a cramp in her side. Sweat coats her forehead. She's paler than the moon.

"You said a graze." I pull her nearer. "You said it barely clipped you." She leans into me. "Bree?"

"I didn't want you . . . to slow down . . . or not go after him." She cringes. "I didn't want you . . . to know."

"Know?" I hold her face in my hands, let my fingers trail over her skin just to confirm she's still real.

"Two shots."

"Two shots where, Bree? *Where?*"

"One graze . . . the other . . ."

She lifts the arm I bandaged just earlier, draws her opposite hand away from her torso. Beneath her jacket, the blood is abundant.

THIRTY-SIX

"OH, NO. NO, NO, NO."

I press my hand against hers, guiding it back to the wound. The blood seeps through our fingers, sticky, warm.

"Emma!" I shout toward the roof.

Bree's breathing is labored. Her eyelids flutter.

"Did you get him?" she asks.

"Yeah. We got him."

She manages the smallest smile, then leans against the wall and groans.

"Emma!"

She's at the top of the stairwell now, looking down on us. "I can try," Emma says. "All I can do is try."

I pull Bree to her feet. She can't hold her own weight

anymore, so I slip an arm beneath her knees and carry her. Emma squeezes past us to lead.

The hospital is full of workers, most of them tending to injured Order members that have been transported back to Union Central from the square. Emma points to a vacant bed and I lower Bree onto the stiff mattress.

"You're fine," I tell her, but I've never seen her look worse. There's so much blood and her skin is too pale and something is off in her eyes. She's half elsewhere. "Bree?"

Her head rolls to look at me. I kiss her knuckles.

Emma shouts orders to another medic. Bree's jacket needs to come off. And she needs a sedative.

"Gray, you have to move," Emma says.

But I don't want to let go of Bree's hand. It might never be warm again. Emma pushes against me. Bree's fingers are sticky in mine.

"Someone get him out of here," Emma yells. "Get him out!"

I'm heaved away by a burly medic and shoved into the hallway. The door slams in my face. When I try the handle, it's locked. All I'm left with is a window view of the chaos. Fists against the glass, throat tightening, I watch.

The sleeve of Bree's leather jacket is sliced open, then freed at the shoulder. Her entire right side, from shoulder to rib cage, is dark with blood. They cut away her shirt and roll her onto her stomach. A medic walks to the window and pulls down a shade.

I slam my palms against the glass, scream Bree's name. The shade remains down. For a long time. Long enough that I quit pounding on the glass and instead slide to the floor. My father, Blaine, now her? It will actually break me. I will come apart at the seams. How many pieces of myself am I expected to lose and still remain standing?

I stare at her blood on my hands.

I can't stop shaking.

Someone needs to tell me what to do. Someone needs to tell me because I'm about to shatter.

You can't sit there feeling sorry for yourself, that's for sure, I hear Blaine chide in my ear. *Frank's dead and everyone's still fighting. Go tell them it's time to stop.*

He would judge me, even now. But haven't I done enough? Sacrificed plenty? How much am I expected to give?

Everything, Blaine says. *Because people believed.*

And right then, the true influence of Bea's work hits me—the stories in the *Harbinger*, the propaganda that's been hung throughout towns, the rumors that have been whispered in quiet streets. I thought they were all lies, but they're not. They'll only become lies if I don't do this, if I choose to make them such.

I'm not the only one who's lost a brother or father or friend.

I'm not the only one who's been wronged. Down in that square, everyone's future is a breath away, or maybe a bullet too close to being taken from them. And if I can't stand with them now, what the hell has this all been for?

I glance at the window to Bree's room. The curtain is still drawn.

This is the last thing you have to do, Blaine promises. *She'll understand.*

There's always one last thing. There will be another after this. That's life.

But he's right. If our fates were reversed, I know he'd already be downtown.

I take a deep breath and stand. Because I must. Because really, when I look at the whole of the matter, there's no other option.

Several blocks from the square there's so much debris in the road I have to abandon the car I took from Union Central and continue on foot. The gunfire is deafening, the world an inferno of flames. I end up cornered in a narrow alley, cowering behind a Dumpster while Order members try to take me out from the roof. I'm an idiot, armed with the same handgun that's been without ammo since I shot Frank's pilots and no plan whatsoever. Somehow, this all seemed a lot easier in my head.

"You trying to get yourself killed?"

I look across the alley and see Elijah's cousin peering from behind a door. He points at a trail of dark liquid on the ground. At first I think it's blood, but notice it's leaking from an overturned Order vehicle at the end of the alley.

Elijah's cousin lights a match and tosses it onto the gasoline. The flames snake up the trail, and when they meet the car, I can feel the explosion in my ribs. The gunfire falters. Momentarily deaf, I dart across the alley beneath the cover of smoke and into the opposite building.

We race up a few flights and find Elijah hunched over a table with a half dozen other Rebels, shouting into a radio. He's covered in blood but he's fully mobile, so the blood can't be his. I tell him about Frank, and he immediately starts firing off orders.

"Someone get a call back to Union Central. I want video of the body ready to go. Two guards for Gray over there." He points to a balcony that overlooks the square. "And get him in a bulletproof vest. I'm not taking any chances."

Before I'm truly ready, I'm stepping onto the balcony with a pair of Rebels at my side. I cringe, expecting a bullet, but nothing finds us. The platform Frank spoke from earlier is overrun. Abandoned cars and broken bodies are everywhere. Some clothed in black uniforms, but nearly as many in threadbare attire. A group of citizens has been beaten into a corner. A throng of teens smash out the windshield of an Order vehicle, drag the soldiers from the car. I can taste blood in the air and see it on the streets. The world is stained dark.

A microphone is handed to me. Elijah says it will be loud enough. They've rigged Frank's original setup to work for our needs.

A high-pitched whiz sounds, and a white trail blazes toward the dome. It explodes in a starburst of blue—a firework, momentarily louder than the shouting and the screams. Nearly as loud as the popping gunfire.

The noise and foreign color are enough to make people in the square falter. They look up, startled, and the wall behind the platform fills with the image of Frank's fallen body.

This is my signal.

"Frank is dead," I say in the brief lull of fighting.

My voice booms through the square. So loud I bet Blaine— wherever he is—can hear me. With this realization, a calm washes over me.

The people turn, trying to locate where my voice is coming from. Some spot me. Others, who have not yet seen the proof of Frank's demise, find it on the wall behind the overrun stage.

"Some of you know me, and the rest of you probably don't trust what I have to say," I continue. "I've been called a lot of things—Expat, Rebel, a fugitive for freedom—but the truth is I'm just trying to get by. I'm trying to make it from one day to the next. Like you."

I realize people are actually listening now. Not all of them, but enough. The soldiers who had cornered their prey pause. The boys dragging men from the Order car let their arms hang at their sides. There are fists, still, and weapons held at bay. But people are listening.

"I know how hard it can be to put down your weapon. I do. Especially when fighting seems like the only way to achieve justice. But those of you fighting for freedom have no reason to keep at it—Frank's gone—and those of you fighting on Frank's behalf are no longer bound by your service to the Order. Not unless you want to be.

"If this continues, we're not destroying the enemy anymore. We're killing neighbors. And I'm tired of fighting," I say. "So damn tired. I want to go home. I want to start living again."

Almost directly below me, a boy puts down a wooden bat. There are two Order members an arm's distance from him, but he lets the bat fall from his hands like a shield he no longer needs. They look at the boy, then their handguns. It feels like it takes an hour, but they holster them.

And then the surrender spreads like a wildfire. Weapons are dropped, fists are uncurled, outward and onward.

Not everyone complies. There are certain Order members shouting, and I can still hear fighting out of sight beyond the square, where people couldn't see a screen or hear my words. But so many have chosen to surrender. They're still watching me. I don't know for what, so I do the first thing that comes to mind. I hand the microphone to the guard and press the Expat salute into my chest. Then I mirror the salute with my other hand, so that my arms are crossed, and both sets of fingers form a letter. E *and* W. East *and* West.

That's when the bullet finds me.

I don't hear it fired, but it hurts like no other when it strikes. It nicks my finger and hits my vest just above my heart. For a moment, I lose my breath.

The guards grab me before I collapse, and pull me into the safety of the building. I catch one last glimpse of the square. Already, a swarm of Order members and civilians alike are descending on what must be the shooter. Those not working to force the stubborn to surrender are mirroring my two-armed salute.

It's beautiful, and I'm exhausted.

I could sleep for days.

I wish you were here for this, I tell Blaine silently. *I think I might have made you proud for once.*

THIRTY-SEVEN

I'M RUSHED BACK TO UNION Central by car. My vest is stripped off, and with the exception of an already-surfacing bruise, I'm uninjured. Elijah still suggests I see a doctor, but there's only one place in the hospital I care about visiting.

The same medic who threw me out earlier is exiting Bree's room as I sprint down the hall. He's got this terribly drained expression on his face, and when he puts his hands up to stop me, I feel my chest rupture.

"Easy, son," he says. "Easy. She's not—"

"Let me see her!" I shout, straining against him.

He grabs my shoulders, shakes me, but I'm already deteriorating.

"I have a right to know!" I feel my knees giving out. "I don't care if she's . . . I have—"

"She's not awake!" he yells. "And she's on a lot of meds. You can't barge in there like a madman."

Not awake. The next breath I draw feels like it feeds double the air into my lungs.

"The bullet entered from the back and was lodged just below her armpit," he explains. "She's lucky she didn't end up with a shattered rib."

"But she's okay?"

He nods. "She might lose some mobility on that side, but she's going to be fine."

I lean forward, trying to peer through the doorway. "Can I . . . ?"

"Just go easy. She's got a long recovery ahead."

Bree's propped up against a pillow when I enter, sleeping. She's wearing a clean tank, and beneath it, her right shoulder is bandaged. They've even seen to her pulled stitches. A fresh piece of gauze covers the corner of her mouth and a good portion of her cheek.

I move quietly into the room, sit on the edge of her bed. She doesn't stir.

"Hey," I say. "Bree?"

Her eyes drift open, and when she finds me sitting

there, I swear she actually glows.

"Hey," she echoes.

"How are you feeling?"

"Tired."

"You scared me, Bree." I put a hand on her thigh and she curls her fingers around mine. "I'd have lost it if you . . . I wouldn't have made it."

"You don't need anyone to get you through life," she says slowly, like the words are a labor to produce.

"I need you."

"No you don't."

"But I *want* you," I tell her. "I want you in every moment. Everything's better with you."

"Greedy jerk."

I shrug.

"No denying that?"

"Not when it comes to us."

She manages a smile, but it looks like it drains her. I give her fingers a light squeeze.

"You know," she says, "I'm not so weak that you can't kiss me."

"You want me to kiss you?"

"Don't make me beg," she says.

So I don't.

The days following the Sunder Rally are an odd bunch. Oddly surreal. Oddly in limbo. Oddly . . . optimistic.

I have a cobwebbed bruise the size of my fist on my chest, and I've never felt more lucky. My announcement of Frank's death was broadcast on repeat throughout Taem and the other domed cities and eventually, the Order stood down. Or maybe they stood up—for the citizens, for the average life they were always supposed to be serving. Turns out many of them had doubted their work for a while, but felt too trapped to do anything about it. The pay was good. Their families needed the earnings. The job gave them access to medical care and water and other goods that weren't easy to come by outside service. Still, by the time the fighting ceased entirely, the casualties were numerous for both sides. So many fallen Order members. Even more average citizens.

Ryder's body was found among the trampled in the public square, leaving Elijah to inherit the role of Rebel commander. Already he has teams working to shut down the Forgery production lab at the Compound, and in the coming days he's set to meet with Vik and high-ranking Order officials to discuss the future of the once-divided country.

"You'll stay and help with the transition, right?" he asks me. "The people will want to see the *fugitive for freedom* playing an active role."

Even before he says *please*, I know I can't. There's a Wall I need to climb, a dusty community I need to revisit. I've only delayed this long because I'm waiting for Bree to be well enough to travel. But Elijah looks so hopeful that I strike a compromise. I'll see to my hometown, and I'll return.

"No promises on how long I'll stay, though," I warn. "I never really pictured myself living somewhere so . . ."

"Free? Liberated? Revolutionary?"

"Big," I say.

Two days after that, Vik shows up wearing a pair of impressive dress pants and a collared shirt. His hair is parted and swept out of his eyes, and when he winks at me, I suddenly know why the picture in Frank's office looked so familiar. That woman's eyes—they are also Vik's. He has her mouth, too. And Frank's chin and polished composure.

Adam said it was just a story, but now I have to wonder if Vik purposely discouraged the rumors.

Vik's the right age—maybe thirty years younger than Frank. He'd have been born roughly a decade after Frank came into power, when the governing methods were only just beginning to grow questionable and the first few generations of the Laicos Project's Heisted subjects faced operating tables.

"Hey, Vik," I say as he shakes my hand in vigorous congratulations. "What's your full name?"

"Viktor Frank LeRoy."

"LeRoy's your father's surname?"

"My mother's. I've never met my father."

Never met him, I believe, but that doesn't mean he's clueless as to who his father is. This always seemed personal to Vik, the fight, the outcome. He lashed out when Frank made contact one too many times, including an attack on Taem's dome just to prove it could be done. Like a boy trying to show his father that he's his own man. And his middle name . . .

Vik leaves to find Elijah for what will be days upon days of meetings, and I decide it doesn't matter. I won't press this. Vik is his own person, and from what I've seen, he's good.

Bree's on her feet again. Despite many warnings, she keeps attempting push-ups, only to be greeted by a searing pain in her shoulder that is followed by an immediate scowl. She doesn't scowl when she apologizes to me though—for doubting me, Harvey, the plan. She speaks with complete sincerity, and I tell her to forget it. It's behind us. It doesn't matter anymore.

"I still have to admit I was wrong," she says.

"Why?"

"Because I was, and you deserve to hear that from me. And also because I don't want you to be able to hold it against me. I'm crafty like that."

We learn that September and Aiden are on their way east. They fared well despite the fighting that broke out in Bone Harbor on Sunder Day, and while I'm anxious to see them, I'll be gone by the time they arrive. Bree's well enough to travel now, and we're leaving in the morning. All that remains is looping in Emma.

Her response is not what I expect.

"I'm staying here," she says when I find her exiting Sammy's room. She has a medical kit in her hands and bandages tucked under one arm. "The hospital's overflowing, and I can't afford to step away, not with so many injured. Tell my ma that I love her, and that I'm here whenever she chooses to follow. You are going to tell them to climb, right? That's why you're going back?"

Not to tell them to climb, but to tell them the *truth*, to let them have what so many victims of the Laicos Project never did: a choice. Still, I nod.

"How's Sammy doing?" I ask.

"Oh, he's a huge baby. He keeps saying he needs bandages changed, and it hurts, and he swears he's getting an infection." She rolls her eyes. "He could have been out of his bed days ago. He had the smallest puncture in his lung from the car crash. So small we didn't even operate. It's healing on its own. The only bandage he does have is on his left wrist—a sprain—and it's certainly not infected."

"He just likes when you visit him," I say. "Hence all the complaining."

"He reminds me of Craw," she says. "Overly fond of girls, cocky, sarcastic. Good-looking and aware of it."

"Yeah, but Sammy really does like you. I've seen it. You don't owe him anything, but I still think you should give him a chance."

"Why do I get the feeling you're looking out for me?"

"Because I am."

How can she not see that? That I might not be *in* love with her, but that I still love her, that I'll always want the best for her. In the same way I never want to see Sammy hurt. In the way I'd have done anything to keep my father or Blaine alive.

"Thank you for everything, Emma. On the roof, in the hospital . . ."

There aren't enough words to express my gratitude. She suffered a lot at my hands. Then she saved me when I was beaten, and Bree when she was down. She saved everyone, really, and didn't ask a thing in return.

"I haven't forgiven you for what happened at the Compound," she admits. "I don't know if I ever will. But I still want to see you happy. Does that make any sense at all?"

"So much."

"Good. Now don't screw things up."

She gives me her typical half smile. Unlike the last time she commented on my feelings for Bree, this doesn't feel like a threat. It doesn't feel like anything but a comment. I wonder if I misread Emma back in Pine Ridge. I've never been able to truly read her, I realize. I can't look at her and know exactly what she's thinking. I can't hear her words before she says them. Not the way I can with Bree.

"I need to get back to the hospital wing," she says. "Maybe I'll see you soon."

"Yeah. I hope so."

It's a good-bye, but not really.

"How can you leave?" Sammy says that evening. We're sitting on Union Central's roof, a drink passing between us as our legs dangle over the edge of the building. "Remember those futures we predicted back in Pike? I'm supposed to be old and fat and living next door to you. I can't do that if you run off as soon as everything's settled."

"That future had me living in some quiet clearing in the woods," I remind him. "Not to shock you, but Taem doesn't really fit that description."

"Do you not see all the grass on that training field?" He points to it. "Green everywhere. It's a downright jungle." He takes a long drink. "It's a shame Harvey's missing this.

He knew all along that he wouldn't make it, huh?"

"I think so. From the moment he spotted the fail-safe in his code."

Sammy whistles. "He never quite looked the part: hero, legend."

"He played it well though."

"That he did."

Sammy lets a bit of alcohol free of the bottle. It rains onto the training field below.

"To Harvey Maldoon," he says.

"And Clipper." I touch the boy's twine bracelet on my wrist.

Sammy tips the bottle again. "To Clayton 'Clipper' Jones."

"To . . ." My voice snags.

"To Blaine Weathersby. Brother, friend, father. Gone but never forgotten."

Sammy continues. With my father, then Adam, and Ryder, and on and on. Back through others we've already mourned, and on to those whose names we don't even know—those who fell throughout the Rally.

The bottle is nearly empty when Bree joins us. She squeezes between us, sitting so her legs hang over the edge like ours, and snatches the bottle from Sammy.

"You're supposed to send your condolences to the stars. That's a waste of perfectly good alcohol."

"Do you have no decency or respect?" Sammy says.

She takes a long swig and cringes at the strength of it. "Bad arm or not, I can still whoop you, Sammy."

"True story," I say.

"And to think I was worried I'd miss you guys." He gazes out over the city. His profile shows a bump in his nose where it didn't heal right after being broken in Burg. That winter feels like it happened a lifetime ago, and to a different group of people.

We sit in silence for a while, the three of us with our shoulders pressed together. Lights wink off in homes as the hours pass. A couple of fireworks blast off down near the square. Somewhere, music is playing.

Much later, Bree calls it a night. She and Sammy give each other an awkward good-bye—part hug, part good-natured shoving—and I'm hesitant to follow. I didn't realize how much I'd miss having Sammy around until the very moment we're about to part ways.

"You'll stay in town, then?" I ask him.

"I spent so many years wanting justice for my father that I barely know what to do with myself now." He rubs the back of his neck. "The bulk of the fight might be over, but there's a long road ahead. I think I should be here, to help Elijah and Vik. Plus, Emma will come around in time, but only if I'm here to come around to."

"She thinks you're cocky," I point out. "And arrogant."

His face pales.

"But also attractive."

A flicker of a smile. "Duly noted."

Sammy grabs my right hand and pulls me into a hug, his other hand clapping my back.

"I never had a sibling, Gray, let alone a brother, so I couldn't understand your pain. Not until now. Don't stay away long."

In the mouth of the stairwell, I pause to glance over my shoulder. Sammy's standing at the edge of the building, the bottle dangling from his fingers as he gazes skyward.

I've lost a twin but gained a brother. Life never ceases to surprise me.

THIRTY-EIGHT

THAT NIGHT MY DREAMS ARE wicked. Shooting Bree, only to find out she isn't a Forgery. Blaine's murder, except I'm the one holding the gun. My father, grabbing my ankle as the *Catherine* goes down, pleading that I not leave him. And blood. Blood and screaming and explosions and an endlessly looping alarm that slowly drives me mad.

I wake sweating. It takes a moment to remember where I am and that Blaine is permanently gone. That my father is at the bottom of the Gulf. That Clipper won't ever see his fourteenth birthday. I thought sleeping next to Bree would help keep the terrors at bay, but maybe it's impossible to hide from shadows in the dark.

I slip out of bed and move to the window. Union Central overlooks the city, and from our room I have a pristine view of dark rooftops and the distant horizon. The sun is just beginning to rise.

I hear Bree yawn, and then she's beside me, looping an arm around my waist.

"Nightmares?"

I nod.

"We could go," she offers. "Might as well, if we're both up."

Elijah sent Raid, the Rebel captain representing Group B, to Dextern. Bree and I have Claysoot to take care of this morning, Saltwater immediately after. An early start makes sense.

"What are you thinking?" she asks.

I grab her chin and kiss her.

"Never mind. I know now." She smiles, and the bandage on her cheek crinkles.

She is beautiful. Radiant. A wildfire blazing. And not just the girl standing before me, but all the intangible pieces, too. I can see the whole of her now, and knowing what's beneath her skin makes me feel so invincible that I wonder how I made it through a single day before her.

I kiss her again.

"I'll get my things," I say.

Her hands trail my forearms, anchoring on my wrists.

"This. Just a moment longer?"

"You say it like it's a chore."

We take a car and a ladder, and Bree drives.

"You first," she says at the Wall.

The smell of the trees is intoxicating—fir and pine and sap—and the sight of clay streets at the hunting trailhead almost brings me to my knees. From a distance, the homes look more worn than I remember, less stable. A goat bleats at us. The young girl feeding him freezes, then flees toward the Council Bell.

We are greeted by arrow tips and drawn bows. The boys holding them look so young. And scrawny. Bree and I show our palms, explaining we mean no harm. It takes a moment, but I'm recognized.

"It can't be." Maude steps through the growing crowd. She's even frailer than I remember. Behind her, Carter is fighting her way between packed shoulders.

"Gray! Where's Emma? Where is my daughter?"

Maude plants her cane in the clay earth, frowning. "I trust you have an explanation?"

The bare necessities will take only the morning, but sharing the whole of the story—explaining *why*—feels impossible. Some experiences can't be fit into words, no matter how many you have at your disposal, or the duration of time you're given to string them together. Still, we try.

A decent number of people climb right away. For others, the news is too much to channel into action. They might leave eventually, but Claysoot is their home. It is all they've ever known. I remember that feeling of uncovering the truth all too well. It was flying and drowning at once, the world exploding beneath your feet. For some, it is paralyzing.

When I finally have a chance to visit Kale, it's nearly noon. My chest is burning. This will be a hello and good-bye in the same breath.

"Pa!" Kale comes running. She's grown like a weed in the months I've been gone. I drop to a knee in the doorway and let her collide with my chest. "Pa!" she says again. "You're back!"

It breaks my heart. The look on her face. The sheer joy. The fact that she can't tell the difference.

"No, it's Uncle Gray, Kale," I say to her. "It's Gray."

"Where's Pa?"

I can barely find my voice. Her eyes are Blaine's. Everything else about her is Sasha, her mother, but Kale's eyes are blue and clear and good and I feel like I'm looking at my brother.

"He's not with me, pea. He's not coming back."

"He's traveling still? Mama said he was. She said to look

at the sky when I wanna talk to him cus he's 'sploring the clouds."

I kiss her blond curls. "Yeah. Something like that."

Sasha appears behind Kale. She's frowning, but it doesn't feel sad. More bittersweet than anything.

"I missed you so much," I tell Kale. "And I know your father, wherever he is, misses you even more."

She smiles.

"I feel terrible about this, but I have to go away for a few days."

"You just got here."

"I know. But there's this one last thing I have to do." One thing. Always one more thing. "I promise I'll be back, though."

"And then you'll live with us forever!" Kale exclaims. "You'll be home."

"Home's here, Kale." I press a finger to her sternum. "And here." I press hers to mine. "The building doesn't matter. It's the people. When you're with them, and even when you're apart, they're still home."

She's beaming. I think she only hears me saying *home*. My eyes sting.

"Don't be sad, Uncle Gray. Here, happy!" She pushes her wooden duck on wheels into my hands and runs off to play with a rag doll.

"Was it quick?" Sasha asks as I stand.

"Faster than a crack of lightning. He didn't feel a thing."

The corner of her lip twitches. "Good," she says. "That's good."

It is late afternoon when Bree and I board a boat on the eastern coast. A stout man takes payment of our labors in exchange for passage, telling us we can start by mopping down the deck.

The work is hard but good, and the feel of a worn wood handle against my palm is a welcome contrast to a gun's grip. To think I was once sick of such standard work. To think I *wanted* to pick up a weapon and race into a fight.

A burst of wind catches me off guard, and I shield my eyes. The smudge of coastline gets smaller. The horizon beckons. There are islanders to visit, a reunion with Heath that Bree's anxious to have. Then a city to return to, and a whole host of possibilities beyond that. I'll take it one day at a time. They may not be visible yet, but the right paths will materialize. The absence of something, I finally realize, does not mean it does not exist.

A pair of gulls screeches overhead, riding the air as though they're made for nothing else. Though the cries are radically different from a loon's, I remember.

"Bree!" She looks up from her work. I clasp my hands

together and blow on my thumbs. The loon call is even more feeble than the one I managed in September's kitchen.

"That was pathetic," Bree says.

"It's progress. I couldn't do it at all a few days ago."

"How are you supposed to get better if I praise mediocrity?" She points a finger at me. "And mediocre is a generous upgrade."

With the mop resting in the crook of her elbow, she whistles a few times to prove her point.

"It's a small miracle I love you," I say.

She grins. "Same."

The captain yells at us to get back to work, and I'm sure to splash Bree with mop water before I do. She curses me. I'll pay for it later, but in the moment, everything is perfect—the birds and the horizon and the boat and Bree. I don't know what comes next, but I know we'll manage. We'll forge our way. We have each other and deep in my gut—at the very center of my being—that feels like enough. *More* than enough.

I feel it, and so I know it.

Some things never change.

ACKNOWLEDGMENTS

Finishing a trilogy is a bittersweet thing. I've spent the last five years in Gray's world, and a small army of people have supported me along the way.

First and foremost, my agent, Sara Crowe. Thank you for believing in this story when it was one of many in your slush pile, and for helping me navigate all the twists and turns in the publication journey that followed. Knowing that you have my back makes all the uncertainties of this industry less intimidating.

I owe an endless chorus of thank-you's to the folks at HarperTeen/HarperCollins Children's Books. My editor, Erica Sussman, has helped me shape this series into the story I wanted to tell—the story I always envisioned but only managed to capture on paper because of her wise suggestions and astute queries. Many thanks also to Susan Katz, Christina Colangelo, Kara Brammer, Alison Lisnow, Stephanie Stein, Kathryn Silsand, the Epic Reads gals for their constant enthusiasm and support of young adult literature (*book shimmy*), and of course, Erin Fitzsimmons, who continues to give my books the most stunning covers and interior pages imaginable.

I've relied on a few trusted readers and critique partners these past years. Susan Dennard, Jenny Martin, April Tucholke: Thank you for all your time and feedback. I owe you guys big-time. To Sarah Maas, Alex Bracken, Jodi Meadows, Kat Zhang, Friday the Thirteeners, the Lucky Thirteens, and the lovely guys and gals of Pub(lishing) Crawl: Writing buddies like you are priceless. I'm so grateful to have been on this journey with you.

I've wanted to be a writer since I could hold a pencil, and I'm only here today because of the support and encouragement of my parents. Mom and Dad, thanks for everything.

My sister, Kelsy, was the very first reader of this series; perhaps its very first fan. Anyone who's enjoyed Gray's story owes her a thank-you as well, because I wouldn't have gotten beyond a few chapters if it wasn't for her constantly asking, "What happens next?" So thanks for all the nagging, Kels. Truly.

Additional gratitude to my husband, Rob, who continues to be supportive of all my creative endeavors. (Also, thanks for putting up with me during that one car ride when I spent three straight hours learning how to make loon calls with my hands. For research purposes.) I love you to the moon and back.

Librarians, educators, booksellers: Gold stars all around. Thank you for getting books into the hands of young readers and for championing my series these past few years.

And perhaps most importantly, a showering of gratitude to *you*, dear reader. Thanks for letting me tell you this story about a boy and a Wall and his quest for answers. I hope this is just the beginning for us. Better yet, I hope to one day be reading something by you. Go forth and dream big. Go forth and write!